BAD SPIRITS

EDITED BY
CLAY VERMULM & TORI V. RAIN

Copyright © 2024 by Clay Vermulm Fiction

All rights reserved.

No portion of this book may be reproduced in any form without written permission from the publisher or author, except as permitted by U.S. copyright law.

Cover Design by Matt Seff Barnes: https://mattseffbarnes.com

Internal Book Design by Dark Forest Press LCC Publishing Services: https://dark-forestpress.com/services/

CONTENTS

FOR SALE BY OWNER Clay Vermulm	1
SHADOWED REALITY Evander Fragoso	17
YGGDRASIL Glenn Dungan	41
AUNTIE LENA Molly Thynes	72
THE BLUE GHOST Taija Morgan	87
STOPLIGHT PARANOIA Kevin Emmons	101
QUIET DESPERATION Clarence Carter	131
DEVILS IN THE DUST J. Agombar	144
BE NOT AFRAID Phil Keeling	163
THE LAST VISIT Tori V. Rainn	185
About the Contributors	223
About the Editors	227

FOR SALE BY OWNER

WRITTEN BY
CLAY VERMULM

THE HUTCH

JAYLYN PACKED up and stored *Azul*, her dad's favorite game, in the family hutch as the misty print of his hand pressed onto the glass of the antique door. It was a question. The same one he asked every morning.

We just played. He can wait until I'm done working. She waited on him all his life. Maybe it was his turn.

She stared through the handprint and into the glass for a long moment, meeting the stare of her father's reflection as he watched her from his rocking chair—*creak, creak, creaking* against the hardwood. Lit from within by a white LED, the intricately carved wooden hutch held a menagerie of board games her parents had collected over the years. Games were the foundation of her family, who'd proven incapable of being in the same room together unless bent over a board or a hand of cards.

A frown crept onto her lips, prompted by the myriad memories those games evoked and by that persistent *creak, creak, creak*. The handprint faded slowly from the hutch as if withering, from her expression. She squeezed out two puffs of the spray bottle and wiped the glass clean, as she had done every day for months.

"I'm busy, Dad," she snapped.

"Always got somewhere to be…"

Jaylyn ignored him. Cleaning wipes in hand, she bustled around the living room polishing every surface, wiping every doorknob clean. She pushed all the table settings to the center, cleaned the table, and put everything back exactly the way it was—a table set for three, just as it had been before her parents passed. If she didn't reset it just right, he would, and she couldn't risk that happening while a potential buyer was in the house.

She finished her cleaning sweep near the kitchen, stopping at an end table with a heavy antique lamp.

Purchased from the local thrift store, just like its predecessors, the lamp stood sentinel against the dim living room. A lone change in the house her father had kept such a tight lock on. Straightening it, she checked to make sure the heavy-duty tape still secured it to the table. She'd cleaned the shattered remains of six lamps since she'd started showing the house. At least her father had never laid hands on her, or worse yet a potential buyer.

I will sell this house, Jaylyn assured herself—trying not to think about the Manila folder on her coffee table. She'd had no issue getting offers, even without the help of a realtor. But none of them had even come to see the house. Those couple people who had were either out of the price-range or looking to do a full-demo, just like the land developers who'd pay in cash and on the day.

"Promise me, Jaylyn…" she remembered her father saying.

Don't think about that.

"Promise me you'll take care of this place. It's what your mother wanted."

Just like dad—defer to Mom or me when he felt vulnerable. When he couldn't stand to ask for something.

That had been one of their last conversations—that longing for legacy echoing through her skull each time she passed his study, slept in their old bedroom, stared at her mother's mural on the wall.

I will sell.

To the right person.

With any luck, the right person was coming today. Jaylyn felt good about it.

She caught a whiff of sour, scalding sugar.

"Dammit," she hissed, dashing to the kitchen.

"Always got somewhere to be…"

Entering a cloud of gray smoke, she quickly wrapped her hands in a too-thin dish towel, pulled the cookie tray from the oven, and dropped it clattering to the stovetop before shaking the heat from her hands.

"Better start over…" Dad said.

Was that voice in her mind, or was he standing behind her? She could never tell anymore.

The cookies weren't ruined. Not all of them. She'd only scheduled one prospective buyer today. She plucked the best cookies from the center and plated them. Frowning, she tossed the burned ones—

charred black, their dough molded into mortar like that of the brick walls around her. Her father and mother spread the mortar, stacked the bricks laboriously upon each other, all for their "real brick house."

"If it ain't right, better start over."

"I know, Dad," she said.

THE DEN

"Hellllooo! You look wonderful! Where did you get that top?" Jaylyn embraced Aria in a hug—warm, but professional. Aria returned the embrace. An enticing aroma of lavender lotion permeated the woman's silk-soft skin.

"Thank you so much," she said, her cheeks coloring as she smoothed her blouse. "I got it online."

Jaylyn winked. "You're a brave woman. Come on, let's get out of the rain."

The younger woman stepped inside. Her Louboutin heels clicked on the dark hardwood. The clean gloss of her perfectly styled hair glinted black in the entryway.

Jaylyn took her buyer's dripping coat and hung it on the rack, wiped her shoes by way of demonstration, and led Aria into the den.

Sucking in her breath, Aria gazed around the room, eyes drifting over the low ceiling, the bright white walls of lath and plaster, the antique couch, and the rocking chair, which had thankfully stopped rocking. The majority of the space was dominated by a large table with six high-back chairs and her parents' prized board game hutch.

"Oh, I love this," said Aria as she strode across the room and peered at the games. "Are these all yours?"

"My parents'. We were a big board game family."

"What a fun way to grow up."

"Yeah." Jaylyn pasted on a smile. "We were never short on fun."

"And, do I smell cookies?"

"Please," Jaylyn said, gesturing to the table.

Aria breathed in deeply and arched a brow. "Oatmeal raisin?"

"They were Dad's favorite," Jaylyn said, pointing to the left half of the platter. "The others are chocolate chip."

Aria nodded, taking an oatmeal raisin. "They're my favorite too." She winked, and Jaylyn felt herself smiling. Usually, most of the oatmeal raisin were doomed to the trash can.

"So, this room is a late addition to the house. As newly-weds, Mom and Dad built this place from the foundation nearly fifty years ago. It used to be half the size. As you can see, it's all real brick."

"You don't see that much anymore."

"Dad always insisted we use brick 'cause it's reliable and fixable. Those were his mantras."

Aria chuckled. "Sounds like my husband. He works in construction. That's part of why he's so excited about this old place. He wants something with some character that we can fix up a little."

A door slammed upstairs, echoing through the halls and rooms. Jaylyn kept her expression flat as Aria's eyes darted to the ceiling.

"Sorry, must have forgotten to close the window up there. I leave them open for the fresh air, but sometimes it gets pretty drafty. This house was built to promote natural air circulation. Never needed AC."

"At least we'll save money there."

That depends on how much you want to "fix it up" I'd imagine.

"Should we have a look at the kitchen?" Jaylyn asked.

THE KITCHEN

The fresh aroma of warm cookies morphed into scorched sugar as they neared the kitchen.

Click, click, click went Aria's shoes, sending echoes fluttering toward the entryway.

"This lamp is beautiful."

"Oh, thanks. Got it at Pristine Antiques on Colby." Jaylyn picked up her pace. It didn't matter. Aria stopped anyway. Jaylyn half-turned the corner to the kitchen and peeked out as her potential buyer ran her fingers along the edge of the lampshade.

Please don't try to pick it up, Jaylyn pleaded to the cosmos when Aria's hand circled the porcelain base.

"The ad said as-is. Are you really selling all of this stuff?"

"I've been wanting to scale down."

Aria nodded, her hand trailing from the lamp. The gold of her watch gave a farewell glint as she made her way to the kitchen.

Gesturing toward the linoleum-lined counters, Jaylyn said, "You've got great natural light, lots of working space, and the old appliances still work great."

"Kurt does a lot of cooking. We'll need a major upgrade in here." Aria clicked her tongue against the roof of her mouth as she strode around the kitchen. Jaylyn listened for any indication of her father's presence.

"He does the cooking and the fixing? You snagged quite a man."

"Well, I make the money, but don't tell him that." She winked.

Jaylyn laughed. "His secret's safe with me. Did you want to look around in here a bit?"

"No, I'm eager to see upstairs." Aria smiled, crystalline-white beaming through ruby lips. "Are there really built-in bookshelves to the ceiling?"

"Yeah, this house is one of a kind." Jaylyn grinned.

This could work. She's actually HERE. She's actually interested in THIS house. Jaylyn tried not to hold her breath, but that flutter in her chest was persistent.

This could work.

THE BATHROOM

Aria gave a little gasp when Jaylyn opened the door at the top of the stairs. The reddish glow from the interior brick walls made the hallway look like something from downtown New York in the heart of Everett, Washington. They stopped at the first of three closed doors.

"Which one's the study?" Aria asked.

Jaylyn pointed to the second door. "Right there."

"The pictures online are phenomenal. I've always wanted a room with tall bookshelves. And that fireplace. Please tell me it's real?"

"It's real, and a lot of work. But I always loved that smell, that heat. Even with the door closed, it filled up the whole house."

"I'm excited to see inside," Aria said.

Jaylyn opened the first door. "Let's check the bathroom out first. It only gets better from there."

Like the kitchen, the lavatory was functional, dull, small—hers. She'd never been good at calculating square footage, but she knew precisely how many Jaylyn-steps it took to cross this room—window to door, tub to toilet, corner to corner, wall to wall—whenever Mom and Dad were at each other's throats, or when she was texting her high school girlfriends in secret, afraid that Dad would rip the phone from her hand and force her to unlock it if he caught her. Concern was painted plain on Aria's face as she entered the room where Jaylyn had paced away her teenage angst. She ran a crimson nail along the old cloth shower curtain, stalked over to the sink, and turned the faux crystal handle. The water spurted out before settling into a low-pressure flow.

"Hmm."

"Full transparency, the water pressure is a little weak in here. But I'm sure your handyman can deal with that?"

"He can do that. I'm more worried about this little shower. I'm definitely a bath girl. We have this Jacuzzi tub at home—"

Footsteps drifted in the hall, soft and barely discernible. Aria stopped talking, her gaze shooting through the wall.

"Old house," Jaylyn said.

"Does someone still live here?" Aria asked, twisting the hem of her blouse.

"Just me. I think there's something in the walls maybe came loose. I hear that sound all the time."

"Is it true that, as a realtor, you have to tell me if someone died here? Like, by law?"

"That's not true in Washington State, and I'm not a realtor, but I won't lie to you. My parents died in this house," Jaylyn replied.

A question seemed to glint in Aria's downcast eyes, but she must have been too polite to ask.

"Cancer got my mom. Dad...didn't do well afterward. They both needed a lot of help, and I was taking care of them instead of doing the whole hospice thing."

"I'm so sorry. They're lucky they had you. I don't know how people do it. I mean, my parents are only in their fifties..." Aria trailed off, maybe seeing the faint streaks of gray in Jaylyn's thinning hair, perhaps thinking of how she'd just mentioned her own mother's death. "Well, what I mean is, that's amazing of you."

"Quit your damn pouting..." Jaylyn's father grumbled from down the hall. She could picture him shaking his head with disapproval—could hear her mother tapping at the door urging her out, lest his scorn curdle into wrath.

"Thanks." She smiled, resisting a shiver. "Time to check out the study?"

"Can't wait," Aria said.

Jaylyn was already walking. "Does Kurt get along with your folks?"

Aria chuckled. "Put my mom and Kurt in the same room, and it's like bringing a new cat home to a one-cat house. Wish they'd get over it." She shrugged. "Crap in one hand, wish in the other."

"My mom always used to joke that any boy who proposed to me would regret it after meeting Dad. That was before she knew I was gay."

"How'd your dad take that?"

Jaylyn froze abruptly, and Aria ran into her back.

"Sorry, that's a really personal question," Aria said.

Jaylyn met her father's stare at the far end of the hall. As always, he stood ominous and tall, dressed in a dark sweater and slacks. The baseball cap atop his head cast a shadow over his face, leaving only the gray bristles of his lower jaw visible. Behind the veil of shade, she knew his face looked stoic, neutral, controlled—just like the perfectly arranged board game hutch downstairs—belying the bridled chaos within.

"Are you alright?" Aria started to step around her, but Jaylyn caught her arm and guided her toward the study, keeping her body between buyer and specter.

"You're going to love this. Best room in the house."

"I hope I didn't offend you," Aria said.

"It's fine. My parents were like lots of parents. They treated me shitty when I first came out. After a couple years, I was comfortable bringing home girlfriends."

"That sounds tough," Aria said, giving Jaylyn's shoulder a little bird-squeeze with her acrylic talons.

"Seriously, it's fine." She turned the study's doorknob and guided Aria in.

THE STUDY

The smell was still in the walls—musk of old books, leather chairs, and three-day-old coffee—blood, marrow, stale feces permeating black-dyed wool.

Everything came back to her in this room. The heat of the wood-burning fireplace. The velvet texture of her father's writing chair and those ever-present sounds of his study—her father's fingers assaulting the typewriter, crumpling paper, clinking a glass. She wondered if the papers or the glasses had killed him in the end.

Not that it mattered.

She gestured Aria in and, with a final look down the hall, shut the door. The soft tick echoed off the vaulted ceiling and bounced off the stained-glass window that looked out toward the forest-cloaked inlets and islands of Puget Sound before falling to rest among the towering bookshelves. Aria walked straight in and felt the worn velvet of Dad's favorite green chair. She ran her crimson-tinted talons over the decorative decanter, picked up her father's prized, collector's edition of *Great Expectations*, and flipped through a couple pages as she wandered toward the fireplace. Jaylyn could picture Aria at night, a glass of wine swirling beneath the stained moonlight as she twirled French-tipped toes in front of the fireplace and thumbed through her Dad's literary collection.

Better they're appreciated. Right Dad? Better than collecting dust. Better than a cold hearth with nothing but ash and sour memories.

She wondered if he could hear her thoughts, if he knew how hard she was trying to do this the right way. How much it mattered that he wasn't forgotten, that Mom wasn't forgotten.

"You look right at home in here," Jaylyn said, loudly.

"I LOVE this room," Aria said, setting her father's favorite book on the windowsill.

Jaylyn thought she actually did. It made her smile. Until she heard the footsteps coming up the stairs. She watched Aria, looking for some sign that the woman heard. She didn't seem to.

The footsteps stopped. A shadow stood behind the door.

Knock.

It was soft enough that Aria didn't react, but Jaylyn heard it.

As Aria stood and circled the room, Jaylyn's gaze darted from the door to her buyer, her breath hitching as she prepared for another sign of her father's shade.

Firmly, but not overly so, she gripped the door handle behind her back, just enough to compress the shake.

BANG.

The force of the blow ran up her arm to her forehead. She shrieked, nearly as loud as Aria. *What the hell?* She stared at the other woman, who'd gone pale.

"What was that?"

There's only one way to stop the knocking.

She turned the doorknob, let the door creak open. Resisting the urge to turn, she focused on her buyer's face. Jaylyn knew he was there; knew what he looked like.

Aria appeared confused. She leaned to the side, as if it would give her a better vantage into the hallway, then leaned the other direction and slowly stalked forward.

Jaylyn turned around.

The man across the threshold met her gaze with bloodshot eyes. A single red line traced its way down the pale topography of his forehead, branching into dripping streams that snaked through his bristly beard. Barely visible in the shade of his hat was a deep black hole that bored its way through his skull. It seemed to watch her, right along with those red-veined eyes, as she stepped through him and into the hall. She willed away the shiver, smelling gun smoke and bourbon. Making a show of looking one way, then the other, she held up a flat palm to Aria. Her buyer obeyed, her heels clicking as she shifted from foot to foot.

"Do you see anything?" Aria asked. Jaylyn shook her head.

"Like I said, it's very drafty up here. Makes the doors slam."

Her father stepped into the room, circling his favorite chair, as Aria walked cautiously around the other side. He picked up the book Aria had set down and took it to his green chair.

Jaylyn kept an eye on him. This was as close as she'd ever seen him get to a buyer. Usually, he just wandered around, aimless in his routine—now, his head tracked the stranger in his study, his mouth turned into a grimace she'd not seen since he was alive.

"Ok, let's see the master bedroom?" Aria asked, a nervous tension in her voice.

"Right this way." Jaylyn eased the door shut behind her with a soft click. Through the thick wood, she heard him mumbling to himself as he sat soundlessly into the velvet, setting the book back in its customary place. Hopefully, he'd stay there a while.

THE BEDROOM

The name *Tara Hutchinson* flowed across the bottom right corner of the mural like a wisp of smoke across water. Taking up the entire back wall of the bedroom, this mural was one of the last remaining pieces of the house that belonged solely to Jaylyn's mother—after she'd gone, so too had the bits of her that Dad could no longer stand to see. The subject was a pen on a plain white piece of paper. A subtle vignette emphasized the pen, broken at the tip, bleeding ink-black-blood across the painted page.

She flicked the light switch up, illuminating the dark-stained wood paneling and floors—the mural's bright whites and reds stood out in stark contrast from the wall behind the master bed. Jaylyn could practically see her mother there, the bed shoved across the room showing a rectangular, dust-free section of the floor which had long been covered by the mattress. Hour after hour, she'd be up on her ladder in her paint-splattered overalls. A happy memory of her father sharing the space flitted through her mind—watching his wife work from his lawn chair as he ate his soup and sandwich. Something about creation—through gaming, through her art, through his keyboard—always helped them find common ground.

Jaylyn looked to her buyer, smiling. That smile quickly receded as she saw Aria's face.

"Oh, that's…very interesting," she said, walking up to the mural and tracing the bottom edge of the wall painting with a finger. "I love…the colors…" She walked the creaky planks, peered closely at the skylight above the bed, and ran her fingers across the arching eaves.

"Did your mother paint this?"

"Mom did lots of painting. This was sort of her final big project."

"I wish I could send it along with you. It must be hard to leave all of this behind."

Jaylyn nodded, unable to find the words.

A bedroom paint job will be high on the list of renovations, no doubt.

Not everyone will love the WHOLE house. Only you could do that, she tried to reassure herself. It didn't mean Aria wouldn't respect the house. She loved the study, she loved—

A door slammed down the hallway. Aria jumped a little.

"Jesus, that's a hell of a draft…"

"Yeah…" Jaylyn went to the door and looked down the hall. The study door was wide open, and there was a scuff mark on the brick wall where the doorknob had slammed against the stone. No sign of her father. "You have to make sure to close the doors."

She heard footsteps. Judging by Aria's face, so did she.

He's never hurt anyone. There's nothing to worry about.

Aria started to reply, but her eyes darted to the doorway.

"Ok," she said. "Do you seriously not hear that?"

He's never hurt anyone.

"I mean, I've lived here for a few years and…"

The footsteps grew louder.

"Jaylyn, I like you. But don't tell me that it's an old house. I can't hear that again. I think there's someone in here."

There was.

She could imagine him lurking just out of the room, peering in—that shadow-veiled face looking like some light-devouring eye. Could picture his hands curled against his sides as he ducked beneath the doorframe, stalked into the bedroom, and made his way toward the woman who would buy his house, paint over his wife's final memory, occupy the study in which he'd lived and died.

Each step squeaked against the hardwood.

"Did you see that?" Aria whispered, pointing to the hallway, where the faintest hint of a lingering shadow stood.

"See what?"

"Nothing," the younger woman said, standing up a little straighter, adjusting her blouse. "I think I've seen what I need to see." She clicked out of the room, sucking in a breath as she rounded the corner into the hallway, a red-nailed hand flying to her mouth.

"What the fuck?" Aria whispered.

It took Jaylyn back, hearing the woman's perfect veneer shattered. Rushing out to join her in the hall, she was met with the disturbing smell of smoke—she heard the crackling of the fireplace, smelled the scent of copper in the air. The hallway seemed to stretch out before them, impossibly far—the only way down was past that study door.

"I thought you said the fireplace was real?"

"It's real."

"So, it's not on a timer or something?"

Jaylyn shook her head. "I think maybe you should get going." Aria looked at her, concern dancing across her eyes, her nervous hands fidgeting with the hem of her top.

"What—" Aria was cut off when the bedroom door next to them slammed violently shut. Both women jumped and Jaylyn immediately headed for the stairs, taking Aria's hand and guiding her down the hall.

Something is wrong. He's never been so aggressive, but he couldn't actually hurt anyone. He couldn't...

As they passed the study, they had just enough time to see the fire crackling in the hearth before that door also slammed shut. In the bathroom the sink spurted on and started running just before that door slammed. Aria was panting now, moving as quickly as her heels would allow. Out of some instinct, she looked over her shoulder just as they reached the stairs, her eyes widening. She didn't have time to scream.

Jaylyn felt a sharp tug at her arm as Aria flew forward, shrieking, straight toward the steep staircase. Shooting out a hand, Jaylyn dug her fingers painfully into the crevices of the brick wall and arrested her own fall. In the same miraculous motion, she managed to momentarily stop her buyer from tumbling face first to the bottom floor. Her shoulder strained against the shock. Aria threw her free hand up for purchase but twisted her ankle and tumbled toward the floor, her fake nails scraping their way free of Jaylyn's palm.

A heavy thump. A groan of pain.

"Are you alright?" Jaylyn called down, descending.

An icy moment drifted through the room as Aria lurched to her feet. She pulled a broken high-heel from one foot, then the other, scanning frantically in every direction.

"Yeah, I...think so," she whispered, her voice guitar-string tight.

She fixed her blouse and rushed for the front door—heels in hand.

Jaylyn got it. That's how she'd felt the first few times she'd seen the apparition. *And he never tried to murder me.* It was that feeling of unseen eyes watching from the dark that had sent people running for safety since the dawn of time.

"I'm glad you're not hurt," Jaylyn said.

Aria didn't respond, just beelined toward the front door.

Behind her, Jaylyn could feel her father. She turned to look the old man in the face, to scorn him, but her words froze in her throat. He was smiling down at her, that smile he wore when he'd won an argument. Her rage coagulated into a bone-deep fear.

"Better start over," he said.

THE DOOR

Jaylyn's breath fogged the glass as she watched Aria stride barefoot to her car, straight past the *For Sale by Owner* sign that dominated the front lawn. The red tail lights glared a firm goodbye to the house. No sooner had she fired up the engine than she was pulling away, flinging a handful of gravel from under her tire.

Clicking the deadbolt home, Jaylyn leaned her head heavily into the window. Through the shroud of her breath, and the blur of welling tears, she saw the bright-red sign. She was so proud when she posted it—so prepared to do right by her family home. If she'd learned anything from her father, it was how to get a job done. All the necessary steps had been taken—permits, inspections, approvals, and contracts. She'd done everything she could to show the house herself, but as soon as she'd started...

The TV came on, blaring static into the empty room. A book flew from the coffee table. The lamp by the hallway shattered on the hardwood. Jaylyn sank to the floor, streaking a red handprint down the window, and noticed her palm was bleeding. A small shard of acrylic nail was lodged in her skin. She pulled it free with a wince and tossed it across the room, hanging her head.

Once she'd realized her father wasn't moving on, once an offer had been placed online and her offer-review date set for the end of this week, the clock had started ticking. She'd saged the house, had a priest bless the place, even paid for a fucking psychic reading. It only got worse with each new buyer, each tour, each batch of cookies.

He.

Would.

Not.

Leave.

"Always got somewhere else to be," Dad said.

Her eyes drifted to the living room table where her Manila folder labeled 'Offers' sat collecting dust. She hadn't been able to add anything to it since the first day she'd put the house on the market. Within the first hour, someone had offered to buy sight unseen.

A demolish and rebuild job. No question.

It took all her will not to sell—leave and never look back.

Jaylyn's hands shook. Forcefully, she denied the tears in her weary eyes—denied the chokes and sobs shaking her ribcage, flowing up her throat, and clogging it like fallen trees damming a river.

"Ok, Dad. Fine," she said, rising to her feet.

The tantrum ceased as she pulled *Azul*, her least favorite game, from the hutch and opened the box on the table. Sighing, she turned her back on the game. She heard her father setting it up, slow and methodical, probably with that little half-smile on his spectral, ageless face.

She grabbed the Manila folder and brought it back to her chair, made her first move on the game without thinking about it, and began leafing through the stack of offers.

Her dad made a move—four reds on one pad to the five spot. It was the obvious best choice. She looked around the room, feeling a weight draining from within her guts like liquid from a freshly lanced boil. Going misty, her eyes wandered listlessly over the living room, over the couch and rocking chair, the television where they'd watched Turner Classic Movies together, her, her dad, her mom—back to the table. She made another move. Smiling across at her father who was focused on his task.

He'd win, she could already tell. Usually, he'd have the game won by the first round, but she'd never wanted to quit. Win or lose, she'd always tried her best to live up to his expectations, to keep her promises. Besides, it didn't matter. She wasn't playing this stupid game for herself.

No more games, Dad, she told herself.

"Your move," she said, directing her sweetest, most obedient-daughter voice to the spectral man who'd joined her across the game board. She could practically taste his arrogant smile as he made his first move.

There would be no *right person*. Jaylyn knew. *Nobody is safe here now.*

Picking up her phone, she made a move on the *Azul* board, dialed the number from her offer sheet, and raised the phone to her ear, clearing the sorrow from her throat as it rang.

SHADOWED REALITY

WRITTEN BY
EVANDER L. FRAGOSO

A BELL JINGLED as Emmett entered the gas station. It reminded him of their cat's collar back home, and he smiled. Luna would always come running excitedly, bell jingling, whenever his wife Kaelyn would come home after a long day in her art studio.

"Welcome," came a gravelly voice from behind the counter.

"How's it going?" Emmett nodded to the clerk and wrinkled his brow at the wide-brimmed hat poking up from behind candy racks before searching for the fridges. They were up in the wintery hills of Michigan, not in an old spaghetti western.

"What brings you out this way?"

"Just a little vacation," Emmett replied.

"Ah, you rented out one of the old cabins then?" the clerk asked.

"Hmm?" Emmett peeked up from the drinks, catching a red glimmer from behind the triangular cut in the rim of the clerk's hat. At second glance, the crimson bead was gone.

"Well, we rented a cabin, but it's a ways out from here," Emmett said as he pulled a tropical-flavored energy drink from the fridge.

The clerk glanced out the window toward the car. "We? There's only the two of us here."

Emmett reached into a cooler for Kaelyn's favorite mango drink. "My wife and I." He nearly dropped the cans when his hands started shaking.

Guess I've been locked up in the house without my meds for too long.

He looked up at his face reflected in the mirrored globe overhead as if the answer to his internal inquiry could be found there, but was greeted by the sight of a dark figure standing behind him. Emmett spun, nearly dropping the drinks, but no one was there—just a cutout of a cowboy eating beef jerky. Emmett took a deep breath, grabbed a bag of jerky and cheese bits, then went to the counter. On the way he noticed sepia-tinted pictures along the large windows.

Missing was written in bold letters above the faded images of teenagers. Their names and information were too blurry to read, but one of the kids almost looked like Kaelyn. He could never get a decent headshot of her though, not like the girl in the picture. The missing girl's smile gave off the same warmth Emmett felt whenever

Kaelyn looked at him. He could picture the missing girl's eyes being that same lovely mix of green and gold as well.

"What's with all the missing kids?" Emmett asked. As he turned to the counter he did a double-take. The clerk wore a weathered dark-brown poncho with a design suggestive of eyes and tentacles. On his chest was a bright-blue name tag that stood out against his clothing. It read *Hello, my name is Pat Turner*.

Remove the tag, wrap bandages around his face, and you've got Argyle, straight from my books.

"You know how kids are, always running off on some grand adventure, looking for other worlds to explore." Pat gave a yellow-toothed smile.

"That's a lot of people to just be off exploring the woods," Emmett mumbled while setting his goods down on the counter, shoving aside thoughts of Argyle, the android turned Bandaged Man.

"It's nothing for you to worry about. Those postings have been up for so long they've become a part of the building." Pat's long, pointed fingernails clicked loudly as he punched buttons on the register. "How long are you and your wife staying?"

"What are you two planning?" Pat asked before Emmett could answer. "The cabins used to be frequented by families looking to get away from the hubbub of the city. After a while, it was just the young folk booking the cabin, looking for a good time. I guess that's just the way of the world, eh? Things change. What was one man's family getaway becomes the funhouse of the young, right? Would you like some condoms to go with these? Or is that all for today?"

Emmett's cheeks flushed. "My wife and I are trying to get some inspiration for our work. Connect with nature, get some good story and art ideas going."

"Oh-ho, a writer then? You know, I thought your face looked kinda familiar." Pat slowly leaned over the counter for a closer look. "Ah-hah, I know you. You write those fantasy books, right? The ones about some warrior running around in an old-west type of world, killing monsters and stuff?"

Emmett stuttered. "Th-that's right." He still panicked when

people recognized him. "*Dark Shadow.*" It didn't help that Pat's attire reminded him of the main villain of the series.

"Ah, that's the name. Great books. How could you let them ruin the movie like that, eh?"

"I flubbed in the contract," Emmett muttered, reaching into his pocket for his wallet.

"Don't worry about it." Pat shook his head, then waved Emmett away. "This round's on me, alright?"

"What? Really?"

"Yeah, with all the hours of adventure you gave me in those books, we're all good. Hell, grab some chocolate on your way back to the car, maybe the ones with caramel inside."

"Thanks," Emmett replied as Pat bagged his goods, "I appreciate it."

"It's no problem at all." Pat nodded. "Just make sure you're careful going up to that cabin. Strange storm we've got here, rolled in out of nowhere."

"It is Michigan after all. We've gotta expect the unexpected with that lake effect. Thanks again."

"Until next time." Pat tipped his hat as Emmett headed for the door.

Emmett stared into the darkened skies, a hand on the gas pump.

"Is your body covered in burns underneath that poncho, or are you hiding something more sinister?" Emmett mused.

"What was that?" Kaelyn asked, suddenly beside him.

Emmett jerked and slipped, barely catching himself against the trunk of the car.

"Woah! Sorry!" Kaelyn helped him regain his balance.

"You gave me a heart attack." Emmett held one of her hands to his chest. "Can you feel that?"

"And here I was thinking I was the one with heart problems," Kaelyn said.

Emmett stuck his tongue out. "I got us some snacks for the rest of the trip." He grabbed the receipt from the pump and shoved it into his pocket before kissing Kaelyn's cheek. "I just have to pee my brains out before we get going again." He wrapped his arms tightly around himself as a strong wind blew through. "Burr, I hope it doesn't freeze on the way out." That made Kaelyn chuckle. Emmett handed her the car keys. "Get in, lock the doors; I'll be right back."

"You say that like you're scared someone's gonna try and take me away while you're in there." She smirked.

"Eh, after the chat with the Bandaged Man, I'm not sure I can trust much of anything…"

"The Bandaged Man?" Kaelyn tilted her head. "*The* Bandaged Man, like, creepy mysterious cowboy, sowing seeds of chaos? Where is he? I've gotta say hi." She chuckled but sobered when she saw Emmett stiffen. "Sweetheart?"

"J-just get in the car, and keep a lookout."

"Wait, you're serious? You really saw something?"

"Something," Emmett said. He could barely make out Pat's broad hat through all the posters plastered on the windows of the small building. Kaelyn glanced at the station with a look of confusion on her face.

"Alright," she whispered, climbing into the car. Emmett watched, waiting until he heard the click of the locks before glancing into the small shop again. He nodded to himself, then walked as quickly as he could through gusty wind and whirling snowflakes toward the outhouse that now felt miles away.

It's just a coincidence. Guy really likes spaghetti westerns, or is just a huge fan of my books.

As Emmett and Kaelyn resumed their drive, the snow beat the car so hard Emmett felt like they were traveling through a snow globe, and whoever was holding it wouldn't stop shaking. He gripped the steering wheel tightly, doing his best to keep the wind from shoving them off the winding road.

"Alexa, lower the volume," Emmett muttered to the voice assistant.

"Whatever you say, Emmett," it replied through the car's speakers.

Kaelyn lightly touched his thigh. "Why didn't you just ask me to lower it for you if the music was too loud?"

"Hm? Oh, you know I like to get as much use out of our voice assistant as I can." Emmett shrugged, then lightly touched her hand.

"It's just silly sometimes."

"Well, neither of us had to mess with the volume."

"Yeah, but…the knob is right there." Kaelyn raised then lowered the volume. "See?"

"Well, maybe I'd rather keep your hand to myself." Emmett gently pulled Kaelyn's hand to his lips and kissed her fingers before quickly grabbing at the steering wheel again, angling against a gust of wind. He groaned and snarled at the torrential snowfall.

"Do you need me to take over, sweetheart? You've driven most of the way already. Why don't you take a break and rest your eyes?"

"It's alright, babe," Emmett replied. "Between the wind and the snow, I rather you didn't hurt your poor wrist." He caressed her scar with his thumb. His heart sank whenever he saw the twinge of pain cross her face from the old injury. A slight moment of distraction was all it had taken to send one young, inexperienced driver hurtling into the side of her vehicle all those years ago. The boy escaped the crash with scratches, while Kaelyn's dominant hand had been doomed to bouts of sharp pain and deep aches for the rest of her days.

"You've gotta save it for all the painting you'll be doing in the cabin," Emmett said. "I've got this."

"Are you sure?" Kaelyn narrowed her eyes.

"Yeah, it's fine. I promise."

"Do you promise-promise?"

"I promise, promise, promise." The wind howled low. "I think you're gonna have to shake me awake tomorrow morning. After all this, I'm gonna crash so hard."

Kaelyn smirked. "Oh, I'll shake you up real good." Emmett loved everything about her face and couldn't help but spare a glance. Besides the fantastic artwork, her lovely visage had drawn him to her at the start.

"Emmett!" Kaelyn squeezed his thigh.

A woman stood in the middle of the road.

Emmett cursed under his breath and tapped at the brake over and over again while steering the car off to the side. He reached over Kaelyn, bracing her into the passenger seat. Kaelyn shrieked as they swerved one way then the other. The car slammed to a stop with its rear end stuck in a mound of snow.

"Are you okay?" Emmett asked through leaden breaths.

"I'm hurting, so I'm still alive," Kaelyn groaned, rubbing at her neck. "I'd be better if you paid more attention to the road."

"What? She came out of nowhere. Who goes out in the middle of a storm like this anyway?"

"Just, go check on them. I'm alright. Just gotta get the wind back in me." Kaelyn unbuckled herself and hunched over, taking deep breaths.

"I'm sorry babe," Emmett whispered. He started to reach out to her but she pulled away.

"Go. It's already getting late, it'd be nice to get to the cabin before sunrise."

Emmett took a deep breath before getting out of the car, falling halfway down the slope of the ditch. The car's rear end was partially buried in a snowbank. It took a bit to crawl out of the freezing wet slide, and by the time Emmett stood on the snow-blanketed road again his joints were aching. His panting breath froze in his mustache and beard.

The woman was gone. He couldn't see any footprints. The sea of white was broken only by his tire tracks. *Did I imagine her? No, Kaelyn had seen her first.*

Something in the back of his mind urged him to get back in the car.

"Hello," he said as the wind howled. "Hello!" Emmett shouted again as he trudged through the snowy mess. "Can you hear me? I'm sorry about almost hitting you."

Emmett peered into the gloom of the trees, squinting hard. He thought he could make out a wisp of hair flapping around a pale white face, but when he blinked, it had vanished. He shivered, more from the eerie feeling than the cold, and hurried back to the car.

"Is she okay?" Kaelyn asked as Emmett opened the passenger door to look her over. "I'm fine." She pulled away from him.

"That look on your face tells me you're hurting," Emmett grumbled.

"Really, I'm used to being in pain. I'm just gonna be a little bruised from the belt. Is she okay?"

"There's no one there," Emmett replied.

"Oh no, are you telling me…" Kaelyn's eyes widened.

"I didn't hit her, she's just not there."

"You think she ran off?"

"I don't know what happened, but there's no sign she was ever there at all, and we need to get out of this ditch."

"I don't think we're getting out of this one on our own," Kaelyn replied, leaning back against the seat's head-rest. "It feels like I'm on a sinking ship. We're gonna need a tow."

"Yeah, well, we can't just sit here. We have to try something." Emmett pulled out his phone. "Besides, the road isn't the only thing this storm is screwing with. There's no signal."

"We'd be fine if you weren't so distracted," Kaelyn said.

"Distracted? I'm just trying to get us out of this ditch."

"We're in the middle of a blizzard and you could hardly keep your eyes on the road."

"Excuse me for adoring you, but that girl just came out of nowhere! And now she's gone!" Emmett stepped away, taking deep breaths, trying to push down his mounting frustration. He made his way around the car and laughed to himself. There was no way of getting out of the ditch with just the two of them.

"Hey! Are you alright?" someone shouted.

Emmett looked up and raised an arm to block out the sudden beam of light aimed at him. *How didn't I notice them?* he thought.

"We're okay, but could use some help getting out of this. Our car slipped and found the one ditch along the highway," he said.

"You're in luck, I always keep a set of straps in the back. Just give me a second."

"Did you hear that, babe? We're saved." Emmett smiled.

"Lucky us." Kaelyn looked away and stared out the window.

Emmett opened his mouth to say something but thought better of it. *I did get us into this mess.*

"Head's up," came the voice from the road. Emmett looked up but couldn't make out anything beyond the flash. The voice sounded like it came from a guy in their late teens or early twenties. A hook attached to some straps thudded into the snow by the car's bumper.

"Thanks man, we really appreciate it." Emmett grabbed the hook and felt under the front of the vehicle for a good place to latch it. "I'm not sure what we'd do if you hadn't passed by when you did."

"No sweat. It's a bad storm. You don't wanna get stuck out in this mess."

"That's for sure." Emmett tightened up the straps then gave a thumbs up. "We're all set down here."

"Cross your fingers." The light disappeared. Emmett hopped into the car and shifted to neutral. The sound of the SUV overhead growled over the wind. He steadied the wheel and clenched his teeth until they were back on the road again.

Emmett let out a relieved sigh and hopped out of the car, approaching the red SUV, but the vehicle's engine roared again. Eyes wide, Emmett jumped back into the car, expecting to be jolted forward by the tow-straps, but the yank ahead didn't come. Before the brake lights vanished into the swirling snow, he managed to make out the license plate. *BNDGDMN.* Emmett turned to Kaelyn, wanting to ask if she'd seen what had happened, but she was staring out the passenger window unawares. Her reflection in the window, the blank stare against the backdrop of the woods, made him feel as though she weren't there at all.

Clenching his teeth to ease the sudden ache in his skull, Emmett turned up the volume of the swancore and continued the drive to the cabin, ignoring the absence of the stranger's tire tracks.

He stiffened as he pulled into the cabin's driveway. Bright light poured from every window, and tire tracks marked the snow. He eased the car behind the only other vehicle in sight. The red paint job was faded and chipped away, exposing rusted parts of its frame. Meanwhile, the tires were flat as if the SUV hadn't been moved in years.

Emmett gaped at the license plate that read *BNDGDMN*, sparkling in his headlights as if it had just been replaced.

"Do you see that?" Emmett asked.

"It looks abandoned." Kaelyn reached for her purse in the backseat.

"The license plate, it's the same as that car that helped us out."

"I think jumping off of your meds is screwing with you. Your brain's trying to adjust, and it's tripping all over itself."

"I know what I saw! I'm not crazy. How could I misread that plate? Look at it, it reads *Bandaged Man*."

"Oh yeah, you're right. You've been seeing the Bandaged Man a lot since going off your meds." Kaelyn leaned on the dash, getting a better look. "Well, that doesn't mean anything. It's just a coincidence."

Emmett shook his head. "Something's not right. Since we left the house, it's like, things just aren't fitting together properly."

"You're just feeling a bit off, sweetheart. Didn't the doc say something about the possibility of seeing and hearing things that aren't there?"

"Are you kidding me?" Emmett closed his eyes tight, clenched his hands into fists, and took deep breaths. "Just, wait here, okay? Let me look around, see what's going on. There shouldn't be anyone here." Before Kaelyn could utter a word, Emmett grabbed the utility knife from the door pocket, shoved it into his coat, and stepped out of the car, slamming the door shut behind him.

In his pocket, the steel corners of the utility knife bit into his cold fingers as he looked the SUV over. The abandoned vehicle was empty. The car tracks beside it looked fresh, but they were lost in the snow drifts only a few feet away. Taking a deep breath, he made his way onto the porch of the cabin and peered into the windows.

A shadowy figure crossed the kitchen, making Emmett's heart stop. After rubbing at his eyes with his palms, he looked again. The shadow stood in the doorway to the kitchen, obscuring the fridge like a human-shaped inkblot. He sucked in a breath of frigid air. In the room just beyond the window, a darkness with long limbs sat on the couch. Its outline was smokey, as if the light were afraid to touch it. The more he stared, the more his brain ached.

Emmett glanced back at the car, but it was gone. The SUV that had been a rusted heap moments ago looked brand new, as it did when it pulled their car out of the ditch. Beside it sat three hot rods in mint condition.

"Kaelyn!" Emmett shouted, leaping off the porch toward the woods. He ran around, looking through the trees for Kaelyn, but there was no sign of her or their copper sedan. The only footsteps in the snow were his. He shouted her name, crying it out desperately to the wind until the light from the cabin window dimmed. Returning his attention to the cabin, he felt his heart sink further.

In the middle of the window stood another dark silhouette, its edges writhing with tendrils of smoke. Another lanky figure came into view, further obscuring the light, and then a third form joined them from another shadowy corner. They had no eyes to speak of, nor any other discernible details. As their elongated shapes twisted, Emmett could feel their attention focus on him.

He bolted, jumping off the porch and slipping through the snow to his knees before running toward the woods. Murmurs followed him as the cabin door opened.

Emmett clung to the side of a tree as four shadow shapes emerged. Something about the dark, featureless silhouettes bathed by the light from within hurt his mind. He desperately tried to see something in those figures, whether it be hair, the glint of eyes, or even just the trace of a smile. His eyes played tricks, placing the features of a face where they should be but the images were fleeting —fluttering ghosts. Emmett couldn't look away if he tried. He stared in fright as the horrors opened the doors of the SUV, started it up, and drove off into the storm.

Emmett slowly peeked around a tree and squinted against the wind. He couldn't shake the trepidation—the feeling of reality twisting and a tingle in the back of his skull like someone was watching him.

He pressed his back to the tree in an attempt to keep the wind from his face and to stop himself from falling over. He closed his eyes, fighting to hold the tears back, thinking of the possibility of never seeing Kaelyn again. There was nothing he could do but whimper into the storm. *I have to find my baby.* He wiped his nose on his sleeve, then slid his hand into his coat pocket and squeezed the utility knife like it was a protective charm.

Alright, Emmett, come on. Wake up! Emmett shook his head, hoping it would jostle him out of the madness, but the shaking hurt. He rubbed at his temples, shivering. *Alright, what if I look at one of my protagonists for inspiration? What would Kurai do in this situation? Would he have run off after his car and wife were gone? No, no way. He would have snuck around the cabin and figured out what in the universe was going on.*

Emmett pulled the scarf over his nose. With a firm grip on the knife, he trekked back to the cabin, ignoring the bloodcurdling growl the howling wind carried with it.

There was no trace of their car and only four sets of tracks in the snow. The impressions were cut off just a few feet from where they began, as if the cars had been dropped off in front of the cabin by a hand in the sky. He'd walked around the surrounding woods with the idea that someone could have moved his vehicle behind the trees and covered up the tracks, and found nothing.

The lights in the cabin were still on; it made his stomach convulse to think that Kaelyn could be in there, with living darkness lurking around every corner.

Gotta stay focused. If this was one of my books...

Emmett laughed. *I'm no hero; I'm a writer of nightmare fuel.*

He rubbed at the utility knife in his pocket with his thumb while staring at the cabin. *Let's not end this with me being sacrificed to some elder god. What would Kurai do?*

Well, for one, he'd sneak in there and use his half-blood senses to figure out what they did to Kaelyn. Of course, I'm just a man.

Who knows what would happen if I tried to grab one of those creatures.

Maybe some sort of gravitational waves would spaghettify me, tearing apart my atoms, absorbing me into their abysmal cores...

Emmett made his way back to the cabin, frequently glancing toward the road. After a cautionary glance inside, he opened the door. With one last look at the cars that were left behind and the spot where his own vehicle had been, he closed the cabin door behind him.

The warmth of the cabin was almost too much of a relief. He needed to sit, warm up, and clear his mind. He hesitated at the couch, then backed away.

A deep impression and a smear of soot stained the cushion as if the creature had sat there for years. Inky-black footprints marked the carpet where they had passed, and splotches of smoky ash showed where they had touched the coffee table. Emmett crossed to the kitchen, avoiding the tainted tracks, while a mixture of scents invaded his nostrils. There wasn't a fireplace but there were hints of firewood ash in the air, mingling with ozone. The cliched paintings of forests and beaches along the wall did nothing to quell the burning in his chest.

Just as he passed the last of the paintings, a rotary phone on the wall shattered the silence. He stared at it like it might bite him. The notepad hanging beside it was scribbled with numbers for the owner and emergency services. He fixated on the last line, *We hope you love your stay.*

What would I even say? Do you know anything about disappearing cars and shadow people?

Twelve rings—he counted. Finally, he caught his breath and lifted the handset, touching the cold plastic to his ear.

"Hello?" Emmett waited. Static came from the other end. As he pulled the phone away from his ear to hang up, someone spoke.

"Hey there, Emmett." A familiar voice came from the other end. It was the gas attendant, Pat Turner. "Hello? Are you still there? Don't up and die on me just yet." His cackle came broken and distorted.

"What's happening?" Emmett struggled to force his words out.

"I guess you're more used to writing about these kinds of things than living them."

"How did you get this number? Where's Kaelyn?"

"Hmm? Who?" Pat's voice oozed with snide, bringing to mind the jagged teeth of *Dark Shadow*'s Bandaged Man.

"Where's my wife?" Emmett's whole body shook as he shouted into the phone.

"Oh, that's right, you said you were heading up there with your old lady! Let's make a trade. You help me, and I'll get her back."

"What do you mean help you? What's going on here?"

"You could feel it on the way up there, right? That sense that something about this place is off? How long did it take for the feeling to crawl over your skin, Emmett? Was it before or after that girl showed up in the middle of the road?"

Emmett paced—to the kitchen, then back—tethered by the phone cord. "This isn't happening," he whispered, out of breath all over again. *I've really lost it. I'm in the car right now, pulled off to the side of the road, eyes closed, going mad. The monsters in my books are reclaiming their birthplace.*

"You're wondering now if you've gone bonkers or if you're in a nightmare. Well, let me tell you something—you've always been a little off the deep end. We both know this. You're a writer after all. Of course this is a nightmare. Most of existence is a nightmare—a pit of suffering that doesn't end until you're dead and buried. Unless some ancient being residing somewhere in the cosmos sees fit to bring you back. Then the torment becomes eternal." Pat Turner laughed. Emmett held onto the handset tighter as if trying to get a better grip on reality.

"Okay, okay," Pat went on. "Let's just put all that aside. Let's say you're not picking up what I'm putting down, eh? You've still just got one option. If this is a dream, you've gotta see it through to the end to get out of it, right? And if this is your new reality, where the things you write into your books have managed to crawl their way into your world, then you'll know following my orders is in your best interest. You know who I am, and what I'm capable of. Do me this favor, and you get to see your wife again."

"Argyle," Emmett muttered under his breath, calling Pat by his true name, the Bandaged Man's name.

"Boy, no one's called me by that name in quite a while. I've gotta say though, it feels good."

"How...how do I know you'll let her go?"

"Emmett, I didn't take her from you. Remember all those missing posters strung up around the station?"

"Yes," Emmett said hesitantly, recalling the girl who resembled Kaelyn.

"Those kids went up to your cabin and disappeared. Remember how your favorite hero, Kurai, once traveled through a forest on the coattails of a vampire? Then the cosmic forces shifted slightly, causing a tear in space-time to open up? That's exactly what happened here. It happens due to the...chaotic nature of the universe. The air opens up, sucks things in, and spits them out in another dimension."

"Are you trying to tell me...that Kaelyn is in another world?"

Emmett took deep breaths and held a hand to his chest while pressing his back to the wall. The thought of the sky opening up and swallowing his wife made his heart ache. There were all kinds of vicious things in his books that made it difficult to survive as a normal human being—giants wielding flame cannons, mutants who appeared human until their bodies split down the middle revealing rows of jagged teeth and sticky limbs, centipede-like creatures that crawled up into a person through the foot to travel along the spine until they got to the brain, where they'd spit out larvae to nest. Emmett sobbed at the thought of Kaelyn in that world.

"Hey now. Settle down, little writer. As soon as we hang up, I'll go get her."

"I'll do whatever you want—just get her back."

"That's what I like to hear," Pat said triumphantly. "I can hear the strength of a hero in you now. Alrighty, Emmett, here's the deal. There's something in that cabin that I need."

"Why haven't you come and gotten it yourself?" Emmett asked.

"Those shadow people and me? You could say we're not compatible. If we came into contact with each other, that'd be very bad for this little planet of yours. The baby, the bathwater, the whole tub. We don't want that, so just listen here. There's an amulet in the basement. When you see it, you'll know. You'll see it, it'll see you—it's a whole thing, trust me. You grab that amulet, hop into one of the cars parked out front, and race your way back to the gas station. I'll be waiting here with your car and your girl, then you guys can go on your merry little way. Just be quick about it—you don't have much time before those shadow people return."

"What does the amulet look—"

"Aren't you listening? Didn't you hear the whole thing about you seeing it and it seeing you? Come on, you're wasting time! Go get it, then head straight over here! I'm hanging up now. I'll go get your girl. See you soon, Emmett."

The line went dead.

Emmett waited for more, struggling to make sense of it all, until the phone digging into his ear felt like it was cutting him. Deep breaths weren't helping. Whatever was happening, having a mental breakdown wouldn't do him any good. He gently set the handset back on the hook before heading for the kitchen.

"Okay," Emmett whispered to himself, "basement. Gotta find the basement and get out of here before those things come back."

The first door he opened was to a fully stocked pantry of cereal, mashed potatoes, and cans of veggies, tuna, and meat.

"They really do stock the place up for a few weeks." Beside the pantry, another door led to stairs going down into darkness. "Ding ding, we have a winner."

Emmett felt along the wall for a light switch but it got him nowhere. He activated the flashlight on his phone, then edged into the narrow door down the creaky steps. A dizzying musty smell assailed him. Random creaks along the entire stairway made him check repeatedly for someone following him.

"The place is just breathing," he whispered to himself.

Oh yeah, breathing alright, he thought, *breathing and getting ready to swallow you whole. Where's the bottom of these stairs?*

As the thought crossed his mind, Emmett missed the last step and stumbled onto the basement floor. He froze from the sound of his own shuffling on the ground. The basement had a very different feel to it, compared to the unsettlingly welcoming living room. There was a moistness to the air that made him feel like he was walking through a misty forest, and he had to hold a hand up to his scarf, pressing it against his nose, trying to keep the scent from seeding his brain. *What if they catch me down here?* Emmett flashed the light around frantically, looking for humanoid shapes in the darkness. He jerked away from a figure in the center of the room, but when he tilted his phone, he found it was just a sewing machine on a small table.

Wooden closets lined the walls further into the basement. Some were closed, while others were open and overflowing with books and toys. It was hard to make out specifics under a thick coat of dust. Mold covered some surfaces, taking him back to explorations of condemned homes as a daring teen. Emmett stepped over a mountain of crusty junk to reach a fuzzy desk. Just as he was about to turn his gaze to a larger shape in the distance, a sparkle of light caught his eye.

Necklaces and rings spilled out over the side of an open drawer. The shapes of the jewelry were barely discernible under dust and mold. Hanging over the front of the drawer from a rusting, beaded necklace, a pendant glimmered from behind the handle of the compartment. Emmett grabbed the necklace and slowly held it up to the light. The piece on the end of the beads remained mostly untouched by the grit and grime that blanketed the basement, protected by the handle it had lain behind. It was a copper shield, slightly smaller than his closed fist, with strange symbols inlaid along the edges. In the center, staring back at Emmett, was an eye. The large iris glimmered like tiny stars, with swirls like a thousand galaxies compressed into a tiny ring around the abysmal pupil. The pupil resembled a mesmerizing black hole as he held it closer.

Something cold and wet brushed up against his leg. Emmett lurched away, falling back against an open closet as he held tightly to the amulet and aimed his phone at the ground. A shriek caught in his throat as he watched a tentacle of black sinew and muscle twitch toward him. He pulled out his knife and slashed at it, but the serpentine appendage snapped at him like a whip, sending the blade whizzing out of his hand. It nicked the top of his ear and thunked into a shelf behind him. Blood trickled down his cheek.

The tip of a desk stabbed into his thigh as he stumbled away and ran for the steps. Things fell all around him. Emmett was too afraid to look back and see what the tentacle was attached to or how many of them there were. It sounded like the whole room was coming alive, with the books spilling out of shelves, toys clamoring on the floor, and articles of furniture knocking into each other.

Emmett moved as fast as he could, keeping the flashlight aimed low to the ground. Had he really walked that far into the big dark room? There was no telling how deep the darkness went. Cursing, he tripped over a tentacle enshrouded by smoke, and jumped over another pair of the fleshy things as they slithered his way.

Taking the stairs two and three steps at a time, Emmett raced for the top while holding back a panicked scream. The sound of the wooden steps and handrails behind him snapping as tentacles gave chase made Emmett gasp. The staircase shook and bent with every loud snap that came from behind, and the sounds of the splintering wood and writhing bodies grew closer and closer. Tears ran down his face.

The chance to tell Kaelyn how much he loved her slipped with each second. He wasn't going to make it.

The light of the kitchen above was a far-away seed of hope. His legs strained from running through the woods earlier, but now they burned like they were being dragged through embers. Emmett screamed as the light grew brighter until he leaped into the kitchen, tumbling across the hardwood floor. He lay against a cabinet, shoulder aching, expecting the tentacles to pounce on him any second. Dark forms swirled just past the edge of the kitchen light, like whirlpools of shadow and smoke. Emmett gasped as a sinewy tentacle reached into the light toward him. Steam hissed from the appendage, and after barely reaching the doorframe leading to the kitchen, the thing quickly retracted. A deep bellowing growl shook the cabin.

"Okay, time to go," Emmett said in between breaths as he struggled to get to his feet. He squeezed the amulet in his hand and rushed for the front door. All the while, he couldn't stop looking back over his shoulder, expecting a tentacle to snare his foot and drag him away, or the shadow of one of those tall humanoid creatures to crawl out from behind the couch to grab him. He froze when he heard the sound of a car pulling up, then raced to the back of the cabin, swearing with every step.

By the time Emmett made it past the couch, the front door had creaked open. He ducked and made for the back door as quickly and quietly as he could. *They saw you, they heard your thoughts. You're dead. You're gonna be one with the void, soon.* Ignoring the pessimistic thoughts, Emmett slowly opened the back door. Laughter echoed from the front of the cabin as he stepped out into the snow, followed by the low growl of the monstrosity in the basement. He sprinted toward the trees, leaving the back door ajar, as the grumbling in the earth intensified. The sound intertwined with that of feet scurrying toward the kitchen. Their pet was calling out to them.

Holding tightly to the amulet, Emmett ran around the house, hoping his legs wouldn't fail him. The basement creature growled louder—loud enough that Emmett could hear the horrid thing over the rushing wind while he raced along the side of the house. He almost looked over his shoulder but the mental image of an amorphous smoke-shrouded creature dragging itself across the snow with a thousand tentacles was enough to keep him running face forward. Kaelyn was waiting for him back at the gas station. She had to be.

Emmett ran past the hot rods and reached for the door of the red SUV, praying to the cosmos that it was unlocked with the keys in plain sight. When the door opened easily, he didn't even give himself a chance to feel relief. He hopped in, checked behind the visor and door pocket before finding the keys in the center console, and jammed them into the ignition.

The rumble from the cabin sounded like an earthquake. Shadowy figures moved about in the windows. Emmett froze as his gaze met the face of one. He could feel its eyes staring back at him like icy daggers. The other three shadows moved away from the window. Emmett turned the key. The shadow people opened the front door of the cabin as the car's engine kicked over. He cranked the wheel and stomped on the gas. The SUV slid back and forth, kicking up snow before he got it to fishtail toward the road.

In the rearview mirror, Emmett could see the living shadows raise their arms against the cloud of white as they started to run toward him, but the traction caught, and he was off, speeding away from the invaders and the cabin. A shiver shot down his spine after driving for a few miles, and the amount of snow coming down grew. The flakes swirling in the car's headlights increased in size, and the deepening sea of snow forced him to slow down, despite the fear crawling across his skin.

Not too bad for some little writer, eh? He kept glancing back into the rearview mirror the whole drive, waiting for the nightmares to give chase or a tentacle to worm its way up to him from the backseat. He tried to calm his breathing, to let go of some of the anxiety and fear, but it was hard enough to keep himself on the icy road. Squeezing the amulet, he turned the corner to the road leading to the gas station, and hopefully, to Kaelyn.

Emmett squinted into the snowstorm. The blizzard kept getting worse, and visibility went with it. The lights around the gas station appeared in the gloom just as he'd started to worry that he had somehow passed it. He started to cry as his copper-toned sedan came into view beside the entrance to the little shop. Emmett almost jumped out of the SUV before putting it into park behind his own vehicle. *Thank the cosmos.* Slipping through the snow, he made a beeline for the driver-side door and yanked it open, only to find that the car was empty.

"Kaelyn!" The only reply to the shout of despair was of the wind howling through the trees. Emmett clenched his hands into fists until his knuckles hurt. His attention went to the small gas station and the sign that read *Pump n' Grub*. Forcing one foot in front of the other, he approached the station.

The jingle of the bell as Emmett entered made his eyes water with thoughts of Kaelyn and their cat running to greet her at the door.

Emmett coughed as the taste of death in the air hit him like a truck. It mingled with the sour smell of spilt milk. The floorboards creaked with every step. Shelves barely held anything but cobwebs. Reluctantly, he approached the counter where he'd talked to Pat Turner, or as he now knew him to be, Argyle—the Bandaged Man—the Cthulhu to his *Dark Shadow* mythos. It was now covered in piles of yellowing paper. The closer he got, the more off-kilter he felt. They were duplicates of the missing posters that lined the windows and walls. The smell of decay grew, inducing a migraine as Emmett reached for one of the tattered sheets on the counter.

"You're here! Sorry about the mess."

He froze at the sound of Argyle behind him. The clopping of the villain's cowboy boots as he made his way out of an aisle and around the counter rooted Emmett in place. Each step was like a nail pinning his feet to the ground.

"W-where's Kaelyn?" Emmett struggled to push the words out. The putrid smell in the air, combined with Argyle's presence, weighed him down.

"There's something I want to discuss before that," Argyle said as he ran his nails across the counter. Ribbons of blood-stained bandages trailed out of his sleeve. The wrappings were also all around his head, as if he were a mummy fresh from the crypt. The only part of his face which remained uncovered by yellowed and crusted linen strips was his right lidless eye. Staring back into it sucked the breath out of Emmett, and for a moment, he was able to reach into his coat pocket with the thought of tossing the amulet and making a run for it.

The Bandaged Man laughed. "Don't." Argyle stopped with his hand below the counter. Emmett struggled to breathe, expecting a gun. Instead, Argyle pulled out a book and held it beside his face. The cover depicted the Bandaged Man, head slightly bowed, looking up through the triangular cut in the brim of his hat.

"This one," Argyle said, "is definitely my favorite."

"Uh, thank you," Emmett muttered, as standing face to face with his own creation, and the book cover illustrating him, caused him to teeter.

"That thing in your pocket, do you know what it is?"

"No."

"There's nothing about that amulet in this book or any of your other stories I'm in. I wasn't lying when I said I was a fan, but I was reading through your work to find some clues as to the amulet's location. You see, the big boss has been sending me around to plant some chaos in various worlds, just as you've written. This origin story here, *Making Contact*, and the collection of some of my exploits across the multiverse, ring mostly true. I don't know who this Kurai halfling is, but it would be nice to know how the story ends, especially if these strings of events were to unfold around me. Tell me, how did these stories come to you? The ones in this book."

"What?" Emmett stared back into his eye. "You want to know... about my writing process?"

Where's Kaelyn? his mind screamed.

Argyle flipped through the pages of the book. "How do you know about my life and things happening in other universes? Do you see it in your dreams? Does a cosmic being whisper in your ear?"

"What are you talking about?" Emmett took a step back, trying not to choke on his words. His throat constricted. Although he had played with the idea of the worlds he wrote being real, the concept was always a fleeting fancy. There were no voices in his head telling him what to write down. The only voice was his own, as far as he knew. The thunderous migraine grew.

"You really don't get it, do you? You really thought the shadow men were just nightmares?" Argyle laughed; it made Emmett's chest tighten as if a hand were squeezing at his heart. The Bandaged Man shook his head and then held out his palm. "I'm sorry, I guess we're just wasting time here. Hand over the amulet, and be on your way."

"Not until you hand over my wife." Emmett squeezed the amulet tightly, feeling the edges of the shield dig into his palm.

Argyle scoffed. "You've really glued the wool to your eyes, eh? I get it. It's tough getting over something like that, blaming yourself for what happened, turning to medications to try and wrangle with the loosening of your sanity. Look at where you are now, mister writer. Open your eyes!"

"What are you talking about?" Emmett took a few steps back, looking around. "Where is she? Where's Kaelyn? You said you'd get her back!"

"Hey now, calm down. I'm sorry, I really am, but I've gotta get going soon."

Emmett stumbled back against an end-cap, sending the shelves clamoring to the ground. He tried to pick himself up but slipped on the metal and dust-caked cans.

Argyle jumped over the counter with ease. "Okay, enough of that. I could snap you like a twig without lifting a muscle. Give me the amulet, and I'll leave you with two gifts: your life, and what happened to your wife."

Sobbing as the pain in his head threatened to blind him, Emmett ran his thumb over the eye set within the amulet. He pulled it out of his pocket and dropped it into the outstretched bandaged palm. As soon as it left Emmett's hand, he found the weight on his chest and pressure in his head ease.

Argyle held the amulet up between his skeletal fingers. "There we go, was that so difficult?" He cackled as he tucked the amulet under his poncho before crouching in front of Emmett.

"Now, mister writer, understand that I'm only doing this for you because I like your work." Argyle's hand became a blur. Emmett felt a prick on his forehead, like being poked by a needle. All Emmett could do was gasp as he felt a drop of blood bubble up and images of his beloved flashed before his eyes.

They were memories of what he tried to forget, flooding back to him. Had it been five years already since their last trip to the cabin? Emmett pressed his palms to his tear-soaked eyes. She was as beautiful as always, his goddess, his wonderful Kaelyn. He couldn't keep his eyes off of her, even as he drove through the blizzard. Something had jumped out in front of them. It was big, whatever it was, and Emmett remembered blacking out from the force of the crash, but when he came to, there was nothing there. He found himself sitting in the middle of the road, hands on the steering wheel. The passenger side door was open, and Kaelyn was gone.

"Where is she?" Emmett wailed.

"Gone." Argyle shrugged and stood. "Whether you get to pill popping or funnel that sadness into a story is up to you."

"No, she can't be. That was just a bad dream, and you brought it back. The psychiatrist visits, those were to keep from going off the deep end, from the growing fame. I just…my brain, it got things messed up." Emmett palmed at his eyes until it hurt, trying to push away the images from that night, but they were only replaced with his desire for answers after the incident. He could smell the pine and feel the snow crunching beneath his boots again, from the search through the woods. There had been no tracks to follow, as if she'd been spirited away. Emmett could still smell her lavender perfume even now. It was the only thing left in the passenger seat and his nostrils clung to it.

"Where's Kaelyn?" Emmett sobbed as his head and heart ached further. "I want my Kaelyn back."

"She's gone. You created a shadow of the woman you loved," Argyle said. He patted Emmett's shoulder. "You can pay me back by making sure they get my character right in the next movie."

YGGDRASIL

WRITTEN BY
GLENN DUNGAN

THE STARTER: foie gras with apple glaze, topped with sunflower seeds, pistachio, and cracked black pepper. Entrée: scallops seared with fennel and shiitake mushrooms, complemented with a sea urchin bisque.

Jude was particularly proud of this dish, and so was the guest, who had asked for Jude to come out and say hello. The man was Sigur Edmunson. Jude recognized him from the various culinary articles and magazines he had read during his commutes on the subway. Sigur was a world-renowned chef who, as of three years ago, became the owner of a famous restaurant in Iceland named Yggdrasil. The man was more than a restaurateur; Sigur was a culinary artist, a man dedicated to his craft. Jude admired this in Sigur, so much so that merely meeting the Icelandic chef fueled his resolve through the busy dinner rush. Jude had worked in a plethora of restaurants, but Sigur was the first person who seemed to understand his own love for the craft, the artistry in the process.

After the meal, Sigur's hulking frame—which seemed weathered with both wisdom and creativity—appeared in the kitchen. Eyes glinting, almost childlike, he placed a plane ticket into Jude's knife-scarred hands along with a sizable amount of kronur.

Within two weeks, Jude was en route to Reykjavik.

As he got off of the plane in Keflavik, reality hit him; he had just left a promising career in Manhattan to pursue a mentorship in the culinary arts—one which Jude gambled would make him a master chef. His Queens-born family had not understood his reasons for leaving, but to Jude, it was more than worth it.

He did not sleep much the night before his first shift at Yggdrasil. Perhaps it was the six-hour jet lag that was still catching up to him or the reality that he had abandoned a promising life in America on some sudden impulse. Perhaps Jude was simply nervous to train under Sigur, and to venture to new culinary heights.

Yggdrasil was even more gorgeous than the open plains of the country surrounding it. Large, industrial windows skirted the front, separating the patio space from the interior. The door was made of Icelandic birch, which was impressive because, according to a statistic Jude had read on the plane, trees occupied less than three percent of the entire country's landmass. A hand-carved tree painted in gold was emblazoned on the door, cut vertically so it split open upon entry.

Jude found Sigur in his chef's uniform, much different than the button-up and tie he had worn in Manhattan two weeks prior. Sigur smiled and shook Jude's hand with a firm grip. He could feel the scars of a life in culinary arts etched like cartography across the man's palm and fingers. When not flushed with wine and a full stomach, Sigur looked hardened from the stone and frost of Iceland—like an old Viking, complete with wispy blond hair that was almost white and an expression so icy it could rival glaciers.

He had half expected Sigur's warmth to be the same as it was in Manhattan, but instead, the chef put Jude in charge of prep work: salads, dressings, potato peeling. Jude felt himself sinking; he had left his nice one-bedroom in a hip part of Brooklyn and a burgeoning career in New York City to peel potatoes—work akin to that of a slightly more competent busboy. He had ventured into a world outside of his own and turned his back on the momentum of the American culinary scene to…what? Follow someone else's recipes and be ignored by the man he had traveled across seas to learn from?

The first two months of working under Sigur were demeaning, but Jude knew his pride would get in the way of his success. He forced himself to be patient as he traveled up the ladder. A couple of months later, after Jude moved up from prep to the line and mastering the dishes, Sigur approached him and, in their first one-on-one interaction in months, asked him to finish up and come downstairs.

"You've proven yourself to Yggdrasil," he said.

"Thank you, chef."

"Do you wish to learn from me, Jude? Actually learn?"

Jude kept himself from smiling, wanting to match Sigur's glacial temperament. "Yes, chef."

"You've got to understand that Yggdrasil does not use conventional ingredients. If it bothers you, or if I think it bothers you, then you take that kronur I gave you months ago and leave tonight."

Jude wanted to question this further but feared the master chef doubting his resolve. Instead, he followed Sigur through the maze of the open kitchen, into the prep area, and past the dish pit. They went into the basement, which was surprisingly immaculate, and passed the inventory of liquor, extra plates, and aprons. At the end was another door; heavy thumping like a heartbeat pounded almost rhythmically from the other side. It sounded as if someone was tenderizing a steak or battering a fresh tuna. Jude had seen this room before and had never seen anyone enter or exit. He had been told by the line cooks and waitstaff that it was a cellar. He had no reason to doubt this. Until now.

Sigur waited for Jude to accept the terms. After a moment of submitting to Sigur's icy, stalwart gaze, Jude nodded and Sigur opened the door. High-pitched sounds of torture screamed out, making Jude's spine tense. The pounding vibrated his bones. Adrenaline began to blossom throughout his body, and he found himself caught between the Venn diagram of fight or flight, but one look from Sigur anchored him, calming the uneasy sea of his psyche.

The room was full of industrial tables, silver and shining underneath, lit only by incandescent bulbs that hung from the ceiling. Jude stepped into a thin layer of blood on the tiled floor, running in little rivers to the waffle drain in the middle of the room. Upon the table were large fish, four feet in length, scaled in effervescent green and blue. Pebbles of melted snow dotted their scales. It was then, as the screams continued, that Jude realized these were no fish but a cluster of women. The most beautiful women he had ever seen, huddled in the corner on the bloodied tiles, their arms tied behind their back, fins folded underneath one another. Eyes that were as blue as the ocean were faded with swollen cheekbones, soft skin splotched with the color of undercooked steak, scarlet hair in tatters on the floor, soft pink lips bloodied and twisted into anguish as they watched their sister.

Two butchers held the mermaid's torso as another took what appeared to be a black gun. Mechanically, the butcher placed the nozzle onto the mermaid's fractured skull, and with extreme precision amid its howls and tears, pulled the trigger, releasing a reverberating *pop* before resetting the piston and moving on to the next table. It was a bolt gun, Jude figured. The kind used to kill cattle quickly.

The creature's eyes rattled in its sockets as it submitted to death in defeated silence. The tails of several mermaids were stacked on top of one another on a table across the room. Several butchers reorganized the stack to add the newly deceased mermaid to the bunch after separating its torso from its waist with a bone saw. They took the torso of the mermaid, its tongue lolling and eyes wide and blank, and tossed it into a large trash bin lined with black bags.

Sigur said, "What do you think, Jude?"

Jude was silent. His hands were shaking and his mouth had gone dry. Sigur had noticed. He gathered himself and put together a series of words that he hoped would pass Sigur's test: "I think that when they die, they look an awful lot like fish."

"Exactly. Mermaid is a delicacy. It is very expensive. We usually sell it for upward of four thousand a dish, depending on the market."

"I didn't know they were real."

Sigur studied Jude's face, then he raised an eyebrow. "It's all real, and you've been serving the meat for months. The tartare, the ceviche...Yggdrasil has a rotating menu. There is a new dish."

"How are we serving her?"

"It. We are serving it with a thyme-maple chardonnay reduction, a side of Brussels sprouts with capers and camembert shavings, and polenta with black garlic and white truffle."

"Brilliant." Jude smiled.

"Now get back to work," Sigur said.

"Yes, chef!"

Jude watched the door close behind him; the many questions on his mind could wait. He belonged in Yggdrasil, and because Sigur believed this, he believed it too.

After four weeks of intense training as an apprentice to the famous Sigur Edmunson, Jude realized that with genius came a certain level of insanity. He also knew that Sigur was as hardened as the glacial air in the Reykjavik streets and had seen his wrath in the kitchen during rushes. It was simple things, really, that awoke

Sigur's ire: too much vinegar in the dressing, not enough chives sprinkled atop the rose-blossom-shaped scrambled eggs to match his seemingly insatiable perfectionism. Jude was not intimidated by Sigur; he was enthralled. Jude could feel Sigur's brain working when his thick brows wiggled during the creation of a new dish, and he noticed the subtle nods of appreciation when his creations were plated with enough presentation to rival the Harpa Opera House. Sigur Edmunson was a prolific artist, and his medium was cuisine. He was the type of culinary master that Jude aspired to become.

Having only gone into the butcher's room a second time to confirm that his eyes were not deceiving him, Jude had become desensitized to their horrible screams rattling in the basement and their battered, fleshy torsos being tossed unceremoniously into a waste bucket. They were no more than freshly caught fish, and, on some weeks, mermaids were more plentiful. It was this pragmatic nature of the restaurant that allowed Jude to lock away any quandaries he might have had, bolting them with a steel lock akin to the one outside of the walk-in freezer.

Sigur captured them every morning off the coast of the Black Sand Beach with methods unknown. He let slip one evening, after a long and successful Saturday night and a celebratory glass of wine, that mermaids were attracted to a special scent. He would not reveal the scent, even after his cold exterior softened with the blush of drunkenness. He did, however, suggest that it was the same scent that attracted ships of men to the sirens of old, miles across the ocean, like blood to a shark.

Jude wondered when Sigur's fascination with these mythical creatures had mutated into serving them. He had never seen anyone stare at and refer to creatures so elegant and magnificent with such detached pragmatism.

As the winter started to regress and give way to crisper, gentler air, the menu experienced that awkward transitional phase of trying to follow the seasons. Jude was now a year in and had graduated from his one-room hostel to a rented studio in downtown Reykjavik, Miðbær. He was starting to make good drinking buddies at the restaurant, who still poked fun at him for being a "burger-eating

American," but this waned when Jude illuminated the Icelander's own love of beer and hotdogs. A server named Cecile had taken a fancy to him, but Jude could not allow himself to get distracted, and could not risk his reputation with workplace trysts.

One day, Jude suggested a gumbo using the mermaid meat with a bone broth base. Sigur thought this was such a clever idea that he gave Jude the rest of the day off to work on the recipe. This caused further butchering of the mermaids in the basement, and the tiles were bathed in so much blood it looked as if they had been painted that way; not a spot of porcelain white shone through. The gumbo consisted of puffins (which were a culturally valued animal in Iceland, but the culinary practice in Yggdrasil had transcended norms in pursuit of art), whale meat, and mermaid. It turned out that mermaid bones made terrible broth, and the product was horrendous. Still, Sigur understood the value of experimentation and instead used whale bones for the base and introduced a new ingredient that he had received from a direct supplier somewhere in the forests of Scandinavia.

"Centaur," Sigur said. "Slow-cooked with pink peppercorns and mustard seed. You're welcome to use some for tonight's dish. Centaur meat is a bit gamey. Consider your applications."

"Thank you, chef."

Sigur's face drew into what Jude assumed was an attempt at a smile, although it was his eyes that reflected the emotions in the Viking chef's weathered visage. Seeing his eyes brighten in Jude's direction reminded him of the first time he had seen the Aurora Borealis.

Sigur said, "You're doing terrific, Jude. Yggdrasil is very fortunate to have you here."

Jude stared over the front of the house, watching the expressions of guests who tried his gumbo travel from curiosity to bliss. His move to Reykjavik had been a good one. With Sigur as his mentor, he had no choice but to become the best.

Summer came, and the ice melted into crystalline rivers to reveal verdant, mossy moors and plateaus. The patio opened, and Sigur hired no additional staff to offset the influx of business that came with the tourists every season. In recent decades, Iceland had become a popular destination for young travelers looking to find themselves, but Yggdrasil did not concern itself with the young, adventurous ilk; the quality of its meals was too luxurious. Instead, Yggdrasil's audience was composed of rich, corporate executives on holiday—clientele wealthy enough to fly on private jets across the world for an evening to spend over one hundred grand on a dinner and then fly back to work on Monday. They did not need staff to accommodate the backpackers, the study abroaders, the lost ones. Seasons did not affect Yggdrasil's audience, only its menu.

Sigur came in one evening holding a metal box. Bandages wrapped around his hands pressed against splotches of blood and pus. He was sweating from his brow as if he had just spent the evening in the kitchen. He held the box gingerly and stepped into prep. The pastry chef gave him a glass of water and a rag to wipe his forehead. A crowd gathered around their master chef, more curious about Sigur's weakened expression than the contents of what he was holding. Jude had never seen Sigur so winded before.

Downing the water and massaging his temples, Sigur said, "I've been waiting for this ingredient. Jude, will you get the fire extinguisher and keep it aimed at me?"

Jude retrieved the extinguisher and stood by Sigur's side.

"Now stand back, all of you."

Sigur opened the box and all four sides dropped down, revealing the cube to be more of a trap, like a carrot underneath a box to catch rabbits. The box was full of straw. The strands rustled, and a sharp chirping noise emanated from the pile.

"A nest," someone said, "for a bird."

"Not just a bird," Sigur said, reclaiming his breath, "a phoenix."

The crowd leaned in just as its tiny, scarlet head peeked from the straw. Some of the servers gushed at its innocent cuteness, but Sigur shot them a hardened look, which straightened their backs to attention. The bird clicked its beak and rustled its feathers. It cocked its head and stared at Jude with dark, nebulous eyes. It was the most beautiful bird he had ever seen. Jude knew that his training had been effective because his first thought was *How can we incorporate this into a dish?*

Sigur struck a match and held it in front of his face, the flames threatening to incinerate his thick, blond-white brows. He said, "I've had phoenix once, when I was a child. It was not the meat that gave me pleasure—it tastes much like quail or puffin. No, it was the ashes."

He lowered the match onto the chick, where it raised its head and opened its beak in expectation of food. Sigur kissed the flame onto the bird's scarlet brow, where it became engulfed in an orb of fire that crackled its bones like popcorn and hissed as it burned the feathers. The chick pipped and squealed in horror as Jude and the staff looked on, hardened by Sigur's own detachment. The bird flailed its head before crumbling like sand into the blackened mess that was once its nest. The flames died, leaving a silence in the kitchen.

Sigur took a pinch of the ashes and sprinkled some onto his tongue. His eyes rolled back and his face relaxed. A bead of sweat fell down his cheek. Jude was not sure if this was actually tears. It was the first time Jude had seen Sigur genuinely enjoy the taste of something, which meant that it was nothing short of magical.

Sigur gestured to the pile of ashes and invited all to try a pinch. The ashes of the phoenix felt almost like soot. They were black and left a residue on Jude's fingers. He placed the pinch on his tongue and immediately understood why Sigur had gone to the labor of obtaining this cindered bird, though he knew better than to ask for details. The ash landed on Jude's taste buds with an explosion of spice. At first, the taste was an unexpected union of paprika and vanilla, then it followed to the sides of his mouth, increasing in intensity until it burned with the aggression of a habanero. Once the spice regressed and traveled to the back of his throat, the taste lingered and turned into salt before returning to its original warming spice—a full loop. Jude felt the ash travel down his esophagus and into his stomach with the smoky burn of a good whiskey, warming his body from the inside all the way to his fingertips. His eyes stung and he wiped away a tear. The ashes of the phoenix were such an intense orgy of flavors that it was almost like covering himself with a blanket.

When Jude looked up, he saw the rest of the crew tearing in euphoria. No one was crying for the dead phoenix. One of the hosts reached into the pile for another taste, but Sigur rapped on his knuckles with a spoon. He took half of the ashes and put them in a mason jar.

"The ashes are a delicacy," Sigur explained. "They are very expensive, and require a lesson for the harvester. To be greedy and take all the ashes is to kill the bird. But we don't want to kill the bird."

Jude asked, "How many dishes can we serve with this amount? Forty, fifty people?"

Sigur shook his head. He put the remaining ashes back in the iron, padlocked cube. "Infinite. There will be a phoenix back by the morning, and we will collect another seven ounces then."

Jude had forgotten the lore of the phoenix—mythical fire birds that rose triumphantly from their ashes. Immortal. He nodded and said, "Something tells me you already have a dish that uses these ashes, chef."

Sigur locked the box. He said, "A rib-eye with phoenix ash rub and mango chutney served with parmesan garlic, fingerling potatoes, and lemon broccoli rabe. For dessert, let's see if we can incorporate the ash into a glaze and put it over our Tahitian vanilla ice cream. Sprinkle it with a touch of sea salt—a touch—and slivers of peaches. Maybe a bit of cayenne, but that might clash with the heat of the ashes. Let's make a dish and see how one of the guests reacts." Sigur turned to Jude with glacial eyes. "Jude, if you feel it's ready to go, send it out. I'm leaving the decision to you."

"Yes, chef." Jude nodded, and set about ensuring that he would realize his mentor's vision.

The employees of Yggdrasil bounced a collective nod. Chefs went to prepare the dishes and the front of the house went about setting up the tables. Jude stood for a moment, paralyzed by Sigur's notice, the gift of agency he had given him.

Sigur personally oversaw the creation of each dish, impervious to any outside influence. He was entranced. Like most things, Sigur's intuition proved correct, and the phoenix-themed dishes sold out faster than Sigur could register. Jude overheard the patrons describe the rib-eye as "addicting," "inspiring," and "incomprehensible in its performance." He thought those were strange words for people who'd spent over twelve hundred on a single meal. The entrée and dessert received such acclaim that their praise circulated the restaurant with as much intensity as a forest fire, and before the night was even half over, their supply of phoenix ash had been depleted. The disdain from the patrons unable to receive the dish was bittersweet; their disappointment a good problem to have.

The following night, Sigur repeated the preparation with the phoenix, both the front and back of house staff stopping to witness this novelty by looking around Sigur's hulking shoulders as they carried trays, plates, sharpened knives. They hovered around Sigur as if he generated a forcefield, like a sculptor at work. On more than one occasion he summoned his booming Viking voice to snap them all back to work.

He placed the box on a stainless steel industrial table and revealed a fresh bird, already chirping and blinking absently in the heavy light of the kitchen. It was almost surreal, like a magic trick. Sigur palmed the ashes into a mason jar and repeated the practice: the remaining ashes into the fireproof box, locked from above and stored in the cupboard to give the bird time to revive. The rest of the kitchen did their best to prepare for the rush of their high-profile patrons, and after the night was over, Jude was asked to open a bottle of whiskey to celebrate the end of a long shift.

Even after a year, the chef showed no signs of waning genius and was unforgiving in his critique, of which Jude was forever grateful. He played no favorites and apologized to no one. Jude was learning much more at Yggdrasil. He had almost forgotten what it was like living in New York, working at places where he felt he had plateaued. The very existence of mythical creatures such as mermaids, centaurs, and the ever-popular phoenix ash was secondary to him. He had never seen a narwhal before, but that did not mean they did not exist. Still, even after these months, Jude was continuously in awe of Sigur and what he had built.

The only fault of the phoenix was that it could not regenerate fast enough to create an additional number of dishes. Anything incorporated with the ashes brought a certain euphoria for the taste buds—one that was not quite addictive but filled the soul with a longing one never knew they had. The shifts at Yggdrasil were like clockwork. The crew arrived and watched as Sigur greeted the newly revived phoenix with the industrial lights and set it aflame, its shrieks of pain and horror no longer shocking for the staff. The sound of its torture became routine, like the dishwasher running or the oven declaring it had been preheated—sounds of a restaurant in full motion. Some of the servers would skip this ritual to get a head start on perfecting the look of their tables. Ashes collected, box closed, workers going home with thousands in their pockets on a Monday night. The mermaid and the centaur meat were still available but had become the reconciliatory option, still exalted, but now no longer "new."

It was in Autumn when Jude came in early for some prep work. He found the words *MUD MEN BUTCHERS* in scarlet ink written across Yggdrasil's oaken doors. Trails of red dripped from its carved branches.

"Mud men," Sigur said, spooking Jude. He was sitting on a bench on the patio, hunched over, as still as a boulder. He shook his head and stroked his beard. "We need to get this cleaned off. Wait here, Jude."

Sigur went into the restaurant and came out with a bucket of water and two sponges. Jude went to the door and began scrubbing alongside him. The brisk Icelandic air bit his soap-covered hand as he raised it above his head.

"Who could have done this?" Jude asked. "I didn't think we had any real competition."

"The mermaids," Sigur answered. "Mud men. It's what they call our people."

Jude paused. It was the first time Sigur had hinted at the ingredients referring to humans as a "people," which implied the inverse as well. It held as much computation as referring to pigs living in a democracy. Jude had spent so much time with their prepped tails that he had forgotten the initial shock of seeing the mermaids butchered and separated from their torsos in the prep kitchen, sometimes not entirely dead. When dealing with their tuna-like meat, it was almost impossible to picture a woman attached. Now knowing that Jude's species were callously referred to as "mud men" signified that mermaids not only had enough intelligence to communicate in English but were advanced enough to devise racial slurs. Who knew those twisted, bloodied lips underneath crooked and snapped noses could form words other than a magnetic Siren's Song from lore?

"What does this mean for us? Should we stop serving mermaids?"

Sigur re-soaped his sponge. "No. I have been serving them for over twenty years."

"Twenty years?"

Sigur nodded. "But I built Yggdrasil four years ago. This restaurant is my culinary church, built on mermaid meat."

Jude was silent. He thought of Sigur as a younger man, with a face less weathered, perhaps with streaks of blond instead of his silver-gray hair.

Sigur said, "Sometimes, the mermaids fight me. But this is as far as they go. Nothing but soundless threats. Icelandic mermaids are no different."

Jude suddenly became very cautious. Using words such as "us" and "them" only made him realize that an entire race of sentient beings hated Jude and his people. It frightened him, but he refused to let his resolve dwindle in Sigur's company. Yggdrasil was a foundation of Icelandic cuisine, internationally recognized. There was no way a collective of mermaids could muster a might as powerful as this restaurant. Sigur must have sensed this in his protégé because he patted Jude's shoulder with calloused hands. Jude thought this was meant to be reassuring but could not help but wonder how much restraint was behind Sigur's hands, how simply he could have broken a collarbone.

"This happens every once in a while," he said, cold eyes staring into Jude's, "but remember they are products. Much like the centaurs or our phoenix."

He went inside. Jude knew Sigur well enough to know that this was the end of the conversation.

Weeks went by, and the restaurant continued to boom. One night in the middle of a rush, Jude was interrupted from calling orders and orchestrating the back of the house. Cecile tapped him on the shoulder, her delicate fingers close to the base of his neck. She balanced a cleaned plate of what was once mermaid steak in one hand and gestured to the windows with the other. When she looked at Jude she looked over his shoulder. It was not the look of a busy worker; Cecile had an issue beyond the mental chaos of a restaurant during rush hour. For a second he wondered if she was going to ask him a question that would have put him in an awkward position; they had been passing glances for weeks.

"Cecile," Jude asked, "I can't go outside now."

"He's asking for you."

"He?" Jude sighed. "I don't have time for this. Get Sigur."

"Chef Sigur is asking for you."

She pointed to the dark abyss outside the restaurant, where the floor-to-ceiling windows were crusted on the perimeter from frost. The black bay looked like ichor, and underneath the kaleidoscopic aura of the famous Icelandic Harpa Opera House and the dancing green of the Northern Lights, the outside looked otherworldly and frightening. The warmth of the kitchen felt more like a blanket to Jude, and suddenly, in his forced comfort, he understood. He put down his rag and pen and made sure the kitchen was alright with their orders. He wiped sweat from his brow and headed out of the restaurant.

The mermaids' heads poked up like the shells of turtles skimming the cusp of a lake. Fiery scarlet strands and hair the color of the sun rose from the black water of the bay, which came to the bridge of their noses, almost so it seemed that the mermaids were stalking prey. If he did not know any better, he would have assumed it was just a group of bold women going for a swim in the frozen waters of Iceland. But he did know better. He knew the girth of their tails that waded to keep aloft in the water, the thick meat that could be tenderized to make the most delicate of fish steaks.

Sigur stood on the basalt in his chef scrubs. He gave Jude a sideways glance when they met at the shore. In typical Sigur fashion, his face was hardened and calloused. He showed no emotion, and when he stood to attention, he gave the impression of an immovable wall.

One of the mermaids spoke from underneath the water. It sounded like wind chimes, a running brook, wind on an open plateau. It was the most beautiful sound Jude had ever heard, and it sent shivers down his spine. A lump formed in his throat faster than he could recognize it, and his eyes began to sting with the advent of tears. It was a visceral reaction, a certain control of his body that he knew was not his own. Sigur had warned him of this once. Even when the fish were not trying for the Siren's Song, every time they opened their gills, it emitted just a little.

"You have received our warning," one of them said. Jude was unsure which one. "Yet, you continue to capture our sisters and consume us."

Sigur said, "I've been doing this for decades, and now you choose to meet me like this? On a Saturday night, when I am making my bread?"

"This savagery must stop, butcher. Your horrors have befallen the centaurs in the forests of Scandinavia. We have heard of you ripping the chicks of phoenixes from the United States. And we have heard of your plights against our sisters throughout the oceans. At first we thought you were a myth, but we see that you have brought your brutality to Iceland. Our children know your name, butcher. You have become the monster that keeps them awake at night."

Sigur remained stalwart. "This is a place of business. Do you harass and defile restaurants that sell lamb or cow?"

"It is not the same," she said.

"Is it not the duty of humans to act their part in the food chain? Do you not dine upon fellow creatures of the sea?"

Their eyes went wide. The water stirred. The blonde one looked at Jude, and he felt his knees buckle. She said to him, and only him,

"And what of this one? Tell me, young one, what would you do if we ate your children?"

Jude stammered, "I don't have children."

The blonde mermaid took a breath. When she spoke, her voice cracked. "And soon, neither will we."

The mermaid with scarlet hair turned her attention back to Sigur. "You have a decision to make, butcher. You end your actions, or we end your life. Make this decision for yourself, so we do not have to."

The mermaids drew their heads back into the water, diving with grace and poise. Their fish tails peeked out of the black lake, like a whale breaching and submerging. The scales were opalescent underneath the green aura of the Northern Lights and the dancing colors of the Harpa. A deft silence invaded by a sudden gust of chilled wind shook him to attention. Sigur looked to Jude, and Jude looked back.

"What are we going to do?" Jude asked.

"Get back to work. The restaurant needs us."

He stepped back, his spine upright, his posture unmoved. Jude looked for any change in his personality that would be caused by the mermaids' threats. He remained as stalwart as ever, like the roots of a resilient tree ignoring the heavy winds of a storm.

Their shoes crunched underneath the black rocks as they made their way from the docks to the back deck of the restaurant, closed due to the sudden drop in temperature. They walked past stacked chairs and cardboard boxes needing to be thrown out. Jude thought Yggdrasil looked particularly warm from the outside. The patrons ate and were merry, their bellies full of wine and delicacies. Flames from the fireplaces licked upward, and the servers moved with such grace they looked like ballerinas. Jude was about to reach for the door when Sigur stopped. Suddenly, he looked very old.

"It's not about the food chain," Sigur said. He gestured to the restaurant. "Although, if one wanted to be pragmatic, it could be. But it's not. It's about the art of cooking."

"But they can think, chef. They speak English."

"So do parrots," Sigur said.

"But parrots can only mimic English. These mermaids—"

"Fish."

"—*understand* English."

Sigur opened the door. The sounds of a busy restaurant flooded in: the clanking of cutlery and plates, the shouting of orders from the kitchen, the hustled communication of the servers as they nestled between the dichotomy of worlds between back and front of house.

"Does it matter?" Sigur said, looking back at him.

Jude returned his gaze to the lake. The mermaids' eyes swam into his consciousness before wading up to the forefront of his mind. It was as if they were still out there, watching him, waiting for his move. Although he could not place it, Jude knew he had been strung into something larger than himself, and that falling asleep with a belly full of Icelandic vodka would not stop their beautiful, haunting eyes from appearing to him in the morning.

"No," Jude said, entering the black rectangle of the hallway because the light had gone out and there was no need to fix it during summer. "No, I guess not."

Jude was settling into his life outside of Yggdrasil. He had found a favorite bar and coffee shop. He was beginning to know the residents of Reykjavik, and they were beginning to know him. The air was cleaner here, much crisper and fresher than the exhaust of New York City. He still was not as used to the quiet, the lapping of waves against the basalt, the smell of that freshly baked Rúgbrauð occupying tiny pockets near the Blue Lagoon.

One night, he got drunk with a couple of coworkers at a pub somewhere on the shopping street Laugavegur and ended the night in an isolated universe with Cecile, whom he had been catching eyes with all night, their movements through the back hallways growing ever closer. It had been long enough at Yggdrasil that Jude felt comfortable navigating whatever this relationship was. He no longer felt displaced, had achieved the respect of his colleagues and Sigur. Plus, Jude had not given himself time to stop and simply exist in this city. He was not getting younger.

Cecile's hair was a natural platinum blonde, and her eyes were as sharp and blue as ice caps. Dimples marked the corners of every flirtatious smile. Well drunk, and whilst leaning on one another outside the pub, Cecile came in for a kiss; without thinking, Jude turned away.

"What's wrong?" she asked.

"Nothing," Jude said.

They tried again and succeeded, but it was neither a passionate kiss nor a drunken one. It felt like nothing more than a handshake. Cecile leaned back, struck, wavering. They stood in a fusion of vodka from their breaths. When Jude looked back into her eyes, he saw the lake outside Yggdrasil again and felt the chill air come through his nostrils and out his mouth, the cusp of water ebbing at the bridges of the mermaid's noses as they watched, half-submerged under the ephemeral green of the Aurora Borealis.

Jude blinked, and he was outside the restaurant. It was three in the morning, and the cusp of sunlight, forever waiting at the horizon due to the curvature of the earth, watched him in his drunken haze. Jude could still smell Cecile's aura on him like a taunting phantom of what could have been, and he was sure his awkward getaway would be felt in the morning. Much like the pain of wounds setting in when the adrenaline ran dry after a dinner rush. He found himself sitting on the docks surrounded by the icy lake and the basalt rocks. He was not sure if he would ever look at fish or women the same way again.

Jude came into work the next day to do inventory. Working his way up from the dry storage to the freezers, he found himself at the end of his two-hour gauntlet of numbers and checking the ounces of ingredients in the basement. The heavy pounding of the butcher's room pierced Jude's eardrums even before he stepped down the musty stairs. It was rhythmic, almost like they were tenderizing a steak. He found his breathing getting heavy as he approached the door, and flashes of those dangling eyes with their lolling tongues swam to the forefront of his memory—the efficient *pop* of the bolt gun between their brows, bloodying their hair, each release a sophisticated machination into a sudden, swift death. That was when they became fish, for in death, as the butchers began the next phase of sawing their tails from their torsos, their faces looked a lot like caught trout.

He opened the door, and the thumping rattled his bones. It

required three men to hold their flailing bodies down and another to steady the bolt gun. Shrieks of horror from the little islands of steel accompanied the flailing of their tails. One by one, the mermaids would submit to the bolt gun and fall limp on the table, where the butchers would move to the next step of removing the tail from their torsos and tossing it into the black-lined garbage pail in the corner. Sigur simply referred to the mermaids' upper half as "bad meat" because the torsos could not filter the mercury in their body as efficiently as their tails, and he would be damned if he made a guest sick. The butchers moved like doctors performing amputations.

Jude stepped over a river of gore along the tiles and ignored the odorous miasma of blood and fish that thickened in the room. He walked to the stack of tails bundled with twine to prevent them from falling. Evidence of spinal cords stuck out like the ends of frayed knots. Counting the tails, he asked one of the butchers where the rest of the inventory was. The man pointed with a blood-stained hand to the pantry.

"Sigur usually does the inventory," he said.

"I'm doing it today," Jude answered.

He stepped over another pool of blood and ignored the screams of protest as the final mermaid attempted to claw her way out of her restraints before succumbing to a deft and final thump of the machine.

The pantry looked like any other in a restaurant: blocky, smelling of cardboard and tin, typical grade. Inside were four mermaids huddled together, arms wrapped around their breasts for warmth, tails curled up. Patches of loose flour gathered on their shining tails and at the edges of their lustrous hair. Blue lips exhumed and prayed in a language that Jude did not understand. They did not even react to him as he entered; they simply looked away, defeated. In the opening of the door, shrieks of another mermaid swept in and the mermaids started to whimper. Jude closed the door, muting the battering of their sisters. He was not sure if he was saving them or himself from the torment. He steadied himself and counted pounds of flour, ounces of phoenix ashes, boxes of cornmeal. He ignored their wavering breathing and they ignored him, although this mutual dynamic was particularly loud because it deafened the horrors beyond the freezer. He made his way about the room, stepping over boxes and tallying on his clipboard. The undying presence of the captured mermaids was thick and cold. Several times, he had gotten his counts wrong.

Jude tried to reason with himself that the mermaids knew they were going to die and that he himself was not slaughtering them. But this did not assuage the awkward guilt that gnawed into his soul. Finally, Jude went to the door and cut through the whimpers of the semolina-dusted mermaids. He looked over his shoulder, and they kept their gaze on the walls, on their huddled arms. Their tails wiggled as they adjusted their claustrophobic positions. Jude put down *four* in his counts.

With the door of the pantry closed behind him, Jude could swear he felt the tremors of their downtrodden and hopeless heartbeats at his back, although he knew there was no way for this to be true. It was their eyes that had shocked him, had become the catalyst for whatever feeling disoriented him. Such human eyes. But Jude had served beef and pork before, and this did not cause him discomfort. Instead, he told himself that the difference was obvious: he served *beef* but he was not a part of the butchery, had not passed the cow on its way down the queue to the bolt gun. Such a revelation would shock anyone, and Jude was not one of the butchers anyway. It was a privilege that Sigur trusted him with inventory, and it was a heavy burden.

The following weeks, Jude felt hollow. He would stay up late and wake up late, leaving only to go to work, which he had slowly begun to dread. His resistance to cook at Yggdrasil crept up on him, like a growing shadow underneath a rising sun. Jude got the suspicion that perhaps these gnawing feelings of discomfort were sourced from an anxiety that he had uprooted his life as a successful chef, in a Michelin New York City restaurant, for Sigur. He had abandoned his old life as fast as he had acquired this new one. This unnamable infraction upon his mind affected his work and invaded his dreams. He was not orchestrating the kitchen with as much proficiency as he had. Weekend rushes caused him as much stress as if he were new to the craft. He passed an opportunity to create a new phoenix ash dish onto a colleague, who was more than happy for the chance to impress Sigur, as Jude had once been.

Jude had the most difficulty serving the mermaid-inspired dishes, although he did not let Sigur notice his wavering passion, still cooking and conducting and creating with as much intensity as before. The weather was in transition from fall to winter, and the air was blistering, morning or night, when the sun hibernated and illuminated the sky for just four hours a day. They served blackened mermaid steaks with tomato remoulade, a side of Swiss chard tossed with olive oil, black pepper, and pine nuts, and diced butternut squash with rosemary and garlic. Sigur's architectural genius of this dish would normally have impressed Jude, but now he was relieved when people ordered the dish vegetarian.

Whenever he would plate the meal, he would recall crystalline eyes floating just above the cusp of the water. With the chilled lake at the bridges of their noses, they asked what he would do if they ate his children, and stupidly, Jude had answered that he had none. The image of the mermaids in the pantry, where no doubt a new group was waiting for their death even now, haunted his dreams and nearly pushed him to vegetarianism. Whenever he would see one of the guests who had paid seven hundred dollars for the dish, Jude would hear screams of their anguish and the forceful snapping of their bones, and the *pop* of the bolt gun as it punctured their temples…the walls of the restaurant began to close around him.

He waited for the dinner rush to subside before switching the orchestration to the line cooks. Under the excuse that he needed air, he stepped outside. Spheres bobbed in the distant, black ichor of the lake. He knew what they were. The mermaids watched him from beyond, protected by the geological miracle of the Northern Lights, gazing upon Jude for weeks as he slowly lost his ability to eat, to sleep, to fuck, to cook. He took off his chef's coat and tossed it on the rocks, where it lay like a dead animal, the frigid air intercepting him as if he had been tackled. Yet, the freedom from its weight forced the cold into submission. His face flushed; the sting of tears blossomed in the corner of his eyes.

"I'm sorry!" Jude yelled.

The mermaids bobbed in the water. They dipped down in unison and appeared faster than Jude could register. They floated before him, just offshore. It was the same distance as before. Their eyes peeked from the curtain of the lake; beautiful crystals adorned with hair the color of the sun, of the night sky, of snow-capped mountains.

Jude fell to his bottom, sitting like a shamed infant and feeling just the same. He picked up his chef's jacket and tossed it farther away, burying his head in his hands. He looked up from his knees and breathed in the cold tickle of Icelandic air.

When the mermaid spoke, the sound was not from the water; it was from the sky itself, bathed in a green aura, coming from the space in between the shore, the holes of each rock once carved by lava now flowing with a river of words. A cosmic echo reverberating into his soul. It was a variation of the Siren's Song, and Jude knew it.

"How many of us do you have? How many of our sisters are alive in that slaughterhouse of yours?"

Jude stammered, "Three, four? Last week it was four, but they are gone now. I'm sorry."

The mermaids stirred. They looked at one another, whispering. Jude heard them.

"Gone now."

"Our sisters."

"No more."

"Our future."

"Monsters."

They returned their attention to Jude, whose tears were now streaming down his face. His chest thumped with each silent sob.

One of them said, "On the morrow, this place will burn. See to it that you are not here."

"Please," Jude said, "please do it when the restaurant is closed. The workers here are innocent."

"None of you are," she said. "You humans are savage creatures, and your butcher does no favors for your kind. But you are not the worst of your ilk."

He suddenly felt more shame than he had thought possible, another blanket that warmed him from the frost-laden air. Between him, a sobbing schmuck, and Sigur the Butcher, these mermaids did not have a good representation of humankind. Then Jude thought of humanity's past wars, bombings, conquests. He felt the shame of a millennia of human evolution and history. He felt it for both him and Sigur because he knew that his mentor would not.

Jude looked away.

"But we will remain resilient, as we always have. We have existed before you and will after you, for we are a part of this world and its magic. We are a part of the primordial roots that your arrogance has made you blind to. You humans have a name for it, our Tree of Life, and you have committed the sacrilegious act of turning a fragment of its beauty into your front door. Tell me, what do you call it? Enlighten us to your bastardization."

Jude looked back at the restaurant, with its warm interior and white-clothed tables. He returned his gaze to the mermaids. "Yggdrasil."

"Yes."

"What do you call it?"

"Ψγγδϱασιλ."

The word was foreign to him, full of strange consonants and sounds that Jude could not even attempt to replicate with his own tongue. It was arcane, a word that he knew he would never hear again. It was one that he could barely comprehend the first time. The mermaids watched him struggle and finally sink into the rocks, aware of his own unimportance, embarrassed of his silence during the butchery of the mermaids.

"On the morrow," one of them said, "right before sunrise. The great council of Ψγγδϱασιλ has given approval."

Jude looked up from his knees. He nodded. The scalps of the mermaids dipped into the black water with great opalescent fins following immediately after, slapping the lake with a splash that echoed in the emptiness of the air. Jude wiped his tears and looked at the chef's coat, all ivory atop the shore of black rocks. He picked it up, felt its weight, and tossed it into the waters before heading back into the restaurant and telling the head waiter that he was going home.

Jude did not sleep that night. He attempted to get drunk at the pub but found his biology unable to submit to the numbing of alcohol. The burning slither of whiskey down his throat failed to warm him from the frosted temperatures outside, nor did it quell the pounding of his heart in his chest. Jude paid his tab and kept his head down, afraid of eye contact. The last time he had gazed into someone's eyes at the pub, he had proven impotent. He shuddered, recalling the mysterious feeling of the real Siren's Song, put on full blast, raping his psyche. Jude feared that their meeting this evening could have ended with him walking into the black waters, freezing his testicles off while they consumed him alive. He shuddered again, embarrassed that he would even think such thoughts when he had seen their anguish, their disappointment at the savagery of his species, of the brutality that forbade them from being something greater. Jude wanted to see the great hall within Yggdrasil—the real one. He wanted to see something beautiful, even though he himself was not, and the appropriation of the restaurant only managed to show him how far away from that beauty he was, that he was nothing short of insulting.

Jude found himself staring at his front door. It was four hours now until sunrise, and he knew that the mermaids would keep their promise. He tried to sleep but gave up almost as fast as his head hit the pillow. He started to pack, haphazardly throwing his clothes—most of which were white and covered with some resistant fleck of resin, sauce, or spice—into his suitcase. It was a funny thing, Jude thought. He had almost forgotten his suitcase existed, for it had turned into nothing more than hidden furniture in his closet. Suddenly, his time in Iceland felt like waking from a fever dream, or perhaps entering one. He was not sure. All he was certain of was that mermaids existed, and they would keep their promise. He was grateful they would not do it when the staff were working and was happy to keep his promise of the knowledge that there were no mermaids currently held in their prisons—currently. Jude paused, thinking of how every morning there seemed to be new mermaids in the fridge. This meant that Sigur might be there now, hefting their unconscious bodies over his shoulder and slamming them into the corner like limp cattle. He hurried out of the door.

It was two hours before sunrise, and Jude was out of breath as he reached Yggdrasil. He unlocked the door and made his way down the stairs, holding onto the wobbly banister and descending two at a time. He entered the butchery, where the tiles were permanently tinted red, resistant to the nightly power washing. The room looked mechanical, like a factory or an operating room. The metal tables, void of bones, gore, and battered flesh, reflected the industrial lamps above. The butcher's tools—mallet, tenderizer, cleaver, bone saw—had been positioned at the right side of each station, ready to be picked up for use in a couple of hours.

The cellar door was open. Jude became flushed both with relief that he had caught Sigur in time and fear that he would have to do something about it. Sigur came out of the pantry, humming an old sea shanty in a low, rumbling baritone, rubbing his hands on his pants, glittering flecks of tail and fin smearing on his denim.

"Jude?" Sigur said. His hulking frame took up the entire door. "What are you doing here this early?"

Jude swallowed the lump in his throat. "We need to get out of here."

Sigur almost growled. "We have to prepare for brunch—it's Sunday."

Jude steadied himself on one of the butcher's tables. He gathered the saliva in his mouth, afraid that his words might fail him. "The mermaids are going to burn this place at sunrise."

"The fish, you mean," Sigur said. "Let them try."

He began to walk away into the back and up the steps to the outside, where he kept his boat. Jude followed him, but not before glancing into the pantry. There were already four mermaids tangled around one another, unconscious, eyes fluttering. Usually, the stock was two to three, but on weekends, especially Sundays, they had more to accommodate the orders. Fucking Sunday brunch. Jude trailed after him, but Sigur paid him no mind. It was like telling an ocean liner to stop by voice alone. He watched Sigur reach into the bed of the boat and, with a heavy grimace, pull another mermaid up and over his shoulder, where he sauntered over the basalt and down the steps, all while Jude attempted to catch his attention. The strength of his mentor was impressive.

"Chef," Jude said, "we've got to stop. Call the staff. Tell them they need to find new jobs."

"Leave me, Jude. Come back in a couple of hours."

Sigur huffed and dropped another mermaid on her shoulder, where she rolled off the freezing flesh of her sisters and tumbled to the damp floor with a painful-sounding thump. As Sigur went to get the final mermaid, Jude stepped in front of the freezer, and suddenly, his six-foot frame felt dwarfed by his mentor's stalwart size. Sigur's hardened gaze, the gaze of a hunter, an artist, a dominator, fell upon Jude—it was a look of ire that Jude was always relieved to avoid.

"Chef," Jude said, "the mermaids are coming. We need to leave."

"If you don't get out of my way, we are going to have problems."

Jude shook his head. He looked past Sigur and saw the mermaids in captivity. "Only if you give up this fantasy of yours. Their threat is real."

"Fantasy?" Sigur grumbled. "I am a prodigy. I built this restaurant with my bare hands and have been cooking since you were learning to chew. This building, and everything it stands for, is art. My great design." He paused and bit his lower lip. The white bristles on his beard bent upward. "How do you know of this threat?"

"They told me."

Sigur put a heavy palm on Jude's shoulder. It felt like the paw of a bear and it surged with ferocious energy. It was different than when, many months ago, a lifetime ago, they had washed off the graffiti claiming Sigur and his staff were *MUD MEN BUTCHERS*, when Sigur spoke to him with a fatherly reassurance. Sigur pushed Jude aside as if he were a turnstile, and even though he tried to hold his ground, he was unable to resist his mentor's strength.

"You're fired," Sigur said. "Go back to the States."

"If you don't call off the staff, I will."

Sigur grit his teeth. "This is my livelihood, Jude. Yggdrasil is my legacy!"

Jude pointed to the mermaids freezing in the corner. The ones from before were starting to stir, flutter their eyes, rub their temples. "It's their livelihood too."

"They are just fish! Do you cry when we eat a leg of lamb? Do you get nightmares from slicing into a steak?"

"Not the same."

Sigur pushed Jude, slamming him against one of the butcher's tables. "It's almost sunrise. Get out of the restaurant." He shook his head, his face souring. "So much potential wasted."

He was right; wisps of sunrise were creeping in through the cellar door. The mermaids would be on their way, or perhaps they were already there, waiting from the cover of the lake. Jude felt behind him, grazing the cold steel of the table, the pedestal of so much brutality. "I'm disappointed in myself too. I'm sorry."

His fingers found their way to the handle of the tenderizing mallet, and in one swing that pulled out his shoulder, Jude slammed the spikes into Sigur's left temple. Sigur stumbled back, holding his face, his hands sticky with blood. He collected himself and charged at Jude, picking him up and slamming his spine on the table. The mallet fell to the floor. Flecks of spit and gore patterned on Jude as Sigur's knuckles crushed his nose, his right cheekbone. Sigur's eyes oscillated between the genius face and the madness lurking within, a brutal creature who used art as a façade to dominate the food chain. Sigur was a predator, a man who refused to become prey to anyone. He punched Jude again, splitting his brow, the force of his hairy knuckles thumping against the metal table. Swathes of black splashed across his vision. Sigur looked down at Jude from the butcher's table.

"Look at you," he said, clearing his face of the blood that ran down his cheek. "You're like one of them now, suspended on the table, half-conscious. Is this what you wanted? To be a fish?"

Jude looked up to the industrial lamps dangling from the ceiling. They looked like suns. He tried to speak.

"Let them come. You can burn with them."

Sigur's jaw dropped and he doubled over, knees buckling. Screams of anguish erupted into the room, and he fell onto the tiled floor. Jude blinked and wiped a spittle of blood that had fallen from his nose, threatening to drip into his mouth like a leaky faucet. To his right, a cascade of opalescence glimmered from the floor next to Sigur's fallen body. Jude turned and saw a mermaid lying on the floor. She held a bloodied bone saw in her hand and propped herself up with the other. They locked eyes, and they were the most beautiful eyes Jude had ever seen. She was the mermaid from the lake, who he'd spoken to. Sigur twitched and held his legs, roaring more in anger than from pain. She had cut his Achilles tendon with the saw, and while that was enough to stop him from murdering Jude, it was not enough to keep him at bay. Sigur roared, caught eyes with the mermaid, and kicked her in the nose with his heel. She doubled back, his strength enough to push her across the tiled floors by a couple of feet, where the back of her head hit the legs of one of the tables. Jude rolled off, his stomach hitting the floor, knocking the breath out of him. He found a bolt gun and struggled to his feet. Taking a deep breath, he dove and tackled Sigur, using the Viking's imbalance to drive him to the ground. With shaking hands, Jude positioned the bolt gun atop his mentor's forehead.

Pop.

The blazing fire in Sigur's eyes went out like a candle in the wind, his head rolling to one side.

Jude dropped the bolt gun and held his chest, heaving over Sigur's lifeless body. He spat some blood on the floor and steadied himself. Sunlight crept through, stretching from the rectangle of the cellar door. The mermaids would keep their promise, Jude understood that. He wanted them to. He stood up, his shoes scraping along the blood that dripped from Sigur's split heel, and picked up the mermaid who still clutched the bone saw in her unconscious hands. She was heavy, but Jude did his best to be tender with her.

Even with a broken nose, she was beautiful. Her red hair fell like drapes and felt like silk on his arm, her tail glittering underneath the rising sun. He walked to the lake, past Sigur's boat, and laid her down on the shore, making sure her head was not in an uncomfortable position among the rocks. He looked at the lake and did not see any heads bobbing in the distance, but he knew he was running out of time. Jude stood and went into the pantry, picked up each mermaid one by one, and limped his way to the shore, setting the mermaids up next to one another. Hopefully, when they woke, they would not be as frightened because they were together. It was then that the mermaids appeared, twenty of them. They watched Jude from the water.

"Please," Jude said. He gestured to the mermaids on the shore and gave them a hard look to communicate that he had just saved them. "Five minutes. I beg you."

The mermaid in the front looked at her sisters lying on the shore then nodded.

Jude went one final time to the pantry to confirm that he had gotten them all and closed the door. Pain was starting to settle in. The strikes of Sigur's brutality were as thick as the blood that painted his face. His muscles were sore from carrying the unconscious bodies of the mermaids. He stepped over the mallet, the bone saw, Sigur's corpse. He pulled out his phone and dialed the assistant managers, telling them that the restaurant was closed for sudden renovations and that he himself was frustrated with Sigur's lack of communication. He called Cecile personally. It was too much to tell them that Yggdrasil would soon be set aflame, and quite frankly, Jude reasoned that the mystery would be enough to keep their sanity and careers intact. He went into the kitchen and turned on the burners one by one as he made his way to the back door, limping, trailing a footprint of Sigur's blood on the carpet with every step.

The mermaids were where he had left them, thirty feet from the shore. The sun had leveled above the clouds now, casting the sky with a delicate white, turning the reflective exterior of the Harpa into fractals of orange and gold across the bay. He was on their time now, and even though their patience came as a gift for his deeds of saving their sisters, he knew his time was limited. The mermaids stared at him from across the water, their faces half-buried at the bridge of the nose. The group had thinned, and Jude understood that, soon, everything around him would be engulfed in flames.

Jude paused. He limped back into the kitchen, past his keys, past the stacks of pots and pans and perfectly sharpened knives that would soon melt into oblivion. He went into the stockroom and swept boxes of flour and spaghetti onto the floor, revealing a faint whisper of a gray, iron box in the back. Jude cradled the container and went back into the butchery, where Sigur lay motionless at the foot of the table.

"Please, two more minutes, two more minutes," Jude pleaded.

He put the box on a counter and opened it to a groggy chirp. The phoenix, more scarlet than the lick of a flame, popped its head out of the ashes that made up its nest, blinking at the sudden disturbance. It was just a chick, and even though Jude was certain it would survive the fire, he was positive it would starve in its metal coffin, or someone as vile as Sigur would find it. The phoenix chick chirped and shook the ashes from its feathers. A certain heat radiated from the box, like having his hand near a stove. He took the box in the crook of his arm and made his way to the cellar door, stopping when he passed an empty mason jar. Jude placed the phoenix on the table, its galactic eyes staring up at him with innocent curiosity, naïve and stupid to the horrors its past lives had been subjected to. Jude shoved some of the ashes into the jar and fastened it tight until his muscles started to hurt. He put the jar in his pocket and limped out of the cellar with the phoenix in his arms, careful not to shake the box too much with his uneven steps. The mermaids were gone. Jude placed the phoenix's box next to the unconscious mermaids, nestling it in between a tiny pit of rocks so it would remain steady for the chick. Perhaps it might even fall back asleep amid all the chaos that would surely ensue.

Jude stood up, brushed himself off, and ignored the pain creeping up on his body. He passed Sigur's boat and gave a fleeting glance at the mermaids and phoenix resting on the shore, their faces so graceful, their tails the color of stars. He looked back at Yggdrasil and turned away, knowing that he would never get the opportunity to walk this way again, to open those golden carved doors shaped to mimic the Tree of Life.

Jude rested on a chair with an icepack on his forehead and fresh bandages on his body. The word of the fire of the great and famous Yggdrasil restaurant of Reykjavik, Iceland, spread as fast as the flames that had burned it to the ground. Sigur's charred remains were easily identified, and it helped that his boat was parked on the shore. When pressed for details, some of the interviewed staff were candid about their suspicions that Sigur's alcoholism had locked away some inner demons and that perhaps the stresses of his lifestyle had finally broken him.

Jude drank tea with some of the phoenix ashes. It tasted almost like a hot toddy. He slept long and good, and the next morning, all his wounds were either healed or had been reduced to light bruises. He took the flight back to New York City the next morning, and when he got off the plane and into the once familiar smog and swears that permeated the Big Apple, he took himself out to lunch before heading into the sublet somewhere in the realm of Bushwick.

He ordered a salad and wondered if his life in Iceland had been a dream or a nightmare. He decided it was both. They were a part of a bigger world, one beyond the realms and perceptions of humans, and even though Jude admitted that he had learned a lot from the monstrous Sigur Edmunson, he would never compromise for his craft. There were better ways to master a passion, though Jude did not exactly know how. Still, as he looked out to the graffitied canvas of New York City, he felt he had returned home, one step closer to becoming the chef he was meant to be.

AUNTIE_LENA314

WRITTEN BY
MOLLY THYNES

THERE USED to be a video channel online. It was called Auntie_lena314. The videos had long since been taken down and even the channel as a whole was blocked.

She posted her first video on May 27. For the first ten seconds, you saw just a teenage girl with sun-bleached hair in a pink cardigan fiddling with the webcam, showing just how inexperienced she was with creating web videos.

"Hello, world! My name is Auntie Lena," she said as she took a seat in the desk chair.

She told the viewers that this wasn't going to be a video channel about boy bands or makeup. Her voice squealing, she told everyone how her nephew, Henry, had just been born yesterday. She created this channel to document the earliest moments of his life.

She was especially excited because her sister, Nan, was going to be moving back home with Henry. She wouldn't be able to keep a baby in the dorms.

"Nan's not too thrilled about moving back home, but at least it's rent-free and she'll have a place to live."

Auntie Lena promised to post a video every few days. She talked about how adorable her nephew was, how she was sure she saw him smile at her. She would film little Henry in the different outfits that relatives sent, chubby and pink with a few strands of almost-red hair. In some of the videos, she appeared with dark circles under her eyes, saying little Henry had kept her up all night crying, or he was struggling with a particularly bad bout of colic. But for the most part, they stayed boring little mundane videos in Nan's little room, and the views never climbed above thirty.

Then, on June 13, she posted a video where she was fidgeting, biting her lip, her hands clenching the seat of her chair. She told the viewers about her sister, Nan. She was refusing to change Henry or feed him, and for the last three days, she hadn't changed her clothes or brushed her hair.

"I've been doing a lot of reading online," Auntie Lena said, her eyes avoiding the camera. "I think Nan might have postpartum depression. I might not be putting up a new video for a few days, because I want to do some more reading about this."

But on June 16, things seemed to be getting worse. Auntie Lena started the video by thanking all her viewers for the articles they had sent on postpartum depression.

"But Nan's been getting worse," Auntie Lena said, holding the camera in front of her face as she walked down the hallway.

When Auntie Lena turned the camera around, she was standing in the doorway to Nan's bedroom. In the center of the room, Nan stood with slumped shoulders, dressed in wrinkled, damp pajamas, her hair stringy and oily. As Auntie Lena moved closer to her sister, you could see that Nan was standing over the baby's bassinet.

"Nan?" Auntie Lena asked as she moved to film her sister's face. "Nan, will you say something to me?"

As Nan's face came into profile, you could just make out her lips moving as she looked down at her baby. If you had your headphones on and the volume turned all the way up, you could just barely hear Nan's words.

"Not mine...he's not my baby...how does no one else notice?"

Auntie Lena spent almost a minute trying to get her sister's attention, even shoving the camera right into her sister's face, but Nan didn't so much as look away or tell her sister to leave her alone. Eventually, Auntie Lena gave up and returned to her room. She set the camera back on top of the computer and settled into her chair once again.

"She's been like this for days. I don't mean just the not taking care of herself or Henry. She's saying all these weird things about how Henry's not her baby. I know that women with postpartum depression say they feel a disconnect from their babies, but this just seems...off."

Reaching off to the side, Auntie Lena grabbed a few sheets of printed paper.

"One of the things I came across in these articles is this thing called postpartum psychosis. Maybe that's what happening, but I don't know. Mom and Dad are trying to get Nan in to see a doctor. I hope it happens soon."

Then, on June 18, anyone who was awake in the middle of the night saw a...disturbing new upload to Auntie Lena's channel. The video opened to pitch black with Auntie Lena fumbling with the camera, as though she was just waking up and trying to remember how to turn it on.

"Do you hear that?"

In the dark frame, you could just make out the outline of Auntie Lena's face, but this wasn't a camera with a night vision function, so pretty much all you had to go on was the audio. You could hear the *rustle rustle* as Auntie Lena kicked off the sheets and climbed out of bed, the soft sound of her bare feet as she ventured out into the hallway.

Finally, you were able to see some light coming from the crack under a door.

"Nan? Are you up?"

Auntie Lena opened the door and held up the camera to show Nan once again standing over Henry's bassinet. In one hand, she was gripping a box of matches. Then the camera picked up a bright flash of light as Nan struck a match and dangled it over the bassinet.

"DAD!" Auntie Lena shrieked as she leaned out into the hallway. From the furthest door down, a silver-haired man bolted out into the hall, nearly crashing into Auntie Lena.

"Nan, don't!"

Their father rushed into the room, pushing Nan away from the baby, grabbing tight around her wrist until his knuckles turned white. Nan lost her grip on the match, sending it flying toward the curtains. Flames raced along the bottom hem, and climbed upward toward the ceiling.

In the struggle, Auntie Lena rushed into the bathroom, pulling a bucket from under the sink. As she filled it with water, you could hear Nan scream from the other room. "It has to die! It has to be burned!"

Running back to the room, she tossed the camera onto the bed. The frame went sideways, but showed Auntie Lena splashing water onto the fire while Nan struggled with everything she had to get away from her father, who was using the whole of his body weight to keep her pinned to the floor.

"Paul, what's happened?" a woman shouted from outside the frame.

"Janet, call 911!"

Auntie Lena managed to put out the fire and looked back toward the bed, as though she had just remembered she had left the camera running. Shooting past her father and sister, she reached for it and the video came to an end.

Why she even posted a video like that, none of her viewers were able to figure out. The host site did have a function where you could stream live video from your camera directly to the site, so Auntie Lena probably had no idea what she was about to walk into. People were trading different theories back and forth in the comment section of her other videos almost immediately after it happened.

On June 19, Auntie Lena appeared on camera, white as a bedsheet.

"Nan's gone."

After Auntie Lena had cut off the video footage, the police came to the house. Even in the presence of men with guns, Nan refused to stop fighting or insisting that her baby had to die. It took both of them to force Nan out of the room and out of the house.

"We just got an update this morning."

Nan was being transferred from the jail to a psychiatric hospital. They were trying a bunch of different medications, but Nan would be staying there until the County Attorney decided what to do with her.

On June 25, little Henry appeared for the first time on camera. Auntie Lena explained that with Nan away, she had to step up and take over a lot of the care of her nephew.

"At least it's summer vacation. Health class was right when they said high school kids aren't meant to raise children."

You see, little Henry was not an easy baby to take care of. He would cry at all hours of the night, and for most of the daytime hours too. He had been difficult to breastfeed, but he wasn't taking to the bottle any better. His skin was loose and it didn't have that baby-soft feel that people went on and on about, and it even seemed to be taking on a blueish-gray color. And Auntie Lena was terrified that the baby was going to starve.

On some level, the more Auntie Lena talked about Henry, the easier it was to see how her sister could have lost her mind taking care of him.

On June 27, Lena appeared on camera with dark circles under her eyes. She was holding her head in her hand, twisting her hair around her fingers.

"I'm wondering…is it possible for babies to go insane? Because I think that's what's happening to Henry."

She said Henry was becoming much more than just a fussy baby. He still cried as much as ever, but the cries themselves had begun taking on an entirely different, more distressing tone. Not the cry of a baby, but…

Auntie Lena listed off everything that reminded her more of Henry's cries. Someone who had had their hand slammed in the door, someone who had a cigar put out on their thigh, a cat having its tail sawed off. The cries of someone who suffered agonizing pain just from existing.

Auntie Lena struggled to detail everything that was happening. She was slumped in her chair, struggling to keep eye contact with the camera. Whenever she did manage to look her viewers in the eyes, you could see the dull luster both her eyes and her skin were taking on.

"What he needs right now is his mom, but Nan isn't going to be coming back for a long time."

For several days, no new videos were posted on Auntie Lena's channel. Instead, she set up a live video feed right in front of Henry's bassinet. On the first night, Auntie Lena got in front of the camera and told the viewers she was going to learn what was happening at night once and for all.

For three nights, nothing happened. Like Auntie Lena said, Henry would cry at all hours of the night. But then on the fourth night, everyone up at three in the morning got to see one of the "crazy fits" Auntie Lena was talking about. From the slanted angle, you watched Henry shake, just a little bit, then begin screaming the most ungodly scream. It didn't stop there. The baby began convulsing, his head bending backward, pushing his little chest upward.

Finally, it all ended with a fit so violent that Henry propelled himself out of the bassinet, where he just laid limp and crying until Auntie Lena stumbled into the scene.

After the live feed, Auntie Lena didn't post anything for over a week. And with the view count on her videos skyrocketing, the comment section began piling up.

Make another video, crazy girl.

Fakey fake fake.

When do we get to see the demon baby again?

On July 1, Auntie Lena appeared on camera once again. For the first several seconds of the video, she did not look at the camera. Her hair was lank, stringy, and unwashed. She was still wearing her pajamas, and from the wrinkles and the stains, she had clearly been wearing them for days.

"Well, you've all seen the livestream of Henry. I've seen it too. I'm...just not sure what it was I saw."

Of course, she told her viewers, she had shown the video of what happened to her parents. Horrified, they took little Henry straight to the doctor. Every test the tiny county clinic performed on him turned up nothing.

"The doctors actually saw the exact same tape you all saw, but even they don't know what's happening right now."

The family would have to take Henry to a larger hospital two hours away if they wanted any kind of medical answers.

On July 5, Auntie Lena posted another video in what felt like a much more eerily quiet house. In her more recent videos, no matter how faint, you could usually make out Henry crying from somewhere in the background, or Auntie Lena's parents pacing the halls back and forth, walking him, rocking him, trying to calm him down. But today, it was just Auntie Lena, her and a book with a blue quilted cover she held in her lap as she played with the fringes along the edge.

"Mom and Dad drove Henry out to the hospital yesterday. The doctors want scans of his brain."

Auntie Lena had chosen to stay behind.

"Please don't send me any more messages. I'm not really interested in what strangers think anymore."

Auntie Lena held the quilted book up against her chest. Still brand new, the tiny details, like the bright-yellow ducks or white airplanes, stood out brightly.

"Besides," she said as she opened the book, "I think I have everything I need right here."

Auntie Lena confessed that she had gone snooping through Nan's room and, shoved underneath the mattress, she found the baby book Nan had bought for Henry. Auntie Lena held it up to the camera. It showed the first photo taken of him at the hospital, the little card that had been on his crib, his hospital bracelet, his little black ink footprints. All the cute little mementos mothers saved after their children were born.

"But here's where it starts getting strange."

She flipped three pages forward, and that's where the actual baby book ended. Instead, the next several pages were filled with writing. Lists, paragraphs, small and large letters filling up the pages from margin to margin. Between that and how Auntie Lena had found it under her sister's mattress, the thing read more like a serial killer manifesto than a baby book. People said as much in the comments.

"Nan wrote all this," Auntie Lena told her viewers. "Let me read some of it to you."

She opened the book. At first, Nan's writing was simply a mirror of what Auntie Lena had been recording in her videos. Henry wouldn't feed; Henry was colicky and fussy. And because of it all, his skin was losing its softness, and his fine little strands of hair were turning sticky and clumping together.

Then came an entry about a horrific nightmare Nan had one night.

"*The entire house was on fire. Somehow, I was managing to avoid all the flames, but then I saw Lena stagger from around the corner, completely engulfed. Lena ran for Henry's bassinet. Then she picked him up in her arms while she was still on fire, and he started to shriek as Lena's flames spread to him.*"

But what was truly terrifying was everything that happened after.

"Even after I woke up, the screams followed me into the waking world. But eventually I realized that the screams were coming from Henry, the sort of sounds a person could only make as the flesh was charred from their bones.

"Since that nightmare, I haven't been able to sleep at night." With all Henry's crying, he never let Nan sleep for more than a few hours at a time anyway.

So instead, Nan would stay up at night, just watching her baby and detailing everything she saw in Henry's little baby book.

She made note of every one of Henry's horrific cries, comparing each one to some horrific pain that could be inflicted on a human being, just as Auntie Lena had done when she first started detailing Henry's disturbing behaviors, before she knew her sister was doing the exact same thing.

"Doctors are always so quick to write off a young, hysterical mother."

The rest of what Auntie Lena read were Nan's speculation on just what could be wrong with her baby. It started off with some fairly mundane guesses—*she wasn't feeding him enough, he had some kind of disease from birth that the doctors missed*—gradually becoming more fantastic—*he had picked up some tropical fungus from the gifts from relatives in Florida*—and horrifying—*someone was poisoning him*—on and on and on.

"Eventually, she just starts writing this same word over and over again," Auntie Lena said, finally looking up at the camera. "Changeling."

After that video, Auntie Lena became much more faithful about weekly postings; most weeks, she posted two or three times. But by now, she had chosen to go in a different creative direction with her channel. Instead of Auntie Lena sitting at her desk in her bedroom, these videos all featured Henry. Gone were the adorable, Facebook-worthy videos, and in their place was something more out of a horror movie. Henry's skin had turned a sickly yellow-gray. His face, his arms, his chest displayed all these crater-like lesions: deep, but none of them were scabbed or bleeding.

In one video, little Henry was on his stomach, lying on the floor, the camera propped up right in front of him. He was bawling his same jarring cry. Auntie Lena's feet paced back and forth behind him across the frame. This went on for about thirty seconds until it was just Henry alone in the shot.

And then...*crash*! A glass pitcher dropped to the floor, right in front of the baby. Shards of glass flew through the air, a few across the baby's face, slicing open his left cheek. Blood poured from the cuts, but that wasn't what people reacted to most in the video. It was Henry's silence—the first silence the viewers had ever heard from the baby. Face still smeared with tears and snot and blood, the baby just stared out at the broken glass, completely transfixed.

That's where the video cut out.

At this point, the comment section exploded with people saying they were reporting her channel, that they were calling the police.

Auntie Lena finally addressed these comments on July 30. For that video, she went back to her old format of her sitting in her room in front of her computer.

"I've been reading all your comments." Auntie Lena's voice was flat. "You can show these videos to the police, but they probably won't believe any of this is real. Nothing I've filmed is anything a baby should be capable of."

She reached for some wrinkled papers on the desk. "And that's exactly what I wanted to show all of you."

With her one free hand, Auntie Lena shifted the camera left, bringing into view the blue bassinet Henry slept in, in her bedroom.

"Nan suspected and she did her best to get the proof." Now Auntie Lena reached for the same baby book she had shown her viewers before. "But I think I finally managed, with these videos, to show that there is absolutely no doubt."

She looked over her shoulder and pointed to the bassinet.

"Henry, the baby you've all been seeing, is not Henry."

Settling back into her seat, Auntie Lena opened the baby book and began flipping through the pages, frantic to the point where she was nearly ripping them.

"In the last parts of Nan's writing, she starts talking a lot about this thing called a changeling," she said. "Babies are taken and replaced with...spirits, demons, or just enchanted objects."

In the background, you could make out the very faintest whimpers and stirring from the bassinet. Auntie Lena ignored them.

"I'm not quite sure when it happened, Nan wasn't really clear on that, but Henry was taken and replaced by that...thing."

Auntie Lena reached over to the side of the desk and held up a stack of wrinkled computer printouts. "Everything I've read says that very often, babies who were disabled or deformed were accused of being changelings, but there are a few ways to know if your baby has truly been taken.

"They cry relentlessly and nothing can console them. Things that normally terrify babies make changelings laugh, or at the very least, stop crying for a few minutes. They are capable of physical feats that human infants are not. And as time passes, they gradually become less and less human-looking."

As if to emphasize this last point, Auntie Lena picked up the camera and carried it over to peer inside the bassinet. Henry lay inside, rasping and jerking unnaturally, like someone on the edges of death.

She turned the camera back to face herself. "There are ways to get rid of a changeling, and some of them even force whoever took your baby to bring it back.

"But..." Auntie Lena looked away, suddenly avoiding eye contact with the camera. "I'm ready to start taking your messages again. If any of you have heard stories about changelings, anything you wouldn't find on the internet, please tell me. There...aren't a lot of good options I've come across so far."

It was this video that brought all the crazies out. People claiming to be paranormal investigators or cryptozoologists in their comments began listing all the gruesome ways Irish peasants would rid themselves of monsters they thought had replaced their children. That's when Auntie Lena's viewers, who had been there from the beginning, began shouting back.

What the hell do you think you're doing?!?!?!

Have you been watching this girl? She's cray-cray!!!

Stop pushing her! This girl's gonna snap! Don't give her ideas!

Then, Auntie Lena posted what would be her last video.

On July 31, she set up another special livestream, opening in the family kitchen. As Auntie Lena adjusted the camera, you could see Henry lying behind her. The room was dark, lit only by the streetlamps outside and the blue light of the moon.

"Thank you all for joining me tonight. Mom and Dad are out… again. To be honest, they really haven't been home much at all lately."

When Auntie Lena moved away from the camera, you could see a large pot on the stove, the kind people used to cook lobster.

"Well, even though it's only been a day, I've received a lot of messages from all of you. But only a few of them were about changelings. Unfortunately, with a few rare exceptions, you don't seem to know much more about changelings than I do."

In the comment section to the right of the video, all of the previous 'experts' were notably absent. Only Auntie Lena's gathering of loyal followers were there, typing a slow trickle of messages, all repeating different variations of asking her just what was going on.

"There are a lot of ways to find out if there is a changeling in your home, but I've only found two ways of driving one out.

"One is with water, submerging the creature," Auntie Lena said, placing a lid over the large pot. "The other is with fire."

She turned the dial on the gas stove and blue flames shot up from the burner.

"Both are supposed to drive the changeling out of your home," she said, bending down to pick up Henry. "Tonight's going to be a very special episode, because we're going to be testing both at once."

Auntie Lena, with her back to the camera, walked toward the counter. For once, the baby's constant cries had quieted to a few soft whimpers. Auntie Lena bounced him up and down until clear strings of steam rose from up under the lid of the pot on the stove. As the rapid bubbling and bursting noises of the boiling water overpowered the hissing of the gas, the comments starting coming through faster and more frantically.

Auntie Lena, what are you doing?!?!
Someone call 911!!!
How?!?! We don't know where she is!!!!!!
Does anyone know how to track the stream?
Lena!!! Don't do something you can't take back!!!!

Auntie Lena lifted the lid from the pot and looked over her shoulder, staring directly into the camera. "You've all seen what I've seen, so you know why I have to do this."

Auntie Lena maneuvered Henry away from her hip, dangling him above the boiling pot. Henry showed no awareness for his surroundings, or of what his aunt was about to do to him; he simply stared blankly out ahead of him, legs hanging limp. Then, Auntie Lena simply dropped him right into the boiling water.

Water splashed and spilled over the stove and onto the countertops, splashing onto Auntie Lena as well. But instead of screaming, like anyone else would have, Auntie Lena slammed the lid of the pot, holding it tightly in place.

The most horrible shrieks you ever heard came from within that pot, which was shaking so violently, Auntie Lena had to stand with the whole of her body weight over the lid just to keep the pot over the burner.

When it finally stopped, Auntie Lena sank to the floor. The previous comments all went dead quiet as silence overtook the kitchen. Then, Auntie Lena reached into her pocket and pulled out her cellphone.

"Hello...my nephew is dead. No, I haven't checked his pulse or done any of that. Because I know he's dead. Because I burned him in a pot. You should send someone here."

For several moments, Auntie Lena just stared up at the ceiling. Eventually, her head tilted slowly down until her eyes stared directly into the camera.

"I told you all this was going to be a very special episode."

Finally, from outside the view of the camera, there came a loud banging on the door. Auntie Lena got up from the floor and picked up the camera.

"Police! Open the door!"

"It's not locked."

The off-screen door flew open and crashed against the wall, and two officers—both young men—entered the frame: Officer Regis and Officer Jamison, from the names on their badges.

"Where's the baby?"

The camera turned toward the steaming pot and showed Auntie Lena pointing toward it.

Officer Regis rushed toward the stove, with Officer Jamison right after him, even though there was no chance of saving the baby after it had been boiling for so long.

"I had to do it. We don't have a fireplace and this was the next best thing."

Officer Regis grabbed the pot off the stove with his bare hands and dumped it into the sink, the whole time shouting as the scalding metal burned his hands and the water spattered over his wrists.

Officer Jamison pulled out his flashlight to examine his partner's bright-red skin.

The injured officer groaned as the water gurgled down the sink. Clearly, neither of them were listening to Auntie Lena, but still, she continued to explain herself.

"He wasn't a real baby, you see. Whatever it was, we've had it here for weeks, and I spent the whole time trying to figure out what to do with it. I don't know how long it will take to get the real baby back."

"There's no baby here."

"What?" Auntie Lena shrieked, running to the sink, taking the camera with her. Inside, instead of the horror there should have been—boiled flesh—you saw bits of wood, pebbles, and pieces of broken porcelain, the color bleached out of it all by the boiling water.

"Miss," Officer Regis said, his voice pained and his whole body shaking, "where is your nephew?"

"I told you, he's dead and I killed him! He's in that pot!"

Officer Jamison reached for his radio and called out, "We need backup. We have a missing child and a possible EDP."

"Where did he go?" The camera swung back and forth as Auntie

Lena searched frantically for whatever it was she had just boiled alive. "Do they just disappear after you burn them?"

"Miss, give me the camera."

Officer Regis reached his blistered hand, with its weeping sores, into view of the camera as he fought Auntie Lena for the device. She fought and screamed, and the camera shook and the audio cracked before it went crashing to the ground.

That's where the video cut out.

The next day, Auntie_lena314 was scrubbed from the host site. I'm sure the police would have been very interested to see what Auntie Lena had been documenting in the first few weeks of her nephew's life, but the host site certainly had good reason not to hand over those recordings which were, essentially, video evidence of a girl slowly going mad and them doing nothing to stop it. But with no actual video, witness statements were worthless.

It also did nothing to tell Auntie Lena's loyal viewers just what happened to her. But if you knew what to type into a search engine, you were still able to follow what happened to her. In rural New York, a fifteen-year-old Lena McCannon was arrested in connection with the disappearance of her nephew, Henry. She insisted she had killed the baby, boiling it alive, but was never able to produce a body. In a hearing, she was deemed incompetent to stand trial. She now resides in the same psychiatric hospital as her sister, Nan, until such time as she is deemed fit to proceed.

The Rockland County Sheriff's Office asks that anyone who has any information about the whereabouts of Henry McCannon to please contact them.

THE BLUE GHOST

WRITTEN BY
TAIJA MORGAN

MARJORIE LIDDELL HAD NEVER SEEN a ghost, but she wanted to more than anything in the world. She tried to sit patiently, but her heart thrummed beneath the starchy white fabric of her dress.

A stout lady with flowing gray locks placed three tarot cards on the table in front of her.

Marjorie wiped her clammy palms on her skirt beneath the tablecloth. The warm, sugary scents of popcorn and candyfloss from the bustling fair beyond the tent flaps permeated every surface. Her gaze lifted to the woman's light-gray eyes, so like Marjorie's father's, and that had to mean something, didn't it? Surely, it was a sign.

"This is your first time," Madame Josephine stated. Not a question, but a comment. Already, this fortune teller could read her. The woman's spindly fingers touched an amulet that adorned her collarbone, a golden pendant shaped like an eye. Her red lips pursed. "And your last."

Marjorie leaned forward. "My last?"

The woman waved a bejeweled hand. "We start with the cards."

"But I only—"

"The cards," the woman said. "Your future. Every young lady wants to know her future."

Marjorie looked away. Her short nails dug crescent moons into her palms as she clutched her hands in her lap. This wasn't what she came here for. She could think of nothing more irrelevant than the future.

"Go ahead, dearie. Flip the cards."

Marjorie's long fingers brushed across the tabletop, then stilled. "Myself?"

The woman nodded. *Charlatan*, Marjorie's father would have called her. He'd be so ashamed to see his only daughter huddled here in this dark tent, surrounded by guttering candles and shiny occult statues. His staunch Catholic upbringing would never have allowed it. But what choice did she have?

Marjorie reached for the first card and flipped it over. It was upside down. *XVIIII* inscribed the top, while the bottom said *Le Soleil*. Two figures stood beneath a blazing sun.

She remembered her own surprise upon seeing the open casket, the slack face within usually so expressive. *How dark he'd gotten*, she'd thought at the time. She'd expected him to be pale in death, the way she'd seen others. But his skin had held the red-brown tinge of sunburn, and she'd imagined the sun beating down upon his back, his uniform soaked through with sweat as he crawled through the dirt. The artillery fire would have been deafening. And how had his face been burned so? Maybe only after hours of lying on his back in the field, bleeding out into the parched earth in his final moments, skin sizzling under the open sky. Marjorie shivered, chilled.

"The Sun card, reversed." Madame Josephine sighed. "Much sadness has enveloped you in your young life. So true of many during the war." She reached out and patted the back of Marjorie's hand. "Your future shows darkness."

Marjorie pulled back, her azure eyes wide. "Darkness?"

Madame Josephine didn't elaborate. "Next."

Taking a breath, Marjorie flipped the second thick, worn card. Its surface was grimy at the edges from a thousand other fingers touching their futures. This, too, she viewed upside down. *XXI, Le Monde*. A small figure stood in an oval. An angel, an eagle, a bull, and a lion filled the four corners.

"The World. Also in reverse," Madame Josephine said.

Yes, Marjorie thought, *the world*. A hungry place with sharp teeth. Cold and insatiable. It was the world that took her father from her. It took, and took, and always demanded more. For God, for country. For the mercurial will of those who controlled it. But she would forgive it all for just one more moment with him, to know that this world wasn't *all* there was.

Marjorie glanced up, meeting the woman's cloudy gray eyes. She wondered for a moment if she were blind—if she couldn't see the cards at all, but rather could *see them*. And if so, what else could the woman see?

Madame Josephine frowned, the action pulling her sagging jowls. "In reverse, it speaks of incompletion. Unfinished business. A lack of closure."

Marjorie gasped. "Yes. Yes, that's exactly it. No closure. That's why I—"

"This reading pertains to your future, dearie. It is what you can expect, not what you are already familiar with."

Sitting back in the uncomfortable wooden chair, Marjorie twisted a long curl of black hair between her fingers. Her mouth was dry, an earthy flavor lingering at the back of her throat. "Are you saying I'll never have closure?"

"The next card, dearie. The last card."

With a huff, Marjorie flipped it over. Like the other two, it faced away from her. X, *La Roue De Fortune*. A wheel surrounded by winged creatures.

Madame Josephine sucked air between her teeth. "The Wheel of Fortune in reverse. Bad luck, dearie." She pulled the cards back, shuffling them into her deck.

Bad luck? What did that even mean? It didn't seem fair. Three bad draws after she'd paid good money for this vague and disheartening insight. "I didn't come to see my future."

"No. You came to see your past. But there is no going back. The past is gone."

Marjorie blinked back tears. "That's not true. He can't be gone. My father—"

"He died in the war."

"Yes!" Marjorie straightened, looking around the dim tent. The shadows seemed to writhe with the possibility of life—life after death. Was he here with them now? Could he see her? Was he trying to speak?

"Everyone has lost family in the war. Every young lady who comes in here. Fathers, brothers, sons, husbands, beaus. They're gone. There's no justice or solace to it, they're simply gone."

She choked, her throat tightening. "But you see them, don't you? You can still see them, so they're not gone, they're—"

"The only ghosts I see are the people sitting at my table."

Marjorie's vision blurred. She swiped at her cheeks and bit down on her trembling lower lip. "But I paid you…"

"I'm sorry to say not every customer leaves satisfied. I wish I could give you peace, but your cards are clear."

She sniffled, cheeks heating. She should never have come here. Crying in front of some stranger, like a child. *Foolish girl.* "That's it?"

The woman stared at her for a long moment. "My dear child, I'm afraid some very bad omens surround you. Your aura is the most peculiar shade of blue. Bright. Unstable. Normally this would suggest creativity, self-expression. But yours..." Madame Josephine shook her head. "The only comfort I can offer is that the end is near for you, and fate will guide your path to the other side of your woes."

Sputtering, Marjorie rose from her chair. Her fists clenched at her sides. Her tongue wanted to unleash something sharp and cutting, but her throat was too tight for words to pass.

Madame Josephine slid Marjorie's coins across the table. "Take them. And good luck."

Had she just been rejected by a fortune teller? Marjorie's mind spun as she slid her money into her pocketbook and stormed out of the dark tent.

The bright sun blinded her. People shoved past. Children laughed. Music played from the center square.

A warm hand landed on her shoulder. Marjorie blinked until her vision cleared.

"There you are. I was looking everywhere." Her friend, Angela, stood beside her in a pink dress, the matching ribbon holding her blonde hair back in a short ponytail. Angela frowned. "Are you alright?"

Rubbing at her wet cheeks, Marjorie muttered, "I'm fine. Forget it."

Tilting her head to one side, Angela looped her arm through Marjorie's and pulled her along. "I was thinking we could go to the dancehall tonight."

"I don't feel like it."

Angela pouted. "You heard the rumors, didn't you?"

Marjorie stopped. "Rumors?"

"About the dancehall. Supposedly, it's *haunted*," Angela said, whispering the word *haunted* as if it were a dirty secret, though her eyes were bright. "Come on, Marj, it'll be a gas."

Haunted. The fist around Marjorie's heart loosened its hold. "Alright. Let's go dancing."

The dancehall vibrated with activity.

Upon the stage, a local band played Sinatra's latest hit, *Five Minutes More*. Behind them, an old mural painted one wall—dancers, hand-in-hand as they wheeled around a blue-and-green Earth.

Couples twirled across the dancefloor. The ladies wore beautiful hats and large bows pinned in their hair. The simple utility dresses Marjorie had grown so used to were still common among the crowd —padded shoulders, nipped-in waistlines, and hems falling just below the knee in a range of colors and patterns—but they were beginning to give way to a new wave of fashion as the world tried to forget all it had lost.

Most of the men wore boxy suits in tweed, but some retained their uniforms even though the war had ended. The many empty, pinned sleeves and crutches attested that the war would never truly be over. Some chose to stay on with the military, either through dedication or because they no longer had anywhere else to call home.

Marjorie's own utility dress was a light blue, simple but clean. Her long black hair hung in curls. If she were honest, she didn't want to be here. There were too many happy people laughing and chatting and pretending everything would be better now. But there was a possibility, however slim, that she might see something tonight. Something to confirm, once and for all, that life continued beyond the veil of death.

"Our cousin Virginia swears she saw it in the ladies' room only last week, and she's been sick ever since." Angela slid a new glass of punch in front of Marjorie as she dropped into a chair. The small, round table was cluttered with empty glasses. "A bright-blue figure. They call it The Blue Ghost."

"A *blue* ghost?" Angela's older brother, Leo, laughed at Marjorie's side. "That doesn't sound very scary."

"It is!" Angela argued. "They say it's a bad omen if you see it."

"Who says?" Leo asked over the loud saxophones and trumpets.

Angela shrugged. "Everybody."

Leo slid his gaze over to Marjorie and rolled his eyes conspiratorially. From the dancefloor, two figures emerged and headed toward their table. Marjorie recognized one as Leo's friend from the war, Ferdinand. The other was an American boy still in uniform. An eagle crest marked him as a volunteer with the Eagle Squadron of the Royal Air Force, someone who would have joined the fight even before his own country committed to the war efforts.

The American smiled at her with bright eyes as he and Ferdinand took their seats. "Arnold," he introduced himself, reaching out to shake her hand. "Pleasure to meet you, miss."

It was at times like these she felt as if she could see the future herself. A warm hand in hers on the dancefloor, those icy blue eyes staring into her own with a whole life laid out before them. But something always pulled her back into herself, and the illusion would fade. The fortune teller had been a disappointment today, but she'd seen Marjorie for what she truly was—a ghost sitting at her table. Ghosts had no future.

Marjorie shook the boy's hand without making eye contact.

"Apparently, a girl died here, back in the twenties," Angela said, continuing their conversation without missing a beat. "And now she haunts the place, still wearing a flapper dress with pearls. If you see her, something bad is about to happen."

Leo scowled. "Don't say things like that, Angie. It's not true. Virginia just caught a bug."

"It *is* true!"

"I believe it," Ferdinand said, earning a grin from Angela. "I met a psychic once. She knew I was a Taurus even before I said anything. She said I'd survive the war." He spread his hands wide. "And here I am. The wheel of fortune is always spinning through our lives."

A hushed murmur rolled over the table.

"Marj saw a fortune teller at the fair today," Angela declared. "Didn't you?"

All eyes turned to Marjorie. She felt her face heat. "*Ang,*" she scolded.

"Tell us!" Angela said, rocking forward in her chair.

Arnold raised an eyebrow. "What did the fortune teller say?"

Images of tarot cards flashed through her mind—worn, the colors faded, foxing around the edges. The Sun, The World, The Wheel of Fortune, a bright future flipped upside down into darkness, incompletion, and bad luck. Her stomach sank.

Marjorie slid her chair back and stood. "Excuse me."

Angela grabbed her arm. "Marj, I'm sorry. I shouldn't have brought it up. You aren't using the lav, are you?" Her eyes were wide. Angela would usually accompany her everywhere, but she looked genuinely afraid to do so now and she certainly didn't offer.

Marjorie shook her friend off and chuckled. "I'll only be a minute."

She could sense Angela's frown on her back as she exited the dancefloor, leaving her friends behind. She followed the signs that led her down a narrow hallway. The din of the music halved as the doors closed, leaving only the tinny echo of voices and instruments.

The fortune teller may not have seen her father, but Marjorie wasn't willing to give up that easily. She had to know. If the lingering spirit of a woman who died more than twenty years ago could still be in this dancehall, then why couldn't Marjorie's father still be around? If strangers could see a dead woman, why couldn't she see her own father?

The hallway was dimly lit. Her low black heels clicked on the off-white tiles. A few women tucked by her on their way back to the dancefloor, giggling, whispering.

As Marjorie stepped in front of the door to the ladies' room, the power flickered out. The dim hallway fell into complete darkness. Something banged on the other side of the door.

Her breath caught in her chest. The music silenced, but she could still hear a muted chatter of surprised voices.

Marjorie shivered, regretting leaving her sweater behind. Her first instinct, in the dark, was to duck and cover, listening for the whine of bombs rocketing through the sky like falling stars.

She tucked into the wide doorway, pressing her back to the thick, lacquered wood. Her heart harbored a hair-trigger as she prepared for the ear-splitting wail of an air raid siren.

Moments passed, but it didn't come.

The war was over. There was nothing to be afraid of anymore. It was just a blackout. Marjorie took a deep breath and stood.

Beneath the muffled voices coming from the dancefloor, she heard something else. She cocked her head, listening in the darkness, listening *to* the darkness. Water. It was the sound of rushing water.

She pressed her palm against the door and eased it open. The sound was louder now and as she took a step forward into the space, her shoes splashed at the edge of a puddle.

A leak, or a broken pipe. Moonlight streamed in through a small window in the far corner. Just enough for her to see that she was ruining her good shoes.

Stomach fluttering, she eyed the stalls. Shadows squirmed in every corner. The stakes seemed higher with the lights out; her craving to see a ghost suddenly more foolish. Just as she was about to turn back, a spark in the mirror caught her eye—bright and blue.

Marjorie gasped. She was here—The Blue Ghost.

Shivering, Marjorie stepped forward.

The lights flickered back on and Marjorie's vision filled with a bright flash. Her muscles snapped tight and rigid. The air froze in her chest. She fell to the floor.

Marjorie's eyes blinked open. She pulled herself up, smoothing down her dress. Her mind stumbled in fits and starts as she glanced around the room.

The power had gone out. It had come back on. She was in the ladies' room at the dancehall. Maybe she slipped in the water.

Marjorie glanced down at the floor. There was no longer a pool of water there. The black tiles beneath her were clean and dry. She could have sworn they'd been white moments ago. Had she hit her head?

Her fingers explored her hairline. No blood. Nothing hurt. How long had she been on the floor? It couldn't have been terribly long—the night was still dark beyond the small window. She stood over the sink, taking in her pale complexion in the mirror.

"*Margie.*"

Marjorie's head snapped toward the door as the phantom sensation of a cold blade slid between her ribs. Her chest drew tight. She was alone. But that voice, she'd know it anywhere.

Her eyes welled. "Dad?"

He'd sounded far away. She rushed to the door and slipped out into the hall. Empty.

Swallowing, she called out for him as she walked down the hallway. The walls looked different than they had before, as if they'd gained a fresh coat of paint. Knowing her friends would be worried about her after the blackout, she headed toward the dancefloor, still listening for her father's voice.

Bodies pressed through the doors to the dancefloor before Marjorie could open them, men and women tumbling out in a mess of bright, colorful outfits. The men wore beards, their hair shaggy and long. The women's skirts were indecently short, hair long and wild. They walked by her through the hall. A costume party? Her mind spun.

"Angie?" she called, stepping into the dancehall.

The music had returned. A new, fast beat. It was a song she wasn't familiar with—a man on stage announced it as *My Generation*. The crowd clapped and hooted uproariously.

This was the wrong room, she realized distantly. Except her table was where she'd left it, the long bar still stretching across one side of the space, the mural of the wheeling dancers and the earth still painting one wall, the windows and exits all in the right places. But the colors were all wrong, the floor shinier. Even the air itself was thick with an odd scent.

Her friends were gone. In their place sat a group of young people in the same strange costumes.

Marjorie walked up to them. "Have you seen my friends? They were sitting here before—"

Speaking amongst themselves, ignoring her, one of the women said, "It's true, Greg. Some girl died here in the forties. Electrocuted in the toilets. They say she still haunts the place."

Marjorie stepped back from the table, her heart hammering.

A man walked through her to reach his seat. Marjorie felt her whole body shift, slide, and snap back into place. She gasped.

The man shivered, turning up his collar. "Chilly in here."

Marjorie ran out of the dancehall.

Her hands trembled, fingers tingling. Tears blurred her vision as she dashed through the front door of the building toward the cool night air—only to find herself standing once more in the ladies' room.

Shaking her head, she tried again to leave, only to find herself back where she started.

Trembling, Marjorie gazed down at herself. She looked the same, felt the same. But something was wrong. This place was so different. And something was preventing her from leaving. Was this some horrible nightmare?

A girl came in wearing a short, shapeless leopard-print dress and heavy eye makeup. She walked past Marjorie and powdered her face in the mirror.

Marjorie reached out, touching the girl's arm. "Please, you have to help me, I don't understand what's—"

The girl shivered violently. Her pink powder case clattered into the sink. Marjorie's hand fell away as the girl grabbed her stomach and leaned over.

The door swung as another woman entered in similar attire. "Hey, groovy chick—whoa, Cassidy, are you okay?" She patted the girl's back.

Cassidy shook her head, still hunched. "I don't feel so well. I think I...I think I saw something in the mirror."

Neither of the women paid Marjorie any attention.

"These mirrors?" Cassidy's friend said. Her rose-painted lips drooped in a frown. "You know this place is haunted, right? Maybe you saw a ghost. It's bad luck to see a ghost here."

Cassidy grabbed onto her friend. "Don't freak me out. Let's just cut out early."

The two turned to leave.

"Wait, I—"

The doors swung softly closed behind them, leaving Marjorie alone, breathing hard.

She sank to the floor, leaning against the wall. They couldn't see her. Something happened when she touched the girl. She'd hurt her. How was that even possible?

Marjorie knew the answer, but she didn't want to admit it. If she was the ghost haunting this place, she'd have to be dead. And if she were dead, then where was her father?

She'd heard the soft cadence of his voice when she awoke, she knew it, but where was he? If this was death, they'd be together.

She wrapped her arms around her knees, rocking.

And The Blue Ghost…For a moment before the flash, Marjorie could have sworn she caught a glimpse of it in here. Her eyes welled. But if this were the afterlife, where had The Blue Ghost gone? Unless…she had taken its place.

Days and years seemed to pass, but the darkness beyond the window never changed. The sun never rose.

After her latest failed attempt to leave, Marjorie paced around the cursed room. This wasn't fair. Her fists clenched at her sides. To be trapped here, to be alone. It wasn't fair.

She huffed out a puff of air, but her lungs burned and she could hardly breathe through her tight throat. She dug her short nails into her palms.

If this is death, where is he?

Marjorie sobbed. She didn't deserve this fate. Trapped in a darkened ladies' room in an endless night. An unresolved past behind her and no future before her. She leaned over, clutching her aching chest.

A metallic whining echoed through the wall behind her, followed by a bang. A spray of water pooled on the floor beneath her feet. Marjorie stared as the pool expanded, the burst pipe clanking. She wiped at her damp cheeks.

This wasn't the evidence of an afterlife she'd longed for. She wondered if death was the same for everyone—a cage. If her father was still on a battlefield somewhere, wandering.

There had to be a way out. She couldn't stand it anymore. The four walls of her prison seemed to constrict, pressing in on her, crushing her.

The lights flickered, then extinguished, leaving the room in shadows.

"*Margie?*" a voice whispered.

Marjorie's head whipped side to side, seeking out her father's voice. Nothing stirred in the darkened corners. "Dad? Where are you?" She choked on a sob.

"*Come home.*"

"How?" she shouted, voice echoing off the tiles.

The door swung open and Marjorie saw a bright light. For a moment, she thought it was *the* bright light, the one she should be going toward but could never find. Then she realized it wasn't a light at all. It was a girl.

The girl shuffled in with her hands out in the darkness. She stepped in the puddle, glanced down, and mumbled, "Oh man. I just got these shoes." Her fingers sought out the cool porcelain sink. She turned it on and washed her hands, sighing.

Marjorie stepped closer. A strange, soft blue glow seemed to emanate from her. An aura, Marjorie realized. Just as the fortune teller had described her own aura so long ago.

Electricity vibrated in the air between them. An invisible pull drew Marjorie closer still.

The girl blindly turned off the tap. A set of dog tags hung around her neck, dipping into the V of her blue dress. A small silver bracelet decorated with winged cherubs dangled from her wrist.

She didn't seem to see Marjorie. But Marjorie saw her more clearly than she'd seen anyone before.

A replacement.

The girl dried her hands, her shoes still touching the edge of the growing puddle.

It was clear to her now. There would always be a blue ghost in this dancehall. But it didn't have to be the same one.

The role of The Blue Ghost must always be filled. Marjorie had been some other girl's replacement after more than twenty years of wandering. And this girl…she would be Marjorie's.

This was her way out.

Marjorie reached out to touch her. Her eyes fell again to the dog tags around her neck. She hesitated.

What had this girl lost already? Marjorie's chest tightened. She knew that pain, that loss, the unending agony of claws tearing and shredding her ribcage from the inside. Was it her fate to be condemned here like Marjorie was?

"*Margie,*" her father's voice whispered from far away.

Marjorie swallowed.

The girl tossed her dark hair back and moved toward the door. Maybe it was fate, after all. Marjorie had been here so long…and the wheel of fortune always turned eventually.

Marjorie's hand landed on the girl's shoulder. She twisted around with a gasp just as the lights flickered on and a blue jolt swept up her body.

The girl crumpled to the floor in a heap.

Marjorie closed her eyes.

When she opened them, she was in a field. The sun had risen and it felt warm against her skin, blanketing Marjorie's cold world in life. Her heart swelled as a man in uniform walked toward her.

"*Margie. I've waited so long to see you again.*"

STOPLIGHT PARANOIA

WRITTEN BY
KEVIN EMMMONS

IT STARTED on a Saturday in April, sometime before 4:29 a.m. I knew it was 4:29 because I was looking at the dash clock when I realized the person in the car behind me had been laying on their horn for at least a minute.

The guy eventually passed, glaring at me through tinted windows. He floored it halfway through the intersection where we had stopped. I watched his tail lights recede into the early morning darkness as I sat in the unmarked patrol car. My insides ached like I'd been forced through an upper GI endoscopy without anesthesia. One of the early ones, with the big camera. I'd been shot once. Kevlar took the bullet, but I got three cracked ribs. This hurt worse.

Little things came to me as I sat in the dark. The police radio buzzed with static, popping and hissing faintly, little louder than the whispering rumble of the engine. The glow from the traffic light filled the front compartment and gleamed off the heavy sweat on my hands. A cardboard sign tacked to the telephone pole to the right of the car read *The liberals are winning. The end is near.* Ahead on the left, a poster in a store window announced preorders for a game called *Ninja Catarina*. The cartoonish woman on the poster had a bit of a Mona Lisa grin, like she'd seen what went down and was waiting for me to figure it out.

I should have been thinking *Wake up, woman. Get it in gear*. Only I wasn't.

When the light turned green again, I shivered, checking the mirrors and side windows for something reaching into the car. Nothing, of course, but I whimpered from the certainty that whatever had bruised my insides was about to start again.

The worst part, looking back on those first days afterward, was how I had no idea where I was, how long I had been sitting like that, or why I had gone there. I remember it now but only because of the dreams and conversations with my boss.

The yellow numbers on the clock read 5:13 when a patrolman finally tapped my window with his flashlight.

Feral gray clouds made passive-aggressive threats of dismal showers on the solitary road where we found the house, like everyone knew it wasn't really going to rain. The electric motor whirred as Wren pulled the car up into the steep driveway just enough to get us out of the road. She parked at the very end as if she didn't consider this her house. I probably wouldn't have either.

Wren shook loose blonde curls out of her eyes and squeezed my hand. "Thanks for coming with me. I know you've got better things to do on your weekend."

"We sick women got to stick together," I said. "Take your time."

Using my detective's voice on Wren felt a little wrong, but one of the things I've learned about myself since the incident at the intersection is that I don't know how to turn it off. I only ever recognize it after the fact. If Wren noticed, she didn't react. Instead, she brushed my shoulder with her knuckles because she knows I don't fist bump. We predate the gesture, she and I. Wren picked it up. I hadn't.

An envelope on the dash drew our eyes. The letter was addressed to Wren from Simeon & Peterson, Will and Trust Attorneys.

"Tell me a funny story," she said. "Like one of those about your grandpa. Those are great."

I stretched my legs and struggled to decide if the moment warranted an anxiety pill. "I'll tell you one that was a little scary, from way back. I was nine or ten. We'd gone out to visit, and grandpa was mowing on the rider. There was a lot of yard between the house and that old red barn. I told you about the barn?"

Wren grinned. "Where he threw you in the grain."

"Right, so he was mowing, and I sat on the porch to watch. He'd make silly faces at me when the laps took him past. Then he hit a fencepost with that shell that covers the blades. What he didn't know was that a swarm of hornets had bored out a nest in a knothole in that post."

I hoped her wide-eyed smile meant at least for a few seconds she'd forgotten why we had come.

"It didn't take but a second before he got off that mower, waving his arms around. It reminded me of a horse's tail when the horse is annoyed with the flies. Of all things, he pulled out a lighter and a can of spray degreaser and shot jets of fire at all the hornets. Then he flamed the nest too."

Wren laughed. "I can picture this. I bet he was a character."

I shrugged. "The part that makes me laugh now is that when it was done, and he came back to the house, sweaty and smelling like that degreaser, he looked at me and said with a straight face, 'Well, that went way better than last time.'"

"Last time?" Wren said. "Wow. I wish I could have known him. My grandpa didn't talk much, but he always had candy in his pockets."

I waited while she stared at the dash, suddenly untalkative. I didn't push. The envelope bothered me too.

Eventually, Wren plucked the keys from the ignition and popped the latch on her door to climb out of the all-electric hatchback. Checking that my walking stick was still folded up in my pocket next to my mask and sanitizer had become a habit. Out of the car, I shivered from the chilly March breeze while we looked up the hill to the wide A-frame with enormous ground-level windows. Wren's daughter had done well for herself for being in her early twenties.

"Amy bought this place down near Brownstown," Wren told me a week earlier. "I don't know how she afforded it. She was sharing it with someone, roommates or something. I really don't understand it."

Wren's curly, blonde hair made rooster tail feathers between her fingers as she held the top of her head like her skull might burst. A bit of chubbiness about her cheeks, combined with the high cheekbones, made her cherubic in the sunlight. I'd dabbled in painting before Indianapolis, before the army and police work. I think I'd have enjoyed painting her face there, in that light. If only the seriousness had been an act instead.

"I guess we better go in," she whispered.

I took her hand like we were old friends and hooked it over my forearm. She glanced at me with a desperate smile that made my awkwardness worth it.

Inside, Amy had decorated with furniture and plants you'd expect in an upper-class home. Wren entered a code into the security alarm by the door, a digital panel with more controls on the display than older, analog models had ever needed. The security panel talked to the refrigerator. How much automation did they need?

We went through the house, Wren taking her time while I kept back and made enough noise to remind her I was there. Periodically Wren shook her head.

"This isn't right," she mumbled at the duck decorations in the kitchen. "I know my daughter."

The enormous bathroom on the first floor had faux flower vases with Chinese-looking scenery. Again, the head-shaking, and Wren's cherubic face broke for an instant.

The first bedroom upstairs had a mirror on the ceiling, a king-sized bed with a surround-sound stereo setup in the headboard, laptop stands and USB charging stations on the sides, and a television longer than some of the walls in my apartment. Probably thicker too.

"This makes me wish I was twenty again," Wren muttered. "Why couldn't we afford stuff like this back then?"

I shrugged. "Army salary?"

The next bedroom was decorated for a pre-teen girl, with crayon drawings on the wall, some little more than scribbles, others more artistic images of unicorns and fairies.

Wren held one hand over her mouth in disbelief. "What kid lived here?"

The upstairs bathroom decor was more spartan, functional, and utilitarian. Three toothbrushes stood in a dolphin cup, one of them smaller, with a unicorn head on the back.

The last room had a queen-sized bed with black sheets saying that thing about wearing black on Wednesday. Posters of punk and metal musicians dotted the walls in no particular order. The desk beside the bed had a folded-up laptop and an assortment of stickers, notepads, pencils, and decorations, all marked with jagged, cartoonish art.

Wren sighed. "This is Amy." She waved her hand at the products on the desk. "I don't know what that is, but it looks like her style. The rest of this—this is definitely Amy."

Both pillows bore the lumpy depressions from use, and different-sized shoes lay in heaps on either side of the bed. A corkboard on the wall had pictures of Amy and another woman at the park, at the mall, arm in arm or holding hands. In some, they were kissing.

Wren gasped. "She's—gay? She never told me that?" Her voice became an angry snarl at the end. She wouldn't look at me, and her face turned red as her head dropped. "I wish she could have told me."

Back downstairs, we returned to the kitchen, where someone had written, in bright-red spray paint across the back wall and kitchen door, *Whatever you do, stay away from that fucking tree.*

The nightmares started three weeks after the stoplight incident. The dreams never play out the same, not exactly, but they're close. Close enough that each time, I find myself pleading to powers beyond human ken that since the beginning is different, the ending could be too.

My desperate prayers haven't worked yet.

The night before I rode down to Amy's house with Wren, the dream started in a diner. I had bacon and eggs and a bowl of gravy over a piping hot biscuit. The orange juice pulp caught in my teeth, but I loved it. My cell rattled on the table as if yearning to grow up into a jackhammer. Kirkland, my lieutenant.

"Boss," I said into the phone.

"A witness just saw Lenny Baker get into a blue minivan and head south. You're down there. See if you can head him off."

Lenny fucking Baker. Pedophiles are more common in my state than anyone wants to admit, and I think it's that way everywhere. As far as we can tell, Lenny doesn't touch kids, but he works for people who do. I'd had him in the station three times already, but he'd always managed to weasel out. I felt scummy and dirty every time I talked to him. Then a witness came forward, agreed to testify, the works. If we could get Lenny, we could get others.

I threw a twenty on the table and ran for my car, the unmarked patrol car with the perfect armrests on the door. The engine whispered to life, and I drove out toward Maryland.

Up until that point, the dreams vary. Sometimes I'm on a date. Yeah, it could happen. There was a waiter downtown I went out with a couple of times. He was finishing a master's in psychology, but he didn't talk like a doctor. He spoke like me. Other times I'm at home, asleep. Sometimes, I'm working a case. The point is, someone calls, and all the randomness leaks out like water squishing out of mud. It evaporates, and I'm on Madison Ave., coming up on that intersection. The minivan is just past the traffic lights. Lenny gets out of his car, walks up to a green Charger. The dream skips faster than a cut video clip, and Lenny's head is gone. I'm screaming, not because I just saw a man die—I've seen that before—but I saw how. Only, that part is what got skipped. I know I saw it. Then the dream jumps again, and the Charger is three blocks down the road.

The ME's report says Lenny met his death at the end of a shotgun, probably a double-barrel with both shots fired simultaneously. When I wake up screaming and sweating like I'm playing tennis under a mad-hot sun, I know it wasn't a shotgun that killed Lenny.

I know it.

My therapist says I'm making it all up to explain the horror of seeing Lenny die in such a gruesome fashion. Maybe he's right.

My skin still crawls when I see a Charger, even if it's not green. I feel cold when I drive through a large intersection with traffic lights overhead.

Something else killed Lenny. I need to find out what in order to prove I'm still up to being a detective, at least, and I'm equally desperate to never ever know what came out of that Charger window and consumed Lenny's head.

Yeah, that's the other part. They never found his head.

Not even fragments.

We bagged up everything in the bedrooms but the furniture. Amy's things went in boxes, and most of that would be going home with us. Wren asked me to take care of Amy's room. It was easier for her to work on the clothes and belongings that didn't remind her of her daughter. The rest Wren planned to donate or sell online. I stuffed and carried bags down to the spacious living room, ignoring how the pressure against my stomach agitated the acid reflux I've had since Lenny and that stoplight.

A little after noon, Wren called for a break. She hesitated when she spoke, like she was second-guessing everything she said.

"Are you okay staying here a bit? I'd like some fresh air and a drive to distract me. I'll go get some food if you want. Yeah, food would be good. I'm buying. You want anything?"

"How about a small salad? No dressing or onions."

"Got it. Look, thanks again, Owena. I owe you big. You've got to let me make this up to you."

I shook my head. "Not at all. I'm paying you back for taking care of me all these months."

"What?" She frowned. "At group? That's nothing."

Nothing? "I was coming apart at the seams. You helped. Lots. This is my thank you. Or part of it, anyway."

Wren glowed. She was pale, like sheets pale, but her cheeks had a lovely blush, even as her face twitched between happiness and despair. "I better get food," she said, finally. "I'll be back in a half-hour or so."

When she was gone, I went back to boxing Amy's things. The pictures on the merchandise showed little black silhouette art of an alien piloting a flying saucer and struggling against other staples of horror like witches on broomsticks, a vampire, a tentacle monster hiding in the barn.

On one end of the desk, a trio of books lay open. The top book was *Collected Ancient Myths* by Adam Carter and showed a section titled "The Carnivorous Trees of Europe." The second and third had similar titles, each referencing flesh-eating plants from the lore of various ancient cultures. The books went in a box with WeirdOut-There.com notebooks.

Out of curiosity, I checked the website on my phone. It turned out to be an investigative blog run by Amy and another woman named

Nicole. Together they tracked down odd stories and talked about them, mixing in excerpts from email and chat conversations, official documents, and transcripts of witness interviews. The website was unprofessional and incomplete but decorated with the same silly, cartoonish art.

While I read, sitting on the end of the bed, my skin began to crawl. No sooner than I noticed the goosebumps, a figure rose from the stairs at the far end of the hallway. I caught the motion out of the corner of my vision. Wren had come back, quiet because maybe she hadn't fared so well with her grief. She needed a hug, and I was the only one around.

When I turned on the bed, Wren's white sweatshirt slipped around the corner. Or her hair. Her blonde sometimes seemed white in the corner of my eye. Maybe she had called out to me for lunch, but I missed it because I was glued to my phone.

I went out into the hallway just in time to glimpse her at the bottom of the first flight of stairs, going around the corner to go down the second. Something off about how she moved defied logic, like she was doing the moonwalk but moving forward instead of backward.

Maybe she felt better after all.

When I got to the kitchen, Wren had left the back door wide open. Outside, a single purple banana plant clung to life in a desiccated garden. A crooked, grotesque oak kept watch farther out over a winter-yellow grass sloping downhill to the east. That must have been the tree to avoid.

Wren was not in the yard. After calling out to her, I closed the door and went to the front, where I found an empty driveway.

I trudged around the house, out halfway to the creepy oak, and then back around the other side. No people, no cars. Just me, the tree, and the house.

The blindness came on the stairs to Amy's room. It often hits when I'm anxious or stressed, and I've never gotten used to it. Sitting on the steps sounded like a good idea, better than pulling out my walking stick. I can't ever get it to unfold all the way without fighting it. After deliberating, though, I fumbled my way back to the bed where I'd been working to sit and wait it out. At some point, the anxiety would wear off and my vision would return. The worst times in the beginning lasted until I slept. I hoped I could see again by the time Wren got back. Taking care of me was the last thing she needed.

I used the voice controls on my phone to have it read one of the blogs on WeirdOutThere.com to me. A post from almost a year ago described Amy's interview with a woman named Trish who had moved in with a college friend and her husband. Everything had been going fine until the woman, Teri, died of cancer. After that, they thought the house was haunted, and not by Teri. I missed some of the middle, where they talked about the tree out back, because I heard something move downstairs. This wouldn't be the first time since Lenny's death that I wished I still had my sidearm.

And my vision.

In the end, it finally clicked that Amy was talking about this very house.

The nightmares made insomnia my constant companion, attending to my every need and more faithful than any lover. The dark circles under my eyes resembled blemishes on the moon if the lights were down. Acid reflux was the family pet. Even the kid who delivered my weekend Chinese paused to ask if I needed help.

My administrative leave ended, but little had changed. I struggled into a suit like Hicks wore, the goth wannabe detective over in vice. My hair looked slept in—because it was—one half of my Oxford hung free, no belt. Had I been a man, I wouldn't have shaved.

Halfway to work on a busy street, I went blind. It wasn't a gradual thing, more like someone flipped a switch. I thought a freak storm had dropped on the city for a second, drowning out the light, and my eyes simply hadn't adjusted. Stomping the brakes nearly got me rear ended by the driver behind me. I flipped my hazards on, gratified by the obnoxious clicking audible over the horns. Somehow I got my phone to dial Kirkland.

"I'm completely blind," I said when he picked up. I needed to scream, demand answers from the sky, and shake someone by the collar all at once. I hit the button to lower the window. Cool morning air helped, even laced with exhaust and the fume of a recently startled skunk.

"What? You mean you really can't see?"

My detective's voice took over. "Boss, I'm on Elton, halfway to the station. It's totally black, and I can't see a thing."

He had to repeat it back to me a few times before it caught. "Sit tight," he ordered. Kirkland has a voice like my detective's voice, but his is closer to a drill sergeant's. "I'll get an ambulance to you and somebody to get your car back home."

And just like that, my last day as a detective ended before it even started.

The sound of a door preceded Wren's shriek. I set the next box to pack aside and hurried toward the kitchen. The stairs made me hesitate in case the blindness returned, and I compensated by getting a good grip on the handrail.

"Wren," I called. "What happened?"

"Down here," she answered. "At the back door."

When I rounded the corner into the kitchen, the back door was ajar, and Wren stood next to it, holding a bag of food and a drink carrier. "Did you leave this open?"

"No," I said. "I thought you had come back a while ago, and it was open then." I didn't mention the blind spell.

Her brow scrunched up as she set the food on the counter. "So it was closed when I opened the front door, right? But when I turned to get my key out, it got lighter. I thought you'd turned on a light, but someone stood in the now-open doorway here. I couldn't make out any details through the glare, and they left. Quick. Like now, I doubt that I saw them at all kind of quick." She paused and turned her crinkled brows my way. "You saw someone too?"

I crossed to the door, checked outside, then closed it. "I thought I saw someone earlier. I thought it was you."

With no better explanation, Wren took the bags of food to the table. We sat on the wall side, where we had a good view of the kitchen door, and I explained some of what I had read online.

"Wait," Wren said, shaking her head. "This was Trish's house?"

"It belonged to Teri and Nigel, and Trish inherited it from them. Amy bought it from Trish, I guess. Oh, and Trish's little sister, Rebeccah, lived with them. That would have been her bedroom upstairs. Amy and Trish met because she was investigating this house after the husband and the little sister vanished, and Trish agreed to an interview."

She frowned. "This is just so confusing."

I took her hand. "It makes you want to cry all over again."

"Was it that obvious? Are my eyes still red?"

"You weren't close to Amy. This has to feel like losing her twice. Also, I can smell the tears." I pointed at her sleeve.

Wren rubbed at a collection of damp spots just below her elbow. "Smell it, huh?" She sniffed at her arm. "Smells like sunsweat."

"Sunsweat?"

She shrugged. "Amy's term, ever since she was little. She noticed people smell differently when they've been outside on a warm day."

"I know that smell. Never really thought about it much. Sunsweat? I like it."

Wren laughed, more of a strong exhale, really. She tried to grin, but then her eyes tightened, and her lip trembled. She picked up her trash, stuffed it in the bag, and then patted my knee.

"I guess I better get back to it."

While Wren bagged up the towels and sundries in the downstairs bathroom, I returned to boxing Amy's things. I was nearing the end, and the last of it was a set of stickers, some for car bumpers and windows, others for laptop exteriors and things like that. The stickers had a variety of phrases. *Make tea, not war. Save the trees. Buy bamboo. Drive for solar power.*

A few of the messages had more profound subjects. One said *I'm not very old, but I can see that basically, the problems in our world come from two things. First is that a little over half of us are perfectly happy with other people suffering or dying needlessly. The second is that most of those in the first group are also screaming the loudest about the Bible and the churches. You say it's not a cult, but stop and think about that.* Another said *We need conservatives and progressives to work together, not stand on either side of a line in the sand and piss on the people on the other side.*

Some of the stickers found their way into my pocket. A part of me said this was something I'd show Wren and ask to keep, but a part of me wanted to latch onto a piece of this woman, Amy, and hoard it miserly, like gold.

I was trying to work out how to approach Wren about the stickers when she yelped downstairs. The stairs riled my anxiety all over again, but I made it down without incident. Wren crossed the living room, pointing toward the back door, now open again.

"Do you see that?" Wren snapped. "We didn't imagine it this time. I've had enough problems that I know when my mind is messing with me. This isn't one of those times. I saw her, Owena. This time I saw her. She ran across the yard, toward that tree."

By that time, Wren had charged out the back door, and I followed. Wren froze just as I saw a woman go behind the oak as if rounding the corner in a hallway. We waited, but she didn't come out the other side or peek back around the right side. After sharing a glance, we tromped through the grass up to the tree, giving it a wide berth.

"Hey," Wren called out. "I'm not looking for trouble, just trying to find out who's been staying here. Let's work something out?"

This is where Amy got it, clearly.

The woman wasn't on the back side when we got to the oak. I circled the bole twice, then three times, while Wren waited, but nothing. Worse, her tracks led through the grass to the tree but ended on the back side rather than running off like I might have expected.

"What is this," Wren demanded, "a magic show?"

We went back toward the house, but halfway, Wren whirled as if hoping to catch the woman sneaking up on us.

"Wait a minute," she muttered. "This can't be right?"

I followed her gaze. "What?"

"Look at the treeline. It's lower on one side of the tree than the other."

Sure enough, the sloping brush thirty meters behind the oak seemed to drop several meters behind the tree. When I moved to either side to get a better view, I did not find a deviation in the treeline that would have explained it. The woods stayed higher on the right side.

"Magic tricks and optical illusions?" I asked.

"I wish I could have afforded to pay someone to clean out this place," Wren whispered. "Who the fuck were these people?"

Three months before what happened at the traffic light, I caught Lenny Baker on a handful of felonies. Petty stuff, but when you want to bait bigger fish, you take what you can get. It was my bust, so I interviewed him.

"Need anything, Lenny?" I asked as I dropped into the seat across the interview table. The plain, scuffed metal reflected both the overhead lights and the department's lack of funding. I set a string-wrapped binder between us, on my side, and just to the left of that, a sweet-smelling latte. I don't drink coffee or anything hot, but Lenny eyed the steam rising from the sipping hole in the lid like he had just come out of the desert.

Lenny nodded. Skinny to the point of looking malnourished, he had his pants tied around his hips with bailing twine. "Yeah," he said. "Can I get a smoke? You've had me sitting here an hour. I'm about to bust a lung."

My grandfather gave me a lighter way back when I was in high school. It was a flip-top, like in the movies, solid gold. Heavy. One side was an eagle from above, and as a girl, I'd imagined the eagle was hunting, and I was following it. Later, after the army and law school, I thought Grandad meant that I was the eagle. Or the eagle was me. I learned how to take care of it and kept it oiled, cleaned, and fueled. I pulled it out, set it on the table, flipped the lid open, then popped it closed again.

"Bust a lung? I've never heard that one before, Lenny. How does that work?"

Next, I pulled out a pack of cigarettes I'd borrowed from a uniformed cop out back to mess with Lenny. His eyes lit up like a kid's at Christmas until I tossed the cigarettes in the corner trash can.

He squinted one eye at me. "It's just a figure of speech, you know? We smokers got to stick together, am I right?"

"I don't smoke, Lenny. Never have. Didn't even experiment when I was a kid."

"Oh? Miss goodie-two-shoes. Lovely. Okay, Dorothy, let's see them red slippers."

It went on like that for a good five minutes. Finally, Lenny leaned as far over the table as his restraints would allow.

"So, you gonna charge me with something, or do I just call my lawyer now?"

I took my time undoing the string wound around the post on the outside of the binder. "You can call your lawyer anytime, Lenny."

"Oh? Really? I thought maybe I had to wait for an invitation or something? You're cute, Miss Detective. Like a little kid with a big new word." His cackle echoed in the plain room. Loudly.

"Sure. Call your lawyer. If you want."

His eyes narrowed. "Wait. You're leading me on here. What? This some kind of deal now? We negotiating?"

"I want to press all the charges, Lenny. And you saw the list. Fifteen years, minimum."

The cackle deflated. "Yeah? And?"

"The DA thinks you're an up-front kind of guy. She says 'lean on him, and he'll talk.'"

"Talk?" Lenny giggled, but his eyes had changed. He wasn't afraid of the DA. Or me.

I shrugged. "She had a lot to say about what happens to snitches in prison. She said, 'He's not going to want to do any time because if he goes in, he's not coming out.' Now, you know me, Lenny. I don't really like games. I think we should throw you in because the law says you go to jail for blackmail and extortion. She's the boss, though, right?"

He looked from me to the mirror and back. His eyes widened, and he shook his head.

"No, no, no. I see where this is going, and I ain't biting. You think I'm fucking stupid?" He pointed at me. "No, don't answer that. But no. No, no, no."

I opened the folder, withdrew a stack of documents with his charges, and lined them up, facing him in a row. The stacks went across the table, and I ran out of space. "Help me out, Lenny. There are people I'd like to put away a lot more than I'd like to see you get stabbed in prison. Think about it? Little risk, big reward, and I get what I want too."

He shook his head. "Listen, Sister. You're barking up the wrong damn dress. You think you got a bead on this?" He pointed at the ceiling with his index and middle finger, then made a circular motion to encompass everything around us. "You got nothing. You don't know shit. You don't even know which corner of the shit house has the worst crap in it."

I watched him, those cold, dead, fish eyes. "I know you get a lot of calls from Harley Conway. I know Harley has a lot of calls with men who kidnap kids and many more calls with people who've been accused of rape, child molestation, and human trafficking. These people are the bottom of the scumbag pond, Lenny. Harley Conway is in the middle of that, and he talks to you. A lot. Give me stuff I can use to put him away, and the DA says I have to go easy on you."

Lenny leaned back in his chair, the fear gone. He grinned. "Lady, you think you know what's going down, but you don't know jack. You've done good for yourself, all high and mighty Miss Detective and all, but this is the really real world, and you think Harley fucking Conway is the top of the food chain? I ain't afraid of him. Not one bit. Not when real monsters are calling the shots."

"Real monsters? Harley's boss? Give me names."

"I'll give you names. Start with Jesus Christ. Start with praying. You see, this road you're looking down, it goes into the desert. The fucking desert. But you think it's just sand and rocks, like Arizona or the Middle East. It ain't. It's like the fifth circle of hell, and you ain't no Dante, and I ain't no Virgil. Get my lawyer on the phone. I'm done with this shit. You'll see. You'll wish you'd listened to ol' Lenny when the real monsters are ripping down your door like a paper sack."

I woke to darkness and Wren shouting.

"...got no right coming in here and telling me I was a shitty mother. No right!"

I rolled onto my feet off the stripped bed in Amy's room. I didn't remember lying down, but sometimes that happened. My medications must have gotten to me, and Wren finished while I was out. I staggered toward the door, then down the hall.

"No right?" I didn't recognize the new voice, but the lady was hostile, the kind of shrieking where I expected hair pulling and fingernails across the face any second. "She was fucking terrified of you. And I can see why. You can't just come into somebody's home and start throwing all their stuff in bags to haul off."

I reached for the clasp on my holster but then remembered I hadn't been wearing a gun for a while now. Instead, I jammed my hand into my pocket, where I found the eagle lighter and a tiny can of hairspray.

"It's not your place. It was my daughter's. Now it's mine. You're trespassing."

The other woman cried out, "No, you're a monster."

I rounded the corner in the stairs and found Wren near the kitchen counter, facing a younger woman at the corner of the couch. From the pictures I'd seen, this must have been Trish. She was wearing a black apron over a maroon polo with a fast-food logo on the breast, and I could smell the burger grease from across the room.

When Wren saw me, she clearly wanted me to step in as the legal authority, but she looked closer and closed her mouth. Trish backed up a step toward the door.

"Hi, Trish," I said. "Where have you been the last three months?"

She blinked. "I've been here. I've been working, and hiding, right here."

"Hiding? From whom?"

"Everyone. Now I don't know why you guys are here, so I suggest you get out of here before I call the cops."

"I was a detective for ten years, Trish. I know that game. But now isn't the time to say people are bad mothers and scream about calling the police. I understand you were close to Amy, and all the paperwork says you sold the house to Amy. Amy's gone, so now it's Wren's. Whether you like it or not, things are changing here, but it doesn't have to be instant. We can make this more gradual, right, Wren?"

Wren had giant tears in the corners of her eyes, but she nodded. "Sure. Yeah. Let the slanderer stay a few more days."

Trish bristled. "Slanderer? Look, lady, Amy's so afraid of you she wouldn't even come out to you. You're nothing but a cruel, bigoted bitch."

Wren shook her head. "I can't believe I'm hearing this. No, I can't believe any of it. I don't believe she didn't tell me she was gay, and I don't believe this nonsense I'm hearing right now."

I raised a hand. "Wren, please, slow down. Kids are afraid of lots of things when it comes to coming out. Maybe you were a little rigid and didn't realize it."

Wren giggled. "Rigid? Stop, Owena. Stop. Rigid? Look, you're a good person, and you're observant, intelligent, beautiful, but you don't see everything. I've been coming on to you almost since day one, but you haven't noticed. I've learned to tell the difference between ignorant and oblivious, and you are definitely the latter." She glanced at Trish while my mouth dropped open. "Look, kid. I don't know what Amy told you about me, and I don't know why. We haven't always gotten along. We've always had problems communicating, but it was never anything like that. Not ever. I married her mother, for fuck's sake. Coming out is just one more thing she didn't talk to me about." She gave me angry, amused eyes. "Rigid? Right. I need some air."

Wren turned to the kitchen door, holding her forehead with one hand. A statue with a burning face, I went over every second I remembered of her and me together. After we met at group therapy, we started hanging out to get away from the stress of our separate but similar circumstances. I had been coming apart at the seams because Lenny Baker died in front of me, and Wren had been troubled by an abusive older brother throughout her childhood. I didn't remember a single thing that didn't seem like plain friendliness.

"Wait," Trish shouted, desperate, when Wren pulled the kitchen door open. "Don't go that way? The tree."

"I don't care about the fucking tree," Wren snapped. "What's the big deal with the stupid, magic fucking oak anyway?"

Trish crossed to the kitchen, reaching for Wren the whole way. "Not the oak. The banana tree. Please, it's stronger in the dark. It can —do things. That's the one to watch out for. Please, come back inside. Go out front if you have to. I'll stop yelling, just please, don't go that way."

Wren frowned, glancing at the dingy purple tree on the patio. "That thing?" Then she shrugged, came back inside, and pushed the door shut.

The door didn't latch.

Wren stumbled away like a drunk while Trish squeaked.

The door creaked open, revealing a shape like a woman, pale on this side, darker on the other. A woman made out of fluid, a little cloudy, like seawater. A mass of ripples hid her face, but the mouth of a shark opened beneath pouting breasts.

It's a bit odd to write that I cornered the coroner.

Mark Havel. I found him drinking in Clarkson's Grill and Bar after hours. He sat at the bar finger painting something only he could see in the grease, moisture, or whatever was on top.

I didn't approach right away. My story had to have made the rounds. I was sure by then everyone on the force thought I had broken. That meant everyone they talked to. That meant Mark Havel.

My therapists just about had me believing it myself. They would have, too, if it hadn't been for the dreams. The nightmares never stopped. They backed off, but I woke in a sweat at least once a week. I had to invest in a mattress pad with a plastic liner. I once joked with Wren that I slept in a swimsuit.

Sooner or later, though, you have to deal. You move on, you grow, or you sink deeper and deeper until you can't breathe. I was ready, but after ten years as a detective, I couldn't just put things down. I needed some kind of closure. I needed to know what the therapists said was closer to the truth than what I kept dreaming, the hints I kept almost remembering. Be the eagle, I'd been telling myself since college. Hunt. Find the answers.

So in proper detective fashion, I stalked Havel. He was a plain guy who worshiped Green Bay despite their reputation. Most nights, he drank himself senseless at Clarkson's, then caught a taxi or the bus home, slept it off, and started all over the next day. On Thursdays and Saturdays, he rented porn from the one movie rental place left in town. Diplomas adorned his office, but no fancy certificates or awards accompanied them. Maybe he wasn't all that proud of dissecting his clients. Maybe he just had too many clients.

After a few days, I decided to approach him. It would have to be public for my protection. I didn't think Havel would be a threat, but I'd seen things go sideways, legally or otherwise, far too often to settle for meeting him at his house or calling him out of the blue. And there was no way I would try to meet him at work. Especially with the questions I had. I'd been threatened with legal action over digging into Lenny's case. Kirkland even suggested my interest implied a more active role in Lenny's death.

That's loyalty for you.

I drank three ice-cold colas to work up my courage. While the situation might have tempted me to try something sturdier, alcohol smells like rotten piss, so there's no way I was drinking any. When the caffeine had twisted my anxiety into finely tangled knots, I went up to the bar.

"Owena Gibson," Mark said with bleary eyes and the slightest of slurs. "What brings you to this fine establishment?"

"Can I talk to you? It's kind of personal."

He grinned. "Yeah, sure. Wanna go outside? We can find a diner or something if you don't like the crowd."

I glanced at the mostly empty bar. "Maybe just a corner booth."

"Sure. Here."

He waved to the lady serving drinks and grabbed his mug. At the booth, he dropped into the seat and nearly fell over. He stared at the table so long I thought maybe he'd actually passed out, but then he straightened and made a flimsy grin.

"There now, Detective Gibson. What can I do you for?"

I slid onto the seat opposite him and shook my head when the serving lady asked what I wanted. When she was gone, I went straight to the point.

"I'm not a detective anymore, Mark. You knew that, right?"

"Oh, that's right. Sorry to hear that. Always felt good, you know, knowing people like you were fighting the good fight."

"You know why I'm not a cop, too, right? I'm—sick. Sort of. That last case really messed me up."

His eyes grew so wide I thought it must have hurt, and he leaned down over the table like we were discussing high treason. "You're here about Lenny Baker."

"I need to know what you found, Mark. Please? I know it's bending regulations, but this stuff keeps me awake at night. I need to know how he died so I can tell myself the nightmares are just stupid dreams."

Mark took a deep breath. "Listen. Just between you and me and the gatepost, this is one whacky case. First, they fire you, then they alter my findings. Peterson up and quits, Rhonda swallowed her own gun, and Addams is in charge now, dressing like a pimp or something. Nothing against pimps. People got to make a living, right?"

I blinked at the onslaught. "Rhonda James?"

That got me a big nod and a disbelieving grin. "Right? Poor Rhonda."

"All over Lenny Baker?"

"Yep. Pretty much. I don't know what all they found, here and there, there and here, but it's wild, I tell you what. It's like a cover-up in a movie. Not as wild as the marks on his neck, though. Nothing that wild. You don't see that every day."

I tensed like I was about to take a bullet. It wasn't supposed to be this way. He was supposed to tell me it was plain, cut and dried, wrapped up neatly with a bow. Lenny Baker died from a shotgun blast that took off his head. Period.

"Tell me," I grated.

Mark shook his head, and his drunken grin got bigger. "You ever hear about the squid attacks down south of Charleston?"

"No."

"I suppose not many have. We all thought they were just urban legends, but when I was an intern, I worked with a guy who did odd jobs for the state. One of them took us out to a barnacle town where two fishermen had been killed. Coastguard found them a few days later, and we got called out to do the autopsies. The bodies had sucker burns on their arms and torsos." He made a ring with his thumbs and index fingers the size of a silver dollar. "But they'd lost their heads, and we eventually determined the wounds at their necks to be from squid beaks. You don't ever forget something like that. Lenny Baker looked like a squid ate his head."

That night, when I dreamed of Lenny's death, I didn't see a squid or anything else. The dream ended like it always had, with me crying and groaning into sweaty wakefulness with a migraine brought on by lack of sleep.

Trish pulled Wren away from the woman made out of water.

"Here, away from the door," the girl said, urging us toward the living room. "That's just a distraction. Amy calls it a geist. The tree's the danger. He's trying to lure you out."

"Lure?" I asked, while at the same time Wren said, "He?"

Trish grabbed a broom from where one of us had left it in the living room and used it to slam the door on the watery apparition without getting too close, like she'd been through this a few times already.

"Look, I don't really have answers," Trish said when she faced us. "I've learned the hard way to stay away from that door after dark. The water lady is creepy, but it's just a trick. Be glad it doesn't look like her."

"Her?" Wren said, in much the same way she'd said "he" a moment earlier.

Trish's voice got quiet. "Teri."

"What are you talking about?" I demanded, pulling Wren toward the couch and away from the kitchen door. Her hand wormed behind my back, and she held me around the waist. I remembered what she'd said earlier and decided I didn't care if this was one of those times or not.

"Sometimes, he makes shapes out the window that look like Teri. I know it sounds weird, and it's weirder to see. Some combination of the water and his leaves. It's another lure. He's hungry."

Wren and I stared at her. She just said the tree, he, was hungry.

Hungry.

Trish pulled her hair away from her face. "Honestly, he's not the worst threat, and Amy has a plan for him."

"Then who is?" Wren whispered. "Who could be worse than a tree that eats people?"

"My sister," Trish said without so much as a blink.

I cleared my throat. "Wait. Your kid sister? Rebeccah?"

Trish nodded. "Well, her people, really. It sounds odd saying it this way, but my sister was way worse than the tree. At least we can outrun the tree. *Bek* gave Teri cancer."

Wren huffed. "How do you give someone cancer? It's not like spreading the cold."

I pinched the bridge of my nose to massage the sudden ache away. "Can you prove any of this?"

Trish leaned on the counter. Her face turned relieved, as if she finally had someone to share this with. "She put chemicals in the food. She laughed when she told me and said she could have done it to us too. After—after she was gone, we found things. IDs. Checkbooks. She had a stash in her room, carved out of the wall. She seduced Nigel, Teri's husband. I know it sounds too hard to believe, but she did. He was into underage girls, evidently, and Bek knew just by watching him. We found chat conversations from months ago where she coerced him into killing some people in Indianapolis and Louisville. We found bank transcripts where she'd rerouted millions of dollars. She impersonated a dozen people. That news reporter, Jerry Filmore? Some lady out of Chicago. A casino owner from Evansville. Then some people she just made up. A taxi driver-drug dealer in New York. Some local guy named Harley Conway. There are probably more."

She paused when I sucked in a breath.

"Say that again," I whispered.

Wren turned to look directly at me. This close, I felt like I was under a microscope. "Which part?"

"That last name? It sounded like—Conway."

Trish frowned. "Harley Conway? Bek had a fake ID with some dead guy's face on it, a whole binder of information about his child kidnapping rings across three states, people he worked with—are you okay?"

That was when I realized I was crying. My eyes stung, and tears slipped hot and painful over my cheeks. "Harley Conway?"

"Look, Bek was a monster, okay? She had me fooled all along, just like Nigel fooled us. Now I have suspicions she might have had something to do with the wreck that killed our parents."

"Monster," I whispered. Killed her parents? What if this little girl was Lenny's *real* monster?

"That's right. But she's dead. The tree got her a couple of months back. It's her people that are the danger now. Friends like Nigel. Rapists. Murderers. At least one former government agent. Truckers, politicians. You name it. I don't even know how to begin describing all the stuff she was doing."

I couldn't breathe. I couldn't think. I had to latch onto something else. "You said Amy had a plan."

"Yeah, for the tree. When she gets back, we're going to get rid of him once and for all. He's a water spirit and there are ways to deal with them."

Wren's face crumbled. She leaned into my shoulder, and I squeezed her.

"Amy's deceased," I whispered to Trish. "Why do you think we're here?"

Trish's eyes went wide. "No, she's not."

I glanced at Wren, not wanting to repeat it in front of her. "They found her on the patio with a self-inflicted gunshot wound."

Trish shook her head and touched Wren's shoulder. "That wasn't Amy. That was her friend, Nicole. The other one, Zed or whatever, he's out in the woods. They haven't found him yet. I can't get involved because I'm doing what Bek wanted, sitting right here. But those guys were snooping around like you are, and that's going to bring Bek's friends. Or *him*."

Wren shook her head. "Not Amy?"

"No. I'm sorry, and I'm sorry you found out this way. Nicole seemed like a nice girl and all. It wasn't a gunshot either. It was the tree."

With trembling hands, Wren took Trish's shoulders. "Then where is she? Where is my daughter?"

Heavy furrows creased Trish's brow. "All I can say is that she's in South America, and she's supposed to be landing in San Francisco next week. If I say any more, I'm putting all of us in more danger."

Wren leaned on me, cradling her head in her hand. "I don't know whether to laugh or cry. You're not lying to me? How did the police get them confused?"

"Animals got to Nicole before the police found her. That helped cover it up. My sister owned people in the police, in the government. Owned them—like you own a poodle. She planned it all out to designs only she understood." Trish laughed, an awkward bark. "It's just that none of us were expecting the tree."

With a glance at me, Wren separated and paced into the kitchen. "She's legally dead. What happens when she gets back?"

Trish shook her head. "Listen, all my sister's plans will unravel, but I don't know when or if someone will step in to take over her operation. It's a mess, and all I know is I have tickets to Cali on Monday."

Wren put her hands together, fingers clasped, and held them at her lips, almost as if in prayer, but she met my gaze. Her brows went up, and hope bloomed like fireworks in her eyes. Could Amy be alive? That was the question, unspoken but loud in the room. I had watched her change these past months from the woman who picked me up and kept me going to a barely functioning, distracted, and remorseful wreck. Seeing her hope just then made me need it too.

The sound of a car door slamming came from the driveway. I went to the window to see who might have come. I saw two cars, Wren's little electric and a dented and rusted Escape, presumably the one Amy described seeing when she first interviewed Trish. I started for the door to get a better view.

Wren made a strangled sound. Trish's eyes widened, and her mouth dropped open.

Across the room, something had opened that kitchen door. It loomed in the darkness, much bigger than the stunted banana tree I saw earlier. The door rumbled as the thing growled, and its geist pulled Wren by the waist toward the door.

I hurdled the kitchen counter—my knee made an awkward and painful pop when I landed—and caught Wren's hand just as she crossed the threshold. The tree flapped its propeller leaves and rumbled like deep thunder. Trish joined me, pulling Wren by the other arm, but the geist still gained ground. So much for being just a lure.

Wren clung to my hand. Her hair stuck to her forehead, and she clenched her teeth, lips opened with the strain. The geist pulled her lower half off the ground, and Wren made a squeaky gasp.

Whatever this thing planned to do to my friend couldn't be good. "Hold her," I shouted at Trish.

When Trish braced, I snagged the folded cane from my pocket and whipped it toward the water woman. As always, the last segment would not lock into place, but I didn't need it to. I flailed at the indistinct face and arms with the stick.

It turns out that hitting a creature made out of water is like hitting the water in a pool. The cane went right through it, splashing out the other side and flinging droplets into the ruin of the garden. Even in my panic, I remember wondering if I could hardly touch it with the stick, how could it pull on Wren so well? The geist flinched, giving us leverage enough to drag Wren back to the house.

With gunshot speed, the tree lashed me with one enormous leaf. It knocked me down, knocked the stick out of my hand, and I cracked my head on the doorframe. I squinted against the pain and lurched for the cane, but root-like tendrils grabbed it first, yanking it close to the tree where more roots enfolded it, snapping it apart.

"Owena," Wren shrieked. The liquid creature was pulling her closer to the tree.

I came to my feet like I had practiced ten thousand times during self-defense training at work, but instead of drawing a pistol, I yanked my gold lighter and a travel-sized aerosol can of hairspray from my pocket. Cracking the lid off the pressurized can with my thumb broke the nail. I held out the lighter, flipped it open and alight in the same motion, and sprayed the hairspray toward the water woman.

At first, the flames had little effect other than making Wren shriek in surprise. I kept the pressure on the spray button—

—and then my vision went.

The tree rumbled. I couldn't see Wren, so I didn't know if I was burning her or not, but I didn't dare let off the spray.

Something splashed, like water hitting the patio. Something jostled me from the side, Wren, I think. Long, cool threads wrapped around my ankle, biting in and yanking me toward the tree. I dropped the hairspray as I tried to catch something, anything.

Wren screamed my name, and then everything stopped with a crunch. Someone grabbed me by the wrist and yanked me toward the door. The rumbling died out, so all I heard were our ragged breathing, groaning, and the sounds of my heels and butt dragging across the kitchen tiles. When we stopped on the carpet in the living room, the bestial grumble of the tree had changed to squeaky whining. More of that odd crunching came as I sank into unconsciousness, followed by the sounds of flames on the patio and one of the others vomiting.

I woke in a hospital in Seymour. The nurses told me a fever had left me delirious for three days. They couldn't tell me what had caused the fever. In a way, I was relieved—no nightmares. Wren was asleep in the chair by the window, and she got up a few minutes later, greeting me with a weak smile. For hours, she wouldn't talk, and then it was just simple answers, yeses, noes, and shrugs.

I haven't been able to decide. Wren's flight out to California to meet Amy is tomorrow, and she wants me to go with her.

The police made a cursory investigation into Trish's life these past few weeks and into her death. I dreaded that investigation, but it dried up. When I commented, Wren would only shrug. "Amy took care of it."

I pulled strings to get a copy of the home security video from the house. The front panel and the refrigerator both had camera footage of that night. It begins as you might expect, right up until the tree and its water minion tried to yank Wren out the back door. There was no sign of either in the video. It looked like Trish and I were trying to pull Wren into the house, and she desperately wanted out. The odd thing about the video, other than contradicting what Wren and I remember, was that in the parts where I fought back with cane and fire, I wasn't attacking Wren. I was fighting something behind her. Something knocked me down, and then the footage shows Wren and me struggling to hold Trish, who was then trying to get to the feeble banana tree. She slipped out of our grasp and collided head first with the tree's trunk. On camera, it looked like she broke her neck on impact.

Wren refuses to talk about that night, other than safe, quiet bits, like the prospect of reuniting with Amy. She doesn't think that meeting is going to go well. Amy believes we're responsible for what happened to her girlfriend.

Maybe she's right.

Last night I dreamed again, the first since the incident with Trish. I began at Wren's house. She made pasta, and we ate and streamed a show. That part really happened. In real life, we ended that night with a conversation. She thinks I'm hesitating to commit to the trip because I blame her for what happened to Trish. That's not it at all. Everything is fine when I overlook her touches and take her grins as signs of friendship. This is the way it's been since we met. I can't ignore those things anymore, though. I'm terrified of opening up to her, and I'm also exhilarated.

But I'm also afraid she blames me. I see it in her eyes, sometimes. Hear it in her voice. Accusation. I failed. The blindness hit me, and I let Trish die.

But in the dream, she took my hand for a minute, and then I went into my apartment, and she went home. As soon as my head hit the pillow in the dream, the phone rang. Kirkland. He gave me the usual spiel. Lenny Baker was driving out of town, and we had a witness. Like in all the other variations, I took the unmarked squad car and chased him down.

I squirmed in the bed, knowing it would be terrible but unable to wake.

Lenny had pulled over, minivan and Charger beside the road, and he was walking up to the car. The stoplight above me turned green—the color of the Charger. The driver behind me was honking and screaming out his window.

The light turned yellow. Lenny leaned down to the Charger's passenger side window. He was grinning, digging into his pocket. He laughed, that skeezy laugh that bothered me even before all the weirdness. More traffic backed up behind me, their horns a cacophonic chorus, a pestilence of sound making me frantic to get off the road, to drive away, to do anything but sit there and watch.

Red flared overhead, two crimson eyes scowling down. Something reached out of the Charger, a shadow too fast to see, and I went blind. The car rocked as if someone heavy sat on the hood. Slick, sticky, wet sounds curled up over the open window frame. It had me an instant later, but I don't remember anything about that. All I heard was Lenny dying in the blur of darkness from the Charger.

The sound wasn't screaming like I expected. It was the same crunch from when the purple banana tree caught Trish.

When I wake after that version, which is almost every night now, the acid reflux is worse.

I still don't know what happened to Lenny. Or Trish. I can't see either death, not in the dream, not in memory. All the reports, all the years of logic and experience leading up to this tell me I'm losing it. I'm imagining or hallucinating monstrous events to bury the crueler, simpler deaths of these two people I barely knew.

Then there's the video of me spraying fire at something behind Wren. A jagged ankle bracelet of scars marks where the roots bit into my skin. I still have esophageal damage from whatever happened at that traffic light, damage none of us have ever been able to explain.

It takes chewing antacids to get through packing tonight. I'm going to California with Wren tomorrow. I'm looking at the gold lighter with the hunting eagle on the side, thinking of Grandad and praying that this time goes better than the last. I tell myself I'm being brave for Wren, but I can't stand the thought of being alone while she's gone. Is that selfish? Of course, it is.

Is it wrong, though?

A taxi pulls up below. Wren gets out and waves up to me.

I don't have the answer, and my skin crawls when I see the traffic light changing from my perch at the window.

QUIET DESPERATION

WRITTEN BY
CLARENCE CARTER

IN A GROUP FULL OF MOURNERS, one man's eyes were dry. He stood amongst them, black suit, head bowed. Inches from the grave sat a table bearing pictures of the deceased. If anyone asked, he'd say he was a family friend. Hank knew nothing of Lizzy McLaughlin other than what he'd read in the paper.

A woman in a black veil sat beside him with a tissue in her hand. She'd cried in low, garbled noises. Her eyes were bloodshot. Hank turned away, evading her gaze.

Rows of headstones covered the rolling greens of the cemetery. Freshly cut grass lingered on the breeze. A canopy on wheels shadowed the grave, suppressing only some of the heat.

The preacher stood at the front, holding the podium. He spoke in a slow, dedicated cadence, perfected by those versed in public speaking.

As the grieving comforted each other, Hank observed the minor details. He noted the cars they drove and the clothing they wore. All of which were signs of wealth. These people weren't Walmart shoppers.

Hank approached the casket to say his goodbyes, which consisted of scouting. He'd attended seven funerals in the past month and dug one grave, or undug, really. With hands clasped in prayer, he surveyed. Through the tufts of gray hair, he saw diamond earrings. A gold necklace hung barely visible from her collared shirt. The shimmering silver bracelet and the diamond ring caught his attention too.

Part of that Henry David Thoreau quote rolled through his mind. *The mass of men lead lives of quiet desperation.* He'd never known desperation like this before.

The woman had enough loot in her coffin to buy him more time before they closed his.

A young man of about twenty made eye contact. Hank couldn't abandon ship, too obvious. His heart thundered in his chest as he approached. By the time the man stood in front of him, he realized he'd been holding his breath.

"Thanks for coming," he said.

Hank nodded a sympathetic nod.

When the man passed, he sighed a breath of relief.

As the crowd dispersed, he crossed the cemetery to his truck. Stepping over every headstone, Hank apologized in his head. Intentionally, he'd parked the truck far away from the family in an effort not to be remembered.

The blazer landed on the backseat. For the millionth time the stack of bills crossed his mind. They were suffocating. If he couldn't provide for his daughter, his ex-wife would take her away. He couldn't live with himself if that happened.

The truck rumbled to life, and he beat the other cars out of the cemetery. Several times he checked over his shoulder to ensure he hadn't been followed.

The brakes screeched outside the bakery he'd frequented for years. He stepped out, looking up and down the main drag for cops. Aside from the previous job being mentioned on the news, he had no reason to believe they were onto him.

Bells above the door jingled as he held it for a woman with a smile. Waiting in line for a cup of coffee, he checked over his shoulder, and then glanced at his watch. If not for its sentimental value, it would have joined his other belongings at the pawn shop.

A sharp pain settled in his lower back, brought on by the hard plastic seats. Sipping his black coffee, fingertip tapping wildly against the table, Hank watched the parking lot. A cloud of exhaust plumed, signifying Jake had arrived.

An average-sized man stepped out of his monstrous truck. The haze dissipated, revealing Hank's nephew, too stubborn to buy something practical or affordable.

Sporting dark ringed eyes and dirty wranglers, Jake looked like he'd been on another videogame bender. Jake's father, Hank's brother, complained about them often. "That fucking *Call of Duty*," he remembered his brother saying.

The woman behind the counter slapped a roll of change against the register. The other windowfront booths were empty, leaving them some privacy.

Hank checked over his shoulder to assure himself the woman

wasn't listening. He'd also motioned for Jake to lower his volume a couple of times.

He leaned in, whispering, "I know there's nearly a thousand dollars' worth of jewelry in that casket."

Jake nodded a couple of times but said nothing.

Gripping tight to his coffee, he said, "Just like last time. We meet at eleven. There shouldn't be any interference."

Jake patted a yawn but kept silent.

On the way out, Hank waved to the woman behind the counter. "See you tomorrow, Rita."

Rita returned the wave.

Elvis played through the speakers of his truck as he tapped his foot. A series of thoughts floated around in his mind, memories of a simpler time, mostly. There'd been a time when he hadn't been dodging a loan shark at every turnaround. A time when he'd been happy. When Rachel had only been a baby.

The truck's lights extinguished. As he walked across the dirt parking lot, he kept an eye out for an ugly Cadillac. He couldn't afford to bump into *him*. His kneecaps couldn't handle it.

Illuminating the entrance to his apartment building was a small light which buzzed. Flittering bugs thumped against it. Hank gave it a wide berth, with a wary eye.

A strong odor of fish wafted through the first floor hallway. New tenants had taken the first apartment. Judging by the array of scents, they ate seafood often. He grumbled his complaints before wandering upstairs.

When inside, he saw the eviction notice he'd thrown away uncrumpled on the table. His daughter, Rachel, had fished it out of the bin. The TV wasn't on so he imagined she'd already gone to bed.

The slow ache of frustration crept across his mind. He wished he'd been better at hiding their dire situation. Once, he could pull the wool over her eyes, but at fifteen she saw through his bullshit. She was a mature fifteen too, the type that got mistaken for an adult too often.

With a click of the remote, the TV flickered on.

The cabinets were bare, as was the fridge.

A saucepan filled with water banged against the burner, followed by a packet of chicken flavored ramen. The water bubbled as he listened to the TV in the corner. A beautiful anchor rambled on about the rise in gas prices. Hank gripped the bridge of his nose, frustrated by the endless inflation.

He had checked the weather obsessively for the past week, ensuring there would be little interference. The last graverobbing had left the news cycle and he patted himself on the back for getting away with it.

He considered going into his daughter's room to talk but thought better of it. Their relationship was constantly on the rocks. Being a single dad had never been easy. Although his landscaping business had failed, he knew Rachel was better off with him than her mother.

After watching the weather, he turned to ESPN where the Celtics embarrassed themselves for the third game in a row. Before halftime he'd drifted off to sleep in his recliner.

The alarm on his phone woke him at ten. The kinks in his back popped as he stretched. Outside the window the skies looked clear. Even a couple of stars poked through the light pollution.

The Keurig rattled and banged as it slowly poured a strong line of coffee. It sputtered, threatening to die. A strong smack to its side brought it back to life until it finished. The alien sticker on his thermos made him chuckle as he tightened the cap.

Careful not to wake his neighbors, Hank tiptoed down the stairs. The odor of fish had been replaced by cleaning products.

From the toolshed behind his building, he grabbed the shovels. Carefully, he lowered them into the bed. His eyes grazed every window, making sure he wasn't being watched.

Driving through town, looking at all the houses, Hank considered how abnormal his life had become. While most people were sleeping, he was digging. He longed for the days when his landscaping business had been on the rise. Back when he had a sense of purpose.

On a dirt road, half a mile from the cemetery, he stepped out of the truck and stretched his legs, looking up at the bright moon above. He'd decided they could dig by the moonlight and spare the flashlight batteries.

As he waited for Jake, he thought back on the eviction notice. He couldn't let that happen. With this score, he'd catch up on the rent and buy himself time. The last thing he wanted was for Rachel to go.

The back-breaking labor didn't bother him. He'd worked in that cemetery many years ago, doing the same thing in reverse.

Another engine rumbled up the dirt road, country music blaring from the radio. It came to a stop twenty feet away. Conway Twitty's voice dropped off. Wearing a camouflage hat and a stupid grin, Jake dropped out of the truck.

Hank slapped a shovel into his nephew's hands. "Did you bring the thing?"

Jake shuffled through the cab before pulling out the radio. He turned a dial, and it came to life. Police squabbled back and forth. Some assholes had dragged an ATM, giving them plenty to do.

Jake smiled. "It looks like we've got time."

The moon shone bright above, lighting the path across the cemetery. Wind rustled the treetops. Off in the distance a lone owl hooted.

With his head on a swivel, Hank crossed the cemetery, mindful of the stones jutting from the ground. He'd tripped on a few during his time there.

Wintergreen wafted through the air, and he knew his nephew had just put in a plug of tobacco.

The shovel dragged on the ground behind Jake as he asked, "Why do you insist on parking so far away?"

Hank paused, long enough to give his nephew a disappointed look. "If we parked near the cemetery people would notice. When we park on the service road, nobody can see the trucks."

Jake spat a line of chew that defaced a headstone. If it wasn't his brother's son, he'd fire him.

Hank loved his nephew, but the boy had no future. His days were spent playing *Call of Duty*, drinking Mountain Dew, and talking about hunting. Since dropping out his sophomore year, his future looked dismal at best.

The layout of the cemetery had been etched into his memory. He'd dug tons of graves and mowed the lawn hundreds, if not thousands, of times. Wind whispered through the trees as they moved toward their destination.

Their tools clashed to the ground. Hank looked around, ensuring they were alone. Crickets chirped distantly. If they weren't about to exhume someone, he might have called it a nice night.

Chunks of sod flew in all directions as Hank pulled them out by hand. The first *schick* of the shovel sank home. Jake had taken his place on the other side of the grave. If he'd trusted another person, he'd have hired a third digger.

They worked diligently with little conversation. Occasionally they'd pause for a drink from the thermos. Conversation between the two of them wasn't fun for Hank. He'd listened to enough of Jake's hunting stories for one lifetime.

Even in the cold night, sweat dripped from his forehead. He imagined himself removing the diamond from the old lady's hand and it sent a chill up his spine. He'd always hated that part, mostly for fear she might grab him. Irrational as it may be, Hank imagined it every time.

Along with his mountain of debt, he tried not to think about the karma that might follow him from disturbing the dead in their eternal slumber. *Anything.* He'd do anything to keep Rachel safe.

Jake paused for a drink of coffee, alien sticker poking between boney fingers. He then hawked a loogy off into the distance. The thermos dropped back into the nearby grass. Before sinking the blade into the dirt again, he spoke. "It's fucking creepy out here."

Hank only grunted in response.

After jabbing and tossing a shovelful of dirt, Jake stopped. "Did you hear that?"

Hank turned his head. "I don't hear anything."

"Exactly."

For a second, Hank leaned against his shovel. The curse words were bubbling up. He wanted to tell his nephew he was being lazy, when he noticed the crickets had stopped chirping. Even the breeze against the trees had lightened.

A rustle erupted from the woods, earning a curious look.

He sank the blade in twice before it happened again, closer.

With dawn lurking in the near future, Hank persisted. There wasn't enough time for ghost stories and tomfoolery.

He'd only sunk the blade halfway before Jake stammered, words fumbling from his mouth. He stumbled a couple of feet before catching his heel and falling into the pile of dirt.

A shaking finger pointed to the woods. His face had gone pale. "R-r-r. Red eyes."

At first, Hank wanted to dismiss it, but his nephew wasn't an actor. He climbed out of the grave and followed Jake's finger to a patch of woods. He saw nothing. To be sure, he shuffled the flashlight from his belt and clicked it on. The beam traced in and out of the trees.

Mounds of dirt surrounded him as he stared off into the distance, following the light with a curious but unamused gaze.

The crickets still hadn't returned.

Hank couldn't hide the apprehension in his voice. "You see, there's nothing out…"

The light touched something before it moved, branches and bushes snapping on its way. He froze, jaw hanging open. Whatever it was, he hadn't gotten a good look at it. "It's probably a deer," he whispered, but even he didn't believe it. *It certainly didn't look like a deer.*

For a long while, Hank's eyes were glued to that spot in the woods. The more rational part of his brain took over and he realized it had probably moved on.

He choked on the words. "We need to get back to work."

After Jake climbed back into the hole, the color returned to his face. With the shovel in his hand, he mumbled, "I got a bad feeling about this."

Without taking his eyes off the woods, Hank pierced the ground. *Thump.* He'd found the lid of the vault. For a second their eyes met, and they both smiled.

The shoveling continued in a hurry before a pattering of clicks erupted from the dark woods. They both paused, staring at each other for a second before braving a look.

Jake asked, "What was that?"

The clicks occurred again, and Hank tried to interpret them, but he'd never heard anything like it before. With a trembling hand, he turned on the flashlight and traced the woods, again. He wasn't sure he wanted to see whatever made that ungodly noise.

In all his years he'd never encountered anything like that before. Judging by the look on Jake's face, he hadn't either.

The flashlight beam danced and raced through the thick woods. It had gone silent again. The flashlight clicked back into his belt, and he reached for the shovel.

In his periphery, Hank saw a man standing at the edge of the trees. He turned to look.

A ferocious flap broke the silence, like a flag in a hurricane. A horrendous shriek followed. The outline of a winged creature blotted the moon before it landed only feet away. Its beady red eyes stared at them. Two antennae jutted from its brows, twitching. Pincer-like things flexed on either side of its mouth.

It stood on two legs like a man, but it was no man.

Its pincers spread. The clicks led into a horrendous screech.

If not for the paralytic fear, Hank would have covered his ears. The best he could do was cringe and try not to scream.

The shovels landed on the ground, and they stumbled out of the hole, feet sliding in the loose dirt.

Their feet pounded against the grass as they broke for the trucks.

Heart in his throat, Hank stole a glance and didn't see it. With his back turned, his foot clipped a headstone and he stumbled. A sharp pain throbbed in his ankle.

A looming fear overcame him. It could land on his back at any second. His fingers dug for purchase in the grass and his legs worked like pistons. There wasn't any time to assess the damage.

Ahead of him, Jake ran without looking back.

Massive wings beat the sky, whooshing as the creature dove for Jake. It plunged, descending hundreds of feet in a split second.

With immense pain ripping in every step, Hank screamed, "Jake!"

In response to his name, Jake swung his head around. For an

instant he'd taken his eyes off the headstones and that's when he tripped.

The creature missed him by inches.

A wave of relief swept over Hank, a fleeting one.

Its massive wings rippled. Regaining height, it let out another ear-piercing shriek. The loudest one thus far. It vibrated his skull, and he swore he felt it in his fillings.

Wincing, Hank clapped his hands over his ears. It did nothing to protect him.

He desperately searched for it, but the woods were just too dark. With every step, unimaginable pain stemmed from his ankle. The vast distance between them seemed like miles as he hobbled toward his nephew.

Jake fumbled to find his feet, looking like a newly born calf.

Its merciless red eyes illuminated from a tree.

His stomach dropped.

From its treetop perch it pounced, gaining in both momentum and ascension. Its rugged wings tore at the sky before it swooped, again.

From across the cemetery, Hank screamed. As if watching a horror flick, he saw the beast descend on his nephew.

Jake couldn't get away in time.

With its massive talons, it shredded into his back.

The screams of agony sent chills racing up and down Hank's spine.

No amount of protest drew its attention from Jake.

Popping and crackling commenced as it swiped at him again, tearing his flesh in tendrils.

Before he reached the monster, it turned to look at him. Those cold red eyes stared as its talons dug and clawed at the meat on Jake's back.

In an instant, it launched into the air.

Unable to track it, he lost sight of the thing.

Lying on the ground, gasping for air, Jake shook violently.

Hank approached. He lifted Jake's head into his lap where he rocked him. Trickles of blood ran over his knees. A few wet coughs escaped his lips before his life faded away.

Every time Hank closed his eyes, he saw those menacing reds glowing from the trees. The flap of its wings echoed in his psyche.

The nightmare seemed endless. As he relived this horror internally, Hank had only been vaguely aware the paramedics stuck him with a needle and dragged him off.

For days reality was hazy.

The clicks. The screech. The flapping of its wings. The bloody soundtrack of his nephew's demise played over and over in his head like a movie with no power button.

Numb, unable to focus, he traveled down a white hallway. The lights shone too bright above. Hank Berryman focused on nothing but the scratchy wheel of his chair as they pushed him into a room.

A putrid smell lingered inside, something like cleaning products covering puke. A couple of people escorted him into a bed against his will. He noticed he not only had no will to fight, but no strength.

A few days passed and Hank got into the habit of spitting out the medication they'd stuck in his mouth when the nurses weren't looking. He'd gained quite the collection between the mattress and the bedspring.

When the fog had worn off, Hank had gone about the room in search of something, anything. What he'd found was a name carved into the wall under the bed. Areum. Something deep inside told him that they'd gotten out and that he could too. He held onto hope.

After what felt like a lifetime, light flooded the room. Someone wearing light-blue scrubs fetched him. As they rode down the hall, the nurse whispered something in his ear. "I'm going to get you out of here." A hint of familiarity rang in her voice.

Under ordinary circumstances he'd be able to recall a voice and a name within seconds. They were both a blank.

They pulled to a stop in front of a door. The nurse leaned forward, and Hank got a glimpse of his daughter's face. Rachel. She wore a blonde wig to disguise her beautiful brown hair, but it was her. A single finger leaped to her lips to shush him.

Someone wearing a white robe walked past, talking to himself.

The man muttered in a low, disgruntled voice but Hank swore he'd said something about pumpkins.

She pushed him into an office where two doctors waited. One of them sat behind a desk while the other stood near the window. A strong scent of old books filled the room. There were two massive shelves behind the desk, littered with psychology literature, undoubtedly.

Neither of them were young men. They both looked to be in their late fifties, skin beaten from years of stress. The man behind the desk ran a hand through his hair. "It's good to see you, Hank," he said.

He didn't reply.

The other man stepped closer. "Seriously, Maverick. He's been here for a week and hasn't said a word. You don't think he'll respond to a Rorschach test."

Maverick lifted a hand to silence him.

The man rolled his eyes, looked out the window for only a second, and resumed his gaze at Hank.

Maverick walked around the desk before sitting on it. He shuffled through some papers and fetched a handful of ink prints. "If you could please tell me what you see here, Hank." He held out the first.

He saw what looked like a man but wasn't a man at all. It had wings and antennae. Two pincers emphasized where its mouth would be and there were two eyes, black instead of red.

Hank screamed.

The two doctors nearly fell over.

"Nurse," Maverick shouted. "Nurse."

The nurse came in and grabbed him. Together they rolled out into the hall, but rather than heading toward his room, they banked left and headed for the door.

His daughter's hand landed on his shoulder. "It's okay, Dad. I got you."

Beautiful rays of sun beat down as the doors clapped shut behind them. They ditched the wheelchair. Stealing a glance over his shoulder, Hank saw nobody in pursuit.

The truck rumbled to life and Rachel slammed it into gear.

Both men were staring out the window with shocked looks on their faces as she burned rubber. They turned onto the main road.

Two nurses flew out of the building and stared at them. Hank had just enough time to flip them off before they were out of sight.

They were on the road for nearly an hour before one of them spoke. She spoke first.

Rachel looked at him from the corner of her eye. "You know out of all of this, I really only have one question."

Hank, who had a million questions of his own, chuckled. "What's that?"

"Why were you robbing graves?"

He stared out the window for a long time. "I didn't want to lose you."

Her soft hand took his. "Dad. I don't care if we have to live in a cardboard box. I'm not going anywhere."

DEVILS IN THE DUST

WRITTEN BY
J. AGOMBAR

DAWN

ISIAH SINCLAIR STIRRED as dawn streaked crimson across the horizon. He hauled up his bulky frame to sit on his bed of empty sacks, sprawled haphazardly across the wooden decking. He rubbed his head with powerful hands before leaving the hut where the others still slept. Shuffling carefully, so as not to wake anyone else, Isiah was mindful of the chains that clasped his ankles as they clanked and scraped across the dusty ground. They were a sign of a recent runaway, but Isiah thought himself luckier than most; other punishments were chained hands, or metal collars with prongs that prevented them from resting, or worse, the metal braces that stopped them from eating. Moving over to the outhouse toilet, he used it before helping himself to a palmful of water from the tap that protruded from the wall of the main house.

Isiah then made his way around the side of the extension where his first duty awaited. A long stretch of mesh wire was clasped onto a wooden frame where the chickens were kept. As he opened a sack of bird feed under the edge of the canopy next to them, they started to scuttle and flap, knowing what was coming. He sprinkled the feed to occupy them whilst reaching a muscular but gentle arm inside each hatch to retrieve eggs for the basket.

The coops faced the sprawling cotton field to the east, bright with glowing spheres. Every morning from that field he dreaded the creature as he felt its gaze upon him. Peering around to the same spot, he saw the familiar silhouette of ram's horns sprouted from a strange head amongst the cotton. It made no noise, it gave no sense of threat, but it watched him, somewhat curiously. His courage was scarce, as were his answers to what this creature wanted, but as the sun rose and warmed the ground, he saw the creature duck down amongst the cotton and heard it slip away out of sight with a faint trot. Isiah felt the creature had spared him for another day.

I

Tambourna House
Shelburn, Louisiana, USA
1861

Three days passed and an amber sun glowed through a thick, hazy sky upon the prestigious house of Tambourna. The trees hung still, and the crickets sang as the slaves worked mercilessly through the heat of the day, pulling cotton from the eastern fields and cutting sugar from the cane to the north. The house was vast, decked out with trinkets and treasures from around the globe. Cyrus McCord rocked in his chair upon the faded wooden decking by the dining room window, a cigar protruding from his rubbery lips. His pinstriped waistcoat was a little tight, as were the chunky gold rings that lined the fingers which gripped the bottle of bourbon on the table beside him. He checked the grandfather clock and smoothed his moustache, knowing that Sam would arrive shortly. Samuel West was a snake that slithered into all manners of morality, but his results spoke for themselves when dirty jobs had to be done.

Cyrus had received a small crate which now lay on the varnished chair by the doorway. It had been posted to him weeks previous and arrived that morning. He took a sip of bourbon before rising with the alacrity of a pig to swill. Taking the crowbar that lay on top of it, he prized the lid off to reveal the glorious antique. A smile beamed from his face as leathery hands hovered down to it like they would to a newborn. He raised the instrument with care, but nearly dropped it as Samuel burst through the door, heavy-handedly.

"Christ alive, Sam! You pray I don't fucking drop this, because it's worth more than what you could earn if you live to be a hundred."

"Apologies, Mr. McCord. What is it?"

"Culture, boy. Culture from the ancient Greeks. A lyre, like Apollo played in the valleys."

The instrument was constructed from a sizeable tortoise shell affixed with two curved horns that were joined at the tips via a tuning block. The block was lined with tuning pegs connected with strings that stretched taut down to the shell. Samuel raised an eyebrow and closed his mouth after realizing he was gaping.

"A liar? So…it don't tell the truth then, huh?"

Cyrus glared at him for a moment before placing the lyre back in the box upon its bed of hay.

"I see such culture is wasted on you, Samuel. A man of the modern world, you are. What did you want to discuss?"

"New workers, Mr. McCord. Replacements for the missing."

"I don't think it's plausible to buy more at the moment, Sam. The trade is slowing at present and it makes it harder to find workers with strong enough backs to persist. How many is this now?" he asked, moving back to the table and pouring the bourbon into two glasses.

"This is the third this month," he replied. "But I have assured them that if any more flee then rations will be reduced for those that remain."

McCord fluttered his eyelids and grimaced as he replaced the bottle on the table.

"I could punish and starve every one of them, but the problem isn't solved. If we feed 'em less, they produce less, and we waste time and money on punishment."

He handed Samuel the glass of bourbon and they both took a sip.

"Sir, surely the fear of God in 'em will force them to work harder. The scheming runaways will think twice before leaving the rest if they know what would happen to 'em."

"Oh, hell, the schemers don't give a horseshit about the ones they leave behind! They know they're bound for nothin', and when nothin' rules men, nothin' stops 'em from being out for themselves."

They both took another sip.

"So what would you suggest we do?" Sam asked.

"Do you have the details of the escapees?"

"Yes, sir. Isiah fled this mornin' after feeding the chickens. He's fled before and is still in cuffs for it. A week ago, a woman named Eliza, and before that, a young boy who used to feed the chickens and run errands for us never returned from Arlington."

"Shit. That's a whole family fled on us," spat the owner.

"They weren't relat—"

"I know they weren't related, Goddammit!" he replied, slamming the bourbon glass on the table, spilling some. He took a few deep breaths in frustration before gathering his conclusions in silence. "The young boy has probably been kidnapped in Arlington, so let's write him off. The woman is a week gone, so probably dead, or in some place much worse by now. But the big fella…I can't let a strong back go easy for nothin'. We'll visit the rest at first light, make an example of one rather than all of 'em. In the meantime, find any other to feed the chickens tomorrow."

"You got it, Mr. McCord," replied West.

II

The following morning McCord and West, along with two other men who conducted business around the plantations, rounded up the workers for inspection. They stood in a line, solemn with few heads held high. The four slavers stood before them, dressed as gentlemen but intent on spreading fear. Samuel West stepped forward to speak.

"Y'all listen up! We have a recent production problem caused by some of you runnin' out on us. Three this month!" He held up three fingers. He paced up and down in front of them, raising his voice gradually. A chicken strayed away from the penned area and trotted over near the workers, pecking at the ground. "I don't know what makes 'em think they're gonna get any better elsewhere, but good luck to 'em. They're probably going to have a worse time than you are." He paused for a moment and changed his footing, placing one hand upon the ivory-handled revolver in his holster. "Question is, what is it that we are doing wrong to make you guys wanna run?"

West pulled his revolver out and the entire row of workers took a step back. He then cranked the hammer back and fired at the chicken, hurling it between the thin legs of a worker and spraying him with blood. The shot caused the whole line to duck and shriek. West paced up to one of the stronger-looking males in the line and pulled him forward by the neck. He hit him on the head with the grip and the man fell to his knees, placing one hand up in surrender.

"Do we not feed you?" he asked him, loudly.

"Yes, sir," the man replied.

Samuel hit him with the grip again, this time in the shoulder.

"Do we not provide you shelter?"

"Yes, sir," he replied, again, cowering.

West kicked him in the ribs, causing him to fall on his side.

"Okay. Our *kind* Mr. McCord provides you everything you need with the money from his own lands and you repay us by runnin' off!?" He raised his voice at the rest of them. "So, can anyone here tell me where Isiah Sinclair went today? Or the girl last week? Or the young boy before that? Huh?"

A moment of silence passed before West ended it by kicking the man on the floor once more into the dusty ground. He raised the revolver toward him to be greeted with whimpers and shrieks from the others but was interrupted by a rustling in the cotton fields nearby. The rustling grew louder and more vibrant as something approached through the plants, bending and disturbing them. Each of the slavers drew their weapon, waiting for perhaps a boar to emerge from the plants. West's eyes widened as the disturbance burst out from the field to reveal a young worker boy of roughly nine years old. He halted his running and fell to the floor, breathing deeply with exhaustion. His arms and back were scratched and bleeding; his eyes were streaming; his pupils were wide and dark with fear. A worker woman from the line, crying and hysterical, ran toward the boy to comfort him. The slavers lowered their guns.

"Where have you been, boy? Not good enough to join the ranks today?" he said.

At that moment, he recognized the dirty faced and trembling boy.

Cyrus McCord appeared from the decking at the rear of the house to witness what was going on. He brought his steel-tipped cane, and limped quickly toward Samuel West.

"Do you know this boy, Mr. West?" he asked.

"Well, shit! I think he's the boy who used to feed the chickens."

West advanced aggressively toward the boy, but McCord held him back by the arm.

"Where have you been, boy?" asked McCord.

The boy answered in his native language. "Eşu wa nibi, ni eruku," he said, trembling in the woman's arms. He uttered some more before McCord cut in and spoke to the woman instead.

"What is he rattlin' about?"

The woman answered him after gathering her nerves. "He says the devil is here. He says that the devil is angry, and will come back for him; for all of us."

The workers were dismissed for the morning and returned to their duties. A searing sun reigned above, turning the remaining grass among the fields from green to amber. McCord let the boy recover from his ordeal; he was cared for by Charlotte, the worker who helped him that morning. He stood with hands on hips by the edge of the plantation, watching as the workers returned to eat by the huts.

"I can't see no devil in the fields. Just many trees and the Lord's many seas behind them. What on Earth would scare a boy half to death out there?"

Samuel West stood next to him, sneered, and tilted his hat.

"Probably a boar, or somethin'. They get crazy ideas in their heads and fucking blaspheme against the Lord."

McCord somewhat agreed with him and commented on how the boy had survived so long. He then turned his attention to more pressing matters.

"Well, as long as we get no more deserters, we should still make the order by Friday."

"Is that when the wagon arrives?" Samuel asked.

"Yeah, dusk."

III

As the day grew brighter, McCord's patience thinned. The boy with the scratched back played on his mind. He wanted to dismiss his words as mindless chatter, but something compelled him to learn what happened. At risk of further filling the workers' heads with stories, he took it upon himself to speak to the boy in his hut. Charlotte turned him around for McCord to see. Apart from the usual nicks and scrapes found on a worker's skin, the boy was scratched strangely on his back and shoulders, similar to claw marks. They weren't deep but enough to hinder his work, and they certainly weren't the marks of a whip or a cane.

McCord attempted to reason with the boy, suggesting it may have been an animal defending its territory, or that he had fallen into thistles, but his explanations seemed so useless that McCord didn't even believe them himself. The boy couldn't describe exactly what had happened after feeding the chickens, but once again, his mention of the devil was not taken kindly by McCord. Subsequently, he dragged the boy out of the hut by his arm to be taken by Samuel West's men into the backwoods to return with proof of the devil.

The men who were given the job were Billy Heath, a skinny unkempt man with gray stubble, and Chris Taylor, a chubbier auburn-haired man whose arrogance was seen through a dumb grin. They rode off on horses, leaving Charlotte crying on her knees. McCord swung a gold-plated pocket watch around on a chain, trying to hide the haunting feeling brought from the image of the dead chicken that still lay on the ground.

Dusk fell once more upon the red earth of Tambourna house, and the grandfather clock in McCord's office chimed seven. A five-arm candelabra flickered in the eyes of the wall-mounted elk above it. A cigar rested in a pewter ashtray on the desk near where McCord had propped up his feet. Beside the large book that lay open before him sat the lyre, tempting him to pluck one of the strings. A faint knock from the door disturbed him before Samuel West let himself in.

"Sam, my boy! You're later than usual. Good day on the cotton?" asked McCord.

West nodded slowly, acknowledging the question, but gritted his lower teeth against his top lip. He took his hat off.

"Something troubling you, son?" asked McCord, palms out wide.

"All is well on the production, sir. But...ah, I can't find Chris Taylor..."

"Taylor! I sent him out with Billy and the scratched up boy earlier."

"I know, sir, but..."

"Well, what does Billy say?"

"He, uh...I can't find Billy either, sir. I don't think they came back."

McCord took his feet off the table, stood, and snatched his cane. "Bullshit! It's been hours. They're probably just dusting off whiskey under some tree because I broke their routine. Idle sons of bitches."

McCord and West proceeded outside toward the open space where the chicken was killed, but only its blood remained on the dry earth. First they checked the hitching rail for the horses. No sign. Then McCord limped up to the workers' huts whilst muttering under his breath. He jabbed his cane on the door of the hut where the young boy resided. The door was opened by a male worker in his mid-twenties. The pair barged past him. McCord was taken by the sour odor of sweat and brought a silk handkerchief to his face as he scanned the room for bedding. Four beds were made up on the floor, all taken, with two hammocks in the back, both empty.

"The boy with the scratches, where is he?" McCord demanded.

Several shook their heads and cowered, but Charlotte, the worker who cared for him, eventually answered.

"You sent him away, Mr. McCord."

"I know that! And he hasn't returned?"

Her head shook again. West stepped forward and grabbed her by her tunic.

"You answer Mr. McCord, bitch! I know you've seen 'em somewhere."

He struck her once with the back of his free hand. Suddenly, an interruption came from outside, the sound of a melody. The two men frowned at each other before bustling back through the hut door to find the source of the music. McCord's outrage balanced with shock as the tortoise shell lyre he had purchased was being played, fluently and accurately, to produce a serene yet eerie tune.

"What in the name of Christ is going on?" West blurted.

The musician was the scratched boy, whose wounds were hard to see in the darkness. A lantern flickered by the edge of the small barn where the animal feed was kept, and was enough to illuminate one side of the boy so they could see his impeccable skill at the lyre. Workers had started to creep out of their huts slowly, and occasional gasps were quickly muffled at the sight of the boy, who plucked with each and every finger of his left hand whilst producing a deeper sound with his right, aided by a cuttlefish bone. In front of the boy was a slumped body. It didn't take West long to recognize the red and white neckerchief that Billy Heath wore as he lay with his blood drying in a dark patch on the earth. The men trembled, and McCord started to stagger, not knowing what to do. He pointed his cane toward the boy in outrage but the boy glanced back at them and stopped playing. His eyes had changed. The dark hues from the tearful and terrified gaze were gone, replaced with an emerald glow and large black rectangular pupils which sat horizontal in the center of each. Samuel West reacted by raising his gun and cocking the hammer. He stood firm but his aim wavered slightly as the boy stood and approached them, lyre in hand.

"By the powers of God, what are you, boy!?" McCord said, warily.

"...Mo wa ni Arcadia...tele ategun ni owuro," the boy replied, expressionless.

The boy started muttering as he came closer, eyes fixed upon McCord.

"...Mo wa ni Arcadia...tele ategun ni owuro."

He repeated the words a handful of times before stopping in front of them. He eyed McCord for a moment. McCord recoiled, frowning. By now West had the barrel of his revolver an inch from the boy's head, twitching for a reason to pull the trigger, but intrigue stopped him. The boy turned, briefly looking West in the eyes, and walked away with lyre in hand, disappearing into the fields. With his revolver still raised, West called behind him toward the small crowd of workers that had formed. Each of them trembled and crouched in anxiety.

"Woman! Where's the woman who knows that boy? Come here!" he wailed.

Charlotte came forward gingerly, clasped her hands; tears streamed her bruised face.

"You heard him, right? The boy. He said somethin'…What did he say?"

"He said, sir…" she responded, "…I was in Arcadia. Follow the trail at dawn."

"What fucking trail? What for?" spat West.

As he spoke, McCord noticed that Billy Heath's body was not as cleanly slaughtered as they had thought. McCord fetched the lantern that hung on the beam at the side of the barn and inched closer to find that Heath's intestinal tract had been pulled away and laid out across the dusty ground. The entrails led toward the fields where the boy had vanished.

IV

The men, restricted by fear, left the body of Billy Heath lying there, guts spilled and strewn. McCord was jittery and Samuel West was in denial, but neither were able to sleep after the evening's strange events. They returned to their rooms to wash and gather arms, and despite the odd nature of the boy's request, McCord believed that somebody wanted a fight and he was willing to step up in order to save the reputation of his household. He changed into a fresh suit and black boots, complete with a bracing buckle and silver spurs. Their anxiety was increased by the sound from deep in the woods that started after midnight. It was different to McCord's lyre and more like pipes playing. The melody increased in tempo and then fell away at certain points, but it was relentless. Occasionally a single note persisted for some time and other clumsy tones tailed off in the moonlight. The two men readied horses and stood over the corpse of Billy Heath just before daybreak, listening to the trilling pipes. West chewed tobacco nervously.

"Damn lowlifes are trying to freak us out!" West cussed, eyes darting across the distance.

"And they're succeeding," McCord replied, expressionless.

"It's gotta be a group of abolitionists in the woods, or somethin', right? Just drifters messin' around."

McCord gave West a tired but bemused look, then glanced at the fetal position Billy Heath's body took upon the ground.

"Are we really taking the bait here?" said West. "I mean, what if this is an ambush, or somethin'?"

McCord sneered in a menacing manner, and raised a vine-etched revolver from his belt. "Then we show 'em why you don't fuck with House Tambourna. Let's go and find our piper at the gates of dawn."

They rode Morgan horses into the darkness of the fields, illuminating the entrails of Billy Heath with a lantern. The entrails were ruptured and torn in places but intact enough to lead them behind the fields and into the woods. Maples lined the fringe, but as they delved deeper, red maple and split bark of hickory surrounded them. They heard only the sound of the crickets' song as the distant pipes ceased. Heath's intestinal tract eventually ended and they circled a small patch of grass stained with blood and bile.

"Is this where it ends?" West asked.

"This better not be a yellow belly trick, Goddammit!" rattled McCord. "Wait here, I need a piss."

McCord then dismounted and took cover behind a nearby hickory. West chewed his tobacco a little slower and drank from a pouch that hung from his saddle. He glanced around at the canopy which now glimmered with shafts of light.

"West..." said McCord from behind the hickory.

"Yeah?" West turned and saw a pale Cyrus McCord standing still, hair wet with blood, and wiping specks from his face with his silk handkerchief.

"I've found Taylor," he replied, face aghast.

West followed McCord's eyes as he glanced above them to find the body of Chris Taylor hanging upside down from a gnarled branch. The left arm and leg of the man were missing, causing the dripping blood, but the men found no sign of the limbs nearby. As West peered closer, he noticed that Chris Taylor had been gutted in the same manner as Billy Heath. His intestinal tract protruded from his body and was hung across several branches above them, leading off a little to the right.

"What kind of animal would do this?" West asked rhetorically.

McCord rubbed his face and tried to find logic amid the horror. "He must have been asleep when they got him. We can't let our guard down. And besides..." He punched a finger up to the hanging corpse. "He's tied with rope, and that's a rolling hitch knot above. This ain't no animal, or devil, but a red blooded mortal man we're huntin'."

McCord staggered over to his horse and mounted with a sudden jittery burst of energy. West took his hat off for a moment in tribute to Taylor. After a moment, he replaced his hat and brushed off the sentiment to join McCord in following the trail of gore above them.

"So long, Taylor. At least I don't have to put up with your dumb grin again," he chanted into the air.

Minutes passed as they followed the winding set of organs strewn above them. McCord squinted and shielded his eyes with a raised hand battling with the light that pierced the canopy. After a while they found themselves in a grove of oak trees that lowered the canopy. Spanish moss hung from them as if they were ancient giant figures wearing cloaks. The men noticed that the sound of the river wasn't faint anymore; it had disappeared entirely. Neither of them recognized the depth of the woodland, let alone where they were in relation to the Tambourna house.

At the deepest part of the woods, a clearing appeared where a nearby oak tree stood. Its giant, limb-like branches looked centuries old, some even touching the dusty ground beneath. It was surrounded by a group of large rocks that lined a small trickling stream behind it. They dismounted and let the horses drink from it whilst they observed the entrails above that ended abruptly over a high branch of the senior oak, allowing blood to drip into the stream. The men scouted the area but found nothing.

"C'mon. What are ya, yellow?" McCord shouted into the air, revolver raised.

"We didn't come all the way down here for nothin'. It's our turn to spill blood ya sick bastards!" West added.

At that moment, a dark, muscular figure emerged from behind the gnarled ancient oak, rags across his waist and holding chains. West recognized him immediately and raised his revolver to fire, but as he pulled the trigger, the mechanism jammed. He fumbled and tapped the bullet chamber to fire again, only to have it jam again. A minute set of vines and weeds had grown inside the hammer. Sprouting at an unbelievable speed, they pushed their way out of the barrel. In a matter of seconds, the gun had solidified with vegetation, rendering it useless.

West launched the revolver at Isiah Sinclair, just to see him avoid it whilst running toward him at an alarming speed. The former worker swung the chains at West, lacerating his face and spinning him around. Sinclair followed up with a tackle, taking West down, and after a short scuffle, he ended by pinning him face down to the ground with a split lip.

Meanwhile, McCord had tried firing his weapon, but the miniature vines had locked the mechanism from inside. Red with frustration, he resorted to throwing his revolver at the hulking Isiah Sinclair, but as he raised it up to do so, his wrist was clasped by a hand. The hand was strong and strange; two large claws and a smaller, opposable thumb claw gripped him with a might he could not surpass, causing him to drop the pistol. He was soon raised off the ground by his arm and then dropped near the ancient tree. As McCord turned, he swallowed hard. The horror froze him. Before him was something half man, half beast. An ancient human body topped the muscular legs of a goat with cloven hooves. Its arms were woven and twisted like those of a banyan and formed the hands of a clawed beast but with human attributes. Its head was also a strange hybrid, caprine in form but with pointed human ears and a menacing expression. McCord stood gaping, and trembling in fear.

"By the mercy of God, what are you?" he stuttered.

The creature let out a huff, much like a horse clearing its nose. It turned, clambered over to the other side of the ancient tree, and sat on a rock by the stream. A small bird briefly swooped and perched on its long curved horns, and then darted away back into the woods. The creature then gestured at McCord to sit on the rock near him with its clawed hand. McCord just remained stunned. The creature growled and gestured again. When McCord eventually relented, the creature spoke in an ancient tongue, slowly, and almost phonetically.

"I…I don't understand…" replied McCord.

"The great piper has been watching you for some time, and sees you have done many wrongs," interrupted a voice from nearby in fluent English. It was the young boy with the scratches, whose pupils had reverted to normal. He carried McCord's lyre in his hands once more. As the creature carried on speaking, the boy translated. "He says your people have turned against each other and punished many who do not deserve it. Your sins against nature and its inhabitants must be paid."

McCord sniggered nervously.

"Sins? Paid, how?" He coughed.

"Paid with blood," the boy said.

"What the hell are you talking about? I don't choose the way things are. I keep it all together and employ many into the safety of my household, including you." McCord stabbed a finger toward the boy and Isiah, who still had West pinned. "Nature don't come into it!"

The boy continued as the creature did. "The great god of the flocks would like to give you a chance to repent. You must join him in a contest."

"What in the name?" McCord ranted.

The goat god finished and breathed heavily enough so McCord could see his sinewy chest rise and fall from distance. The creature eyed him relentlessly, but McCord could not meet his wide-set yellow and black eyes.

V

The boy brought the lyre and cuttlefish over to McCord and invited him to go first. At that moment the woods around them fell silent and still; not a leaf fell in anticipation of the event. A group of figures appeared slowly from the woods. As they came closer, it became clearer they were not local, but somewhat otherworldly. Five, six, seven naked ivory-skinned women gathered closely to watch the contest. Each had divine figures with hair of gold and auburn that glowed under the canopy which moved as if floating underwater.

They sat on the nearby rocks. All eyes, including the creature's, stared at them.

McCord blinked rapidly, and when all eyes turned toward him, he eventually raised the cuttlefish to pluck the strings of the lyre, one by one at first, and then bowing with reasonable accuracy for a beginner. His chord sequence clashed a little but the slow vibrato-infused sound he produced caused the spectators' heads to drift lightly in melancholy trance. He ended his performance and the creature was the first to produce applause. The naked women followed suit and seemed to commend him.

The hybrid creature then raised a set of pipes to his lips and played them with an enthusiasm that spurred the ladies of the woods to dance in the grove around them. An energetic narrative trilled from his bound reeds, and animals of the woods such as birds, lizards, boars, minks, and squirrels came running from their habitats toward the sound of the pipes. Energetic key changes forced the ancient creature's hands to tire and gradually slow to a halt, ending his performance. The same applause followed, started by the scratched boy this time, who stepped forward.

"The contest is now finished, and I am pleased to announce that the winner is…the great spirit of nature and the protector of flocks."

McCord shook his head and placed the lyre down, feeling confused and ridiculed. He rubbed his legs in frustration and searched his body for the answers to the strange events around him. His busy eyes scanned his boots, which sparked a reminder for him. Meanwhile, the boy continued.

"However, he would like to commend you on your performance and effort in the contest, and offer you a trade."

McCord frowned, and glanced at the devilish creature.

"One of you may live, but one must be sacrificed to repent the sins of the white men. You may choose to stay yourself, or trade your freedom for the life of your friend," he said, gesturing toward Samuel West who still struggled under Isiah's grip.

"Sacrifice? Horseshit! What is this, some kinda pantomime gone crazy?" McCord blasted as he stood, pacing toward Isiah and West.

On his approach, he pulled a dagger from a sheath concealed in his boot and lunged for Isiah Sinclair, wounding him below the shoulder. He lost his grip on Samuel West, allowing him to wriggle free and stand. A bellowing growl, almost a roar, erupted from behind the men, and all the animals and divine women scattered back into the woods. The creature sprang from the rocks and bolted toward the men. McCord felt the thud of the ground as the creature approached him and so swung recklessly around with the knife, just to be caught by the wrist once again. He dropped the knife as the clawed grip tightened and was forced to stare into the eyes of the snarling creature. Its eyes glowed and scowled as it uttered another line with powerful, echoing vocals. The boy translated once again as West ran in retreat for the horses by the stream.

"Men weep over the blood of the bird, but not the blood of the fish. The god of the flocks protects and weeps for the vulnerable, but rarely for the blood of man," the boy stated.

McCord's horror was over when a set of claws were thrust toward his face and neck. Isiah Sinclair stood slowly, wounded. Years of lacerations across his back had numbed him somewhat. He glanced to find the goat god standing over the body of McCord, which stained the dust with blood. He then returned his gaze toward the fleeing Samuel West.

A line of workers in rags and chains stopped working and watched warily from the cotton plants as a horse galloped from beyond the treeline and into the fields before them. Samuel West was the rider, holding a whip in his hand and ready to use it. Then another horse bolted from the brush, once ridden by Cyrus McCord; Isiah Sinclair followed West closely, unarmed.

West dismounted, cracking his whip to make the workers disperse. He ran to the barn and snatched a pitchfork that leant against it. By the time Isiah had dismounted, West was poised with the tool, wary of another attack. He cracked the whip, catching Isiah's chest.

"Your time is over, Sinclair," he shouted, and turned to the rest of the surrounding slaves. "All your little games are over. You're on my territory again!"

He cracked the whip again as the workers encircled the two men. One of them whistled and threw Isiah a scythe to defend himself. West cracked the whip again, catching Isiah's arm, and advanced, swinging the pitchfork, but missed. Isiah then swung the scythe, tearing West's arm at the elbow. West recoiled and dropped the pitchfork, but retaliated by repeatedly cracking the whip and pushing Isiah back toward the cotton plants. Isiah switched stance and swung the scythe low from his other arm, catching West at the back of the knee. The new gash caused him to yelp and stagger, but he remained standing. He limped over to the enclosing workers and grabbed a young woman no older than twenty. Holding her hostage, he faced Isiah and wrapped the whip around her neck in a stranglehold.

"I'll kill her, you Satan worshipper! You hear me?" he shouted.

The girl choked as she tried to pull the whip from her neck. Her veins bulged as she gasped and lost her voice to scream. Isiah was forced to drop the scythe and back away.

"That's right, boy. You're not that stupid are y—"

His words were drowned by the blood he suddenly vomited, which partly soaked the shoulder of the young woman as she wriggled free and ran. The whip fell to the ground as West splayed his arms out wide and was lifted off the ground by a screaming slave who had pierced his lower back with a pitchfork. He grimaced through crimson gritted teeth as the prongs pushed through his abdomen. When he eventually fell to the ground, the one responsible was revealed: Charlotte, her expression desperate with hate.

DUSK

A large empty wooden wagon pulled up outside House Tambourna. It was led by a dark, polished, armored stagecoach where an inspector stepped out and greeted Isiah Sinclair. Isiah opened one of the many sacks to show him the bundles of fresh cotton they had collected. The inspector nodded and signaled the ten surrounding workers to load the cart.

"Is Mr. West around to receive the payment?" asked the inspector, who held his bowler hat under his arm.

"He is unwell. Mr. McCord has asked me to bring him the payment today," he replied.

The inspector twitched his substantial gray moustache and glanced toward the house. He then eyed Sinclair before handing him a large sum of cash tied with string. After stepping back into the stagecoach, he leant close to the barred windows.

"Where are you from, son?"

"Arcadia," Isiah replied.

"Never heard of the place," the inspector replied as the wagon pulled away.

BE NOT AFRAID

WRITTEN BY
PHIL KEELING

JOANNA WAS six years old when the angel came. Six and a half, she would have been happy to remind anyone, as her birthday had been an entire week before the angel arrived. So even a day after her sixth birthday, six became "six and a half" just like that. Like magic. So, bearing all of this in mind, Joanna was six and a half years old when the angel came.

Joanna shared a house on Chapel Street with her mama and daddy, with no sisters and brothers to keep her company. Other adults would come to visit and tell her parents how lonely Joanna must be, right in front of her, which she found to be rude. Talking about her as if she wasn't there.

"Shouldn't she have a brother or sister to play with?" they'd ask. Or sometimes, the obtuse "When are you planning on making Joanna a big sister?"

They would ask these questions while smiling, but Joanna would notice that Mama and Daddy didn't smile back. Or if they did, it was a different kind of smile; one that didn't use anything but the lips. When those adult friends came by, Joanna would squirm a bit in anticipation of the questions. It was different when Uncle Stuart came to visit, which, sadly, wasn't often.

Uncle Stuart was Daddy's brother but looked completely different. Where Daddy was barrel shaped with a booming laugh, Uncle Stuart was as thin as a green bean, and chuckled politely to himself, as if certain jokes and insights were meant especially for him, and he was enjoying them the way Joanna might enjoy the first bite of a peanut butter and jelly sandwich. Slowly and gratefully.

Uncle Stuart was visiting the night that Joanna met the angel. She knew that company was coming because her mama had ordered her to the backyard to clean up her toys and gather sticks to be thrown in the fire. She paced the yard, pretending not to notice the remains of her toys, waiting for the appropriate moment to go inside and see her uncle.

She stepped over a tricycle and made her way in the back door. However, since she knew that she hadn't finished her chores and felt some residual guilt about this, she sneaked in quietly. Already she could hear the boom of her father's voice, with the clear inflection of her uncle following close behind. She glanced around the corner of the kitchen to find Uncle Stuart already at the table with her father, each holding glasses of swirling red liquid.

Part of the reason it was comforting to see Uncle Stuart was that he always wore the same thing: an all-black suit with a funny white collar. Her mama had said it had something to do with his work, and why they didn't see him all that often. As the two men stared solemnly at each other, Joanna's mama stirred something in a pot, filling the kitchen with the smell of onions and garlic. Stuart looked sad and excited. He sipped again from his glass and Daddy mirrored the movement, as if to encourage her uncle onward.

"I'll tell you," Uncle Stuart said, his eyes bugging out as if he were attempting to make a funny face, "it was the damnedest thing I ever saw."

Joanna didn't like that part. It sounded like something that the older boys would get in trouble for saying.

"It was something in the sky," Uncle Stuart was saying. "It was there, and the prop plane hit it and then *pfbbbt*, both of them were gone."

"Another plane?" Mama asked as she set the table around the two men.

"No, not another plane. Some *thing*. Something with wings."

"A plane's got *wings*." Her father chortled, and the ice in his glass clinked together like an exclamation point at the end of his laugh.

"Not those wings, not plane wings, feather wings!"

Her dad was laughing for real now.

"*Feather* wings."

"Like a *bird's* wings! Don't laugh, Paul, this is serious. A whole plane just fell out of the sky."

At this her father stopped laughing.

"Yeah, you're right," he said. "That's true. It's terrible."

"So this plane hit a bird and exploded?"

This was her mom, now spooning food onto the plates. Joanna noticed a place was set for her, but she dared not move in too soon; she didn't want them to stop talking.

"It wasn't a big plane," her father clarified. "Little two-passenger prop plane."

"But it wasn't a small bird," her uncle said. "Would take more than a goose to bring something like that down."

"But it's *happened*," her Mama said, ever the voice of reason. "Flocks of birds get stuck in engines, I've read about that."

"What flock of birds?" Uncle Stuart was asking, sipping his glass again. "It's November, Nicki; the birds are all gone south."

"There'll be an explanation eventually, I'm sure," Daddy said. "Things like this happen, and the first couple of days, people panic. The explanation comes around eventually."

"Sure," said Uncle Stuart.

"But it's true!" Daddy said.

"Enough of that," Mama said. "If it had happened above *your* church, you'd be shaken up, too."

"But what am I supposed to think happened?" Daddy asked.

"Do you *need* to think anything happened at all?"

"It's my town. It's *our* town," Daddy was saying, his hands up and out like he was giving up a game of baseball. "We have a right to know what's happening."

"You know," said Uncle Stuart, "there are some people saying that it's…"

He trailed off and then shook his head, downing the last of his glass with a look on his face that seemed to say "It's stupid."

Uncle Stuart liked to do this. He would trail off before something extra interesting or funny, and want you to ask "What? What?" Mama called it "taking the bait" and she hated doing it. True to form, she just rolled her eyes as she opened a bottle of wine and placed it on the table.

Daddy liked this game, though.

"What?" he asked. "What are people saying?"

And Stuart chuckled and looked down at his lap, as if the bait really was stupid this time. Finally, he looked up.

"They're saying the plane hit an angel."

The three adults said nothing for a moment afterward, looking at each other in strained silence. And then, a switch flipped, and the three of them laughed as if it was the funniest thing they'd ever heard. Joanna didn't understand. Her uncle loved telling her stories about angels. They were all over the books he brought her on birthdays and holidays. An angel tells a lady she's going to have a super baby. Angels releasing people from chains. Crazy men wrestling with angels. Joanna liked angels. She didn't understand why Uncle Stuart and her mama and daddy would laugh at the idea of one getting hit by a plane. It left her with a heavy feeling in her stomach.

When she joined them at the dinner table, no one brought up the plane or the angel or even birds. But Stuart drank more from his wine glass and told funny stories, though they made less and less sense as dinner went on, and her mama didn't laugh at them as much. It didn't really matter to Joanna, though, and her rapid-fire laughter only encouraged her uncle to ham it up further and drink more heavily from the glass beside him. Eventually her daddy told her that it was time to tell her uncle bye, and by that time she'd forgotten all about the angel and the plane. Stuart hugged her close, and Joanna thought that he smelled sweet and sour, like juice left out in the sun too long. He said goodbye and then turned his head on her shoulder, speaking directly in her ear now.

"Keep an eye out for angels, wouldja?" he asked before straightening up. Mama told her to finish cleaning up her toys before the sun went down, and that made Joanna happy. Not that she cared for picking up her toys, but it gave her a few more minutes outside before bedtime.

It felt like even more leaves had fallen since she had come inside for dinner, and the more she searched, the more toys she found. A plastic rake, several wiffle balls, and even an apron that her mother had bought for her when she took up an interest in pretending to make muffins. Joanna was considering the consequences of "forgetting to clean the play kitchen" when she heard a voice somewhere beneath the leaves.

Please help us, the voice said in a tone that was somehow both powerful and weak; a boom that wavered. It didn't sound like anyone she'd ever heard before. It was cold enough that anyone speaking would have puffed out clouds of steam, and Joanna thought this would be a good way to narrow down where the voice was coming from. She glanced over the fallen leaves, which had come down in frumpy layers of various thickness all along the house's vinyl exterior. No steam. Joanna frowned.

Plastic rake in hand, she began to sweep away clusters of oak leaves, imitating her father in seasons gone by. She began to think that she was no closer to uncovering the source of the voice, when it spoke again.

We offer you peace. Nothing but peace.

Well, that was a weird thing to say.

She hadn't considered that whatever was talking to her meant to do her any harm. So why all this talk of peace? The kids at school only said "I'm not gonna hit you" if they planned on hitting you. It unnerved her enough that she considered going to her father for help. But she decided against it. If she went to Daddy, it wouldn't be hers anymore. Daddy got to drive in a car and went to a job almost every single day. Daddy made the fires in their fireplace and climbed up the tall ladder whenever the gutters got full or Joanna's frisbee went too high. He went on adventures all the time. This was going to be *her* adventure. And she'd let Daddy or Mommy in on it after she'd had some fun. Or if she got into trouble. But in the meantime, she kept raking, seeking out that voice.

It wouldn't take much longer. Eventually she dragged away a clump of wet leaves, revealing something that wasn't matted grass.

Was this an angel? Mom and Daddy and Uncle Stuart had mentioned an angel. At Sunday School, the books were filled with pictures of angels; great, muscular people with enormous, feathered wings and golden circles framing their pretty faces. Sometimes they even wore armor and carried swords. And while this creature definitely had wings, they weren't attached to the back of a movie-star-handsome man or woman. Past the broken and dingy feathers, in fact, Joanna couldn't see its body at all. They were beautiful, though. Rather than the same dull white she'd seen in pictures, they were countless pale shades; from ivory to cream to striking bright white. If not for the blood that matted in the delicate folds of the plumage, the creature's color would have struck her as perfect and pure.

It watched her with too many eyeballs, each one a different color or shade. Some unlike anything she'd ever seen before. Which was a silly observation, she realized, because *nothing* about this angel was like anything she'd ever seen before. A single eye, larger than the rest, focused on her, its iris a deep indigo color like her mother's African violets. The pupil dilated, and Joanna thought she could see something deep in the blackness; clockwork pieces whirring and rotating in unison, like the insides of her mechanical toy cars. The strange symmetry of it, the *wrongness* it gave off, all of it left Joanna with a terrible pit in the bottom of her stomach. It was getting heavier and heavier, to the point that she worried the weighted mass of panic would tear through her insides and splatter to the floor, anxiety juice bubbling at her toes and burning her feet. She found it harder and harder to breathe the more she looked upon the angel. She felt like she might scream.

Be not afraid, the angel said.

And just like that, Joanna wasn't.

It took a minute to get the angel into the root cellar. It would have taken longer if her father ever remembered to lock it. Her parents had always talked about using the dark spot beneath the house as the perfect place to store canned foods, the moment they got into canning. But that was years ago, when Joanna was a baby, and they still hadn't shown much interest in the root cellar or the hobby that was meant to go along with it. Instead, it had become a repository for tools, gewgaws, and various other items that they would set into the cellar for safekeeping and promptly forget about. There were countless empty flower pots, several enormous bags of potting soil, and a brand new maul axe with an untouched price sticker.

It wouldn't be till the end of winter that Daddy and Mommy would start considering gardening as a hobby again; buying another bag of potting soil and cursing themselves for idiots when they made their way to the root cellar for their gardening tools only to rediscover that they'd purchased a bag last year, and the year before that. And by the time that all happened, Joanna intended to have the angel all patched up and wrapped in gauze and sent on its way.

Her first attempt at picking up the angel had been thwarted by the awkwardness of its many wings.

"You're too big," she said to the angel. It responded by sliding its wings beneath the central core of its body. Folded this way, the creature was a little bigger than the size of a trash can lid. After the angel closed its large, central eye, Joanna was able to carry it more comfortably. She felt the structure of bones beneath the down-covered mass in her arms, and she felt its body sink into her, the way she did when her father picked her up at the end of a long day. When she sat the angel down on the softness of the potting soil bag, she got a better look at it.

"Categorically speaking," she told the angel, "you look pretty good for something that just got hit by a plane."

Her mother liked to use the phrase "categorically speaking" a lot. Joanna didn't know what it meant exactly, but something about it conveyed authority. It sounded strong, and she decided that that was how she needed to sound.

A plane, the angel said. Not a question. Barely even an acknowledgement. Just repeating the word.

"Yes," Joanna said, moving another bag of soil to the ground in case the angel needed more room. "Are you warm enough?"

It was chilly and damp in the root cellar, and Joanna was only just starting to notice.

Faith is all the warmth that I require, the angel said.

That was another weird thing to say.

"Okay," she said, running her forearm across her upper lip, where her nose was slowly beginning to run. "But do you, like, need a sweater?"

She felt silly asking that of a creature that didn't appear to have arms or legs. But it was the first thing that came to mind.

No, thank you, said the angel. The politeness made Joanna smile.

Now we're getting somewhere, she thought.

"Do you eat?" Joanna asked the angel.

In a manner of speaking, she heard it say in her head.

And she was certain of it this time: the voice was definitely in her head. She considered the mass of feathers and eyeballs in front of her again. Shouldn't she be more scared? She had felt something terrible inside when she'd looked at the creature initially, but its voice had soothed her somehow. That voice that zinged inside her head like the static on the end of a shrieking radio signal. Uncomfortable and sharp, but not so bad after a while.

"Do you..." she started, then trailed off, unsure if she'd get into some sort of theological trouble asking what she was about to ask.

"Do you...you know?"

The dreamy multicolored eyes regarded her silently, and she made a brief, if accurate, mimicry of someone squatting down, straining, and perhaps releasing a bowling ball from their pants. The eyes of the angel almost imperceptibly widened momentarily, then returned to their usual, almost sleepy demeanor.

No, the angel said simply.

And that was that. She wiped her nose again and turned, reaching for the cellar door. Startled, she stopped still, noticing for the first time a crimson stain on the back of her hand.

Her nose hadn't been running. It'd been bleeding.

Joanna returned to the root cellar the next morning as soon as she'd finished breakfast, muttering to her mama she was going to visit some friends at the nearby youth center.

The angel was where she'd left it. Even its eyes were still open, regarding her as she approached. She didn't know what to say, so she tried, "Hey, angel."

The angel didn't say anything back, so she tried again.

"How are you feeling?" she asked, coming closer to observe the bloody stains in the angel's plumage. The crimson liquid wasn't as bright as yesterday; most of it had reduced to a splotchy rust color.

"Are you hungry?" she asked.

The angel's eyes dilated and refocused on her.

Yes, it said, and Joanna was thrilled to be rewarded with the tingly sensation of its voice in her head again. Food! This was something she could work with.

"Do you want eggs?"

No answer.

"Pancakes?" She wasn't even sure she knew how to make pancakes, so she was a little relieved when the angel kept silent. The silence, however, remained for sausage and peanut butter and cookies and bologna sandwiches. She was starting to get frustrated when the voice returned to her head, ringing like a copper wire pulled taut.

Sing to me, the voice said. *Sing to me. Please.*

The angel had been weird before. But now Joanna couldn't help but feel like they were going into a new region of strange. She had heard the stories of stranger danger and avoiding men in unfashionable glasses and windowless panel vans. All of that she understood. It wasn't that there was anything overtly *wrong* with the request. It just felt odd; like the ice cream man asking you to do jumping jacks. You couldn't quite put your finger on it, but the request felt unsettling.

"I don't know what to sing," she said.

*Why not try…*The angel paused for a moment, as if considering. Suddenly, Joanna felt a sharp sensation behind her eyes for a moment, as if a bright light had been shone directly into her pupils, and then it was gone.

You Are My Sunshine, the angel said.

It was a good song. Joanna felt instantly at ease, and stood before the angel, suddenly happy to make a performance of this moment.

She sang *You Are My Sunshine* the way that her mother used to sing it to her. It lacked all the dancing and bombast of the way that Joanna was fond of singing, but being more solemn and thoughtful seemed more appropriate. Partway through the song she found it difficult to focus. She was unsteady on her feet and before she could get to the end of the second chorus, she stumbled and fell into the many soil bags she'd assembled for the angel. Her face pushed through a curtain of its shimmering white and cream feathers, smudging the thickness of what she already knew was blood in the divot underneath her nose.

Tiny fireflies popped before her eyes and she shook her head in an attempt to clear her thoughts. She stood before the angel, who, for the first time, had closed all of its eyes. There was a violent flash of red on its feathers that she knew was her fault. Her blood mingled with the dried sanguinary marks of what she assumed was the angel's own life fluid.

There didn't seem to be anything left to do, so she made her way out of the root cellar and back into the house, where her mother stood poised over the sink.

"Back so soon?" her mother asked.

"I didn't..." Joanna started, but couldn't finish. Her head was swimming with tadpoles; a complete mess.

"I didn't go," she said, plopping into one of the chairs at the breakfast table.

"And why was that?" her mother asked, glancing up from her cleaning. The sight of her daughter's bloodied face startled her, and she dropped the dish with a scraping crash to the kitchen floor. Joanna hardly seemed to notice. Her mother kneeled next to her, strained and worried, trying to keep control of her voice.

"Joanna?" she asked. "Are you alright, baby?"

Joanna looked up at her mother through bleary, bloodshot eyes. She admired her mother's face, backlit by the overhead lights of the kitchen. She smiled, revealing a mouth full of the missing teeth of a six year old. In this moment, however, her bare gums and ridged baby teeth felt warped and unnatural, and the gesture sent a tremble up her mother's back.

"So shiny," Joanna cooed up at her mother, her sunken eyes rolling horribly back into her head. "So good."

And then Joanna collapsed to the kitchen floor.

Joanna's mother had never babied her. Even at such a young age, she'd trusted the girl to make sound decisions and be smart about people. Joanna had always shown good instincts and carried herself as someone who knew what she wanted. For a six year old, she was a very headstrong kid, and her mother had encouraged that. Sure, go out and fight and play and come home beat up and covered in grass stains. That's how it ought to be, right?

But with her daughter lying down in the pediatrician's office, she wasn't so sure. The doctor had asked her where Joanna had been, and she'd answered, honestly? She didn't know. The girl had told her she was going to the youth center, and she'd believed her. That was good enough for her, and it should be good enough for anyone, *Goddammit...*

She took a breath and steadied herself. The doctor hadn't *meant* to seem judgmental, not as far as she could tell. He was doing his job. He was asking the questions that a doctor *should* ask. She was scared. Joanna was a healthy, normal enough girl. In fact, she was downright athletic, something she herself had the knack for at Joanna's age. To see her collapse like that had been a moment straight out of hell. She didn't think that Joanna had lost consciousness at any point exactly. Her crimson eyes had been rolling in her skull, even as her head bounced horribly with every speed bump or pothole they drove over.

Joanna's eyes were red because she'd blown several blood vessels in each.

By the time Joanna's father arrived, her breathing had returned to normal, her face didn't look quite so shrunken, and she was even sitting up and asking when she could have lunch. Or dinner. Or a snack. The main issue right now seemed to be that she was hungry.

The doctor offered several explanations, all safe and understandable. Blood sugar. The onset of a flu. Even garden variety anxiety. But none of the adults, including the doctor, felt very reassured by this reasoning.

"Did you meet anyone out there?" the doctor asked Joanna, stooping to her level. "Did someone give you something or do something to you?"

The doctor made it very clear that Joanna would not be in trouble if the answer was yes, but Joanna still responded by pursing her lips and shaking her head *no*. This was a relief, but Joanna's mother couldn't stop herself from wondering if she saw a flicker of doubt on Joanna's face. She wondered if the doctor saw it, too.

"Most likely it's just some sort of caloric crash. Kids are funny like that. But just in case…" He lowered his voice for their benefit. "Consider keeping her inside when she comes home from school. For a few days, tops. Arrange a board game night or something like that; whatever you have to do."

"What are we looking out for, exactly?" asked Joanna's father.

"I'm not honestly sure," admitted the doctor. "But just keep an eye on her."

Joanna was happy to be back home, and even happier when her mama and daddy informed her that she'd be taking Monday off from school.

"Just a couple of days off," her father had said. "Just until we know you're all better."

That also meant she'd be able to check in on the angel again. She didn't have time when they got home from the doctor's office. She could feel the eyes of Mama and Daddy at any place she was in the house. It really wasn't like them to be so protective; it made Joanna feel weird. She'd need to figure out some way of getting away from them. Some sort of excuse, anyway. She didn't want to give up her adventure, not *now*. It had only just gotten started, and she didn't like the idea of it being ruined because she'd had a little tumble. People on adventures got cuts and bruises; that's how it *worked*.

Dinner and the rest of the day went normally. They watched a funny game show while her mom scratched her back, but not long after a story from Daddy and two goodnight kisses, she could hear a rumble. Not a big one, the way earthquakes sounded on the TV, but low and drawn out, like the growl of her neighbor's Great Dane. Before she knew why she'd done it in the first place, she was out of bed and marching down the stairs. She thought at first that she was in control, but no. The sound *demanded* her presence.

"I'm not asking you," Joanna remembered her mother once saying to her. "I'm *telling* you."

She was moving toward the root cellar.

By this time, it was dark outside, and while it wasn't the coldest night, she wished she'd been compelled to put on her shoes *first*. And maybe even a sweater.

Her teeth chattered as she approached the root cellar door. The rumbling rattled the inside of her skull more the closer she got, to the point that she knew her poor brain must be slamming around inside of there. Her hand trembled with the chill as she reached for the door latch, only to find that it wouldn't open. Her father must have remembered to lock up the door that day.

All she wanted was to get inside to the angel. To sing to it again. For a moment she considered where her father's keys were. Hanging up on the hook near the front door. The key to the root cellar had to be there. She considered this for a moment, but was suddenly jarred with the realization that she *has to get into the root cellar right this minute. There isn't time to wait for the stupid keys. I need to get in there now.* The wood was heavy beneath her shoulder, but she knew it would work. This wouldn't take long.

Joanna's father had already been having trouble sleeping. Something in the air was settling behind his eyes with a dull, low frequency. It gave him the sort of headache that he'd come to expect when he'd had too much whiskey or a tooth needed to be pulled. He rolled onto his side, and blinked through the darkness to look at his wife. She was asleep on her back, eyes closed, which was the stance she normally took when she was trying to sleep and having little success. He considered shaking her so that the two of them could screw around. That always managed to put them to sleep.

Well, it always managed to put *him* to sleep.

But before he could tug at her side of the covers, he heard a thump outside. It wasn't like the dull tone in his head; it was far more real and visceral. He stood up, pulling on a pair of gym shorts on his way downstairs.

He stopped on the staircase, trying to remember where he'd left his baseball bat, but ultimately decided it wasn't necessary. The neighborhood he and his wife had chosen was safe and sound. They'd moved there specifically for that reason. Burglars and serial rapists and arsonists were other people's problems. That sort of thing didn't happen here. Most likely it was a dog that had escaped its yard, or...

He stopped. Framed in the sliding glass door that led to the backyard, a flash of pink fabric had shot into his view and then quickly out again.

Thump.

A familiar piece of fabric. One that he knew. It came into his view again, and then...

Thump.

It disappeared.

He tugged open the door, gasping in the sudden cold and then at the sight before him. Joanna in her pink nightshirt backed up for enough space, and then charged, slamming her little shoulder into the wood of the cellar door. She collapsed into the dewy grass, her tiny arm hanging uselessly. He was on his knees, gathering her up like a little bag of leaves. Her eyes were closed and spattered with bright red that gleamed in the moonlight.

"What happened, baby? What are you doing out here, baby?"

And then two fat drops of blood appeared on Joanna's face, splattering like a Pollock painting. Joanna's father reached up and touched the underside of his nose. He was bleeding. As he stared at the blood that coated his fingers, he could feel the strain of his daughter's body beneath him. Weak with exhaustion, but still coiling her muscles to leap out and strike the cellar door again. By the time his wife found them in the backyard, the dull rumbling in his ears had crescendoed to a feverish roar, like waves of blood crashing against his eardrums.

Like with the incident that put her in the doctor's office, Joanna had eventually regained herself on some level, exhausted but otherwise fine. Her father put her in bed and she slept for a while. They used their smallest voices to speak to each other, like children afraid of getting into trouble. What could make a child act this way?

They were both experiencing headaches at the same time, and at first put that off to stress. The same with the nosebleeds; it was getting cold, after all. Skin dries out, skin cracks. Nosebleeds are normal.

But the root cellar. What was in there that could cause their little girl to attempt some stunt like breaking down the door? They resolved to take a look in the morning, as they didn't want to leave Joanna alone. But it was also clear that neither of them wanted to be the one to turn that key. To see whatever their crazed daughter had been trying so desperately to get to.

Joanna's father had locked the root cellar door the morning of the incident. He'd been on his way to the shed to get the lawnmower for one last pre-winter trim of the grass, and had noticed the lock hanging open in the latch. He'd bent down and clicked it shut. He hadn't even considered opening the door for a peek inside. He wondered what he would have seen. Whatever was responsible for all of this? Or were they all just exhausted and put into hysterics by the darkness? Nothing good happens after dark; it was something that the human body knew instinctively. How many horrible things evaporated in the daylight?

Most of them. Most.

Joanna's father watched as she slept and couldn't help but believe that *this* night wasn't going to fall under that category of "most."

As they began to fall asleep, the tone started again. The same low, trembling sound traveled its way up their legs and into their heads, where it left them wincing with the dull ache of it all; like every one of their teeth had sugar packed into infected cavities.

"Do you hear it?" Joanna's father asked, and in truth her mother wanted to deny it. Treat her husband like he was some sort of lunatic. *Of course I don't hear anything.* It would have been simpler.

She *wanted* it to be simpler.

"Yes," she said. "I can hear it."

At that moment, Joanna woke up.

Still dreamy and lethargic, she responded to the tone like a rat following a piper. She tossed her legs over the side of the bed lazily, as if they didn't belong to her. Her feet didn't quite touch the floor, so she was almost silent in slipping out of bed. It was only when she slid between her parents, each dozing on uncomfortable dining table chairs, that they realized Joanna was even awake.

If awake was what you could call it.

Her eyes were open, but her movements, her gaze…

"It's like she's on autopilot," her father said. He reached out instinctively, taking her arm. The force that Joanna pulled away with was unreal and disturbing. He tried to match the pull, but was afraid that he'd hurt her. He let go and put both hands around her ribs, lifting her into the air. Joanna's scream was otherworldly and painful. Not only painful to listen to, but clearly painful to make. It was a shriek to herald the death of an angel; a screeching banshee brought to life. With the help of his wife, Joanna's father managed to pin his daughter to the top of the bed, where she howled and shook like a child possessed. Joanna screamed so violently that something tore in her vocal cords, and a mist of blood coated her father, her mother, and the pillows beneath her head.

And then it stopped.

For a moment, if one could ignore the blood, the horror of the evening might never have happened in the first place. Cautiously, Joanna's parents stood up, slowly dropping their grip on their daughter. Joanna's face was pale, her eyes closed. Where just a moment ago she had been a creature of vicious strain and agony, she now resembled nothing so much as any other sleeping child. Just another kid.

"She's cool," her mother said, placing her hands on Joanna's cheeks and then back again to her forehead. She didn't know what that meant, or if it meant anything at all, but it was something to say. Something to observe.

Joanna's eyes opened. She didn't direct her gaze at either of them, but instead stared into the ceiling above her bed, a tired but somehow bemused expression on her face.

She began to sing in a weak voice; her mother recognized the lyrics to *You Are my Sunshine*. But after a few lines, Joanna closed her eyes again, and finally drifted off to sleep.

"Tomorrow," Joanna's mother said to her husband in as steady of a voice as she was capable, "I want you to call your brother."

"She could be mentally ill," Stuart said.

"You didn't see her," his brother said. "You didn't see how she looked. How she sounded. She screamed until she tore something in her throat."

"I'm not a doctor," Stuart said.

"That's not why we called you," said his brother.

"Demons?" asked his sister-in-law. "Is there such a thing as demons?"

"Yes," Stuart said, tugging a bit at his collar.

"Do you think it could be a possession? Aren't there still priests out there that do exorcisms?" Joanna's mother asked.

"This doesn't sound like a possession. It sounds…" Stuart flipped the thin pages of his Bible incessantly now. "It sounds like you're describing a temptation. Like a being is calling out to Joanna, and compelling her to join it."

"And then what happens?" his brother asked.

"I don't know," Stuart said. "Perhaps it's calling her for indoctrination. Or maybe…"

He paced, wishing he had the good sense not to think out loud.

"Maybe what?" his sister-in-law asked.

"To feed on her," said Stuart.

"What could feed on her? I've never heard of that. I've never heard of a demon needing to feed on a little girl." His sister-in-law was ranting now.

"I've never heard of a real demon *at all*," Joanna's father said.

Silence.

"We're a little out of our league, here," admitted Stuart. "But that doesn't mean we give up."

By the time they were outside the root cellar door, the low tone had begun again, and Stuart could feel what seemed like twisted pins worrying their way into the softest parts of his brain. Whatever wanted Joanna was behind this door. Based on what little knowledge he had of demonology, he assumed it wanted her because it was weakened in some way. Hurt, maybe; otherwise it wouldn't bother with children. That weakness, he told his brother- and sister-in-law, could make all the difference.

His own confidence waned. His entire arsenal was a canning jar full of water from the sink, and his Bible. He had blessed the jar of tap water, and kept his thumb sandwiched between the pages to hold his place; a verse from Isaiah. If you had asked him the day before if he believed in the sanctity of the water, he would have said yes. But the longer they spent preparing for this dubious spiritual warfare, the less convinced he'd become. Nothing wrong with humoring the family at first. And then, when they opened the door and there was nothing inside, they could discuss some sort of therapist for Joanna. In the dark of the night, it was easy to be afraid of demons. But in the cold light of day, practical decisions needed to be made. That was the sort of priest Stuart was. All the same, he wanted to be prepared; to satisfy his family in knowing that he didn't think they were nuts. That he was willing to give them the benefit of the doubt in all things; even this.

His brother unlocked the door and stood back. Stuart opened the pages of his Bible, his palms sweating. He knew the verse by heart, but still checked to make sure he got it right.

It began:

Do not fear, for I have redeemed you;
I have called you by name.

If he could remember that, he could get through the rest. Even if he would, ultimately, be speaking to an empty root cellar. It *would* be empty. The door opened, and Father Stuart strode inside, mouth and jar opened to deliver the Word and the Blood.

He could not speak when he saw it.

The herald of hell was awe-inspiring to look upon, and immediately Stuart wanted to wretch, to pour the contents of his stomach onto the earthen floor beneath the floating being of endless, inky eyeballs and tattered feathers. His poor Joanna; she wasn't the slave of her imagination or a faulty mind. She was the thrall of a creature not of this earth. And here it was, staring him down with a thousand eyes, a low, rolling tone registering from nowhere and sending spears into his mind. Blood poured down Stuart's nose, lips, and chin, dripping to the floor with a steady *tap*.

Be not afraid.

He heard the words in his head, his limbs, and his stomach. They reverberated in his soul. He stared into the eyes of the beast, and somewhere in the darkness behind them, he could see turning; ethereal gears and wheels ticking in some infernal clockwork mechanism. It clicked and snapped into position in rapid-fire succession, creating the low, steady drone that even now burned its way through his skull. He threw a splash of the holy water. It beaded and fell from the oily feathers of the beast, and the force in his head only tore deeper. He risked another glance into its eyes, and could see the wheels turning faster, faster, *faster*.

Stuart couldn't look away. The multitude of eyes rolled back, exposing whites and purples and reds. The central eye, however, stayed focused on him, never allowing him to stray from its gaze, even as he attempted to tear himself away. The creature had him frozen in place, its many voices whispering through his skull.

Still locked in place, Stuart opened his mouth to speak the Word.

"I have called you…by your name."

For a moment, the force echoing off the beast stopped, and each of its many eyes turned slowly toward him again. The fully dilated pupils regarded him like an insect under glass.

I, the demon said, *have called YOU.*

And then everything in Stuart's mind disappeared forever. His body, now a fully empty shell, crashed to the floor of the root cellar.

Joanna's mother kneeled over Stuart, weeping.

"We need you to get up," she begged. Slowly, the creature drew closer to her, its eyes focusing on her trembling body. She wouldn't look up at it; couldn't.

Be not afraid, she heard in her body and mind. It rattled her ears and the hairs in her nostrils, and she knew its power. She felt the oily feathers brushing against her bare shoulder.

I am your tonic and your salvation.

She continued to tremble, feeling the low tone worm its way into her sinuses. She felt the first drops of blood as they trickled their way past her mouth. But in that moment, it wasn't the monster that she thought of. It wasn't her dead brother-in-law, or even her own safety that swamped her mind. It was Joanna; helpless and enthralled, prowled upon by this hideous beast.

Be not afraid, the demon said, and Joanna's mother met its massive central eye in full. She took two handfuls of the creature's musty black feathers and pulled it closer, watching the locomotion of gears hiccup in the blackness behind its eye.

"I am *not* afraid of you," she said truthfully, even as she trembled. Mimicking her, the creature began to shake and vibrate, as if it had one final psychic blow to offer.

And then it stopped.

She felt the weight of the demon fall against and past her, and the sound of her husband's grunt. Suddenly relieved of the pressure and the weight that had held her in place, she scrambled away from the creature like it was made of hot coals. Pressed against the earthen walls of the root cellar, she watched her husband standing over a mass of blackened feathers and weak, watery eyes. The axe; the one that they had bought several seasons ago, back when they were convinced they would use it every day to split wood. Back when they were trying to "get back to the land" and grow their own food in the backyard of their little suburban neighborhood. The steel head of the axe was slammed into what she could see was just an oil slick of black feathers and tiny, beady goat eyes. The demon was now something smaller, punier.

Not a real monster at all.

Her husband and his axe rose and fell. Rose and fell. Rose and fell. And the liquid that dribbled from the imp's body was dehydrated and gelatinous, the color of a bird's droppings. In a flash, all its power, all its infernal majesty, was gone. Replaced instead by something that crept in the shadows and hid from the light.

And, maybe sometimes, was hit by passing prop planes.

Her husband smeared the horrible stuff left on the axe against his pant leg, where it would stain permanently. Finally, when it was clear the thing was dead, he turned to look at her. He stepped past the fallen body of his brother and sat on the bare floor. She joined him, and he took her hand almost forcefully.

"It's finished," he said, and attempted the barest ghost of a smile. "It's done."

THE LAST VISIT

WRITTEN BY
TORI V. RAINN

THE BLARING horn revved Mateo's nerves. The space beneath his compressed brake pedal shook as the steel worm crawled along the tracks ahead of him. A missile the size of that train would be a welcomed distraction, anything to stop him from crossing this path and going back to that place.

Mateo propped the side of his head against his palm, trying to concentrate on his sister's words.

"Dad's getting older. We need to consider this."

The train horn blared once more, scattering his thoughts into oblivion.

"I can't do it," Mateo said. "He'll die there."

The red rearview lights of the car in front of them outlined the creases around his sister's dark eyes. She huffed. Both siblings shared complexions the same shade of brown. She inherited Mom's thick black hair. Unfortunately for him, he had Dad's light brown, though he imagined Dad's was all gray by now. Sibling three was not here, or even in the same state. There was no telling what Hector's life looked like nowadays.

If his father hadn't decided to have kids when he was fifty-something, Mateo and his sister might not be crammed in a car with no AC. Now at thirty, Mateo was stuck with the decision of what to do with his father, a choice he couldn't begin to swallow.

"Then he'll live with you?" she said.

His hand tightened around the steering wheel. "You know he can't."

She flung her hands up. "What a surprise. We're back to square one."

When the final railroad car passed and the gate arms moved to their upright positions, Mateo wasted no time reaching the tracks.

"Watch out!" Elena shouted.

The gate arm swung back down like a gauntlet. Mateo slammed on the brakes, but the arm still nicked the bumper. The driver behind him landed on his horn as if Mateo was the reason the arm decided to malfunction.

Elena cursed. "Everything is always broken in this town. Hurry and go around it before the other car beats you to it."

Mateo had a better idea. *Turn around and never come back.* The gate arm was trying to save him, but instead, he ignored the warning and listened to his sister.

Sweat gathered in his pits. Mateo bore down on the gas pedal, gripping the steering wheel tighter, and the engine roared. The vehicle sped up, edged closer to the yellow lines, and broke the fifty-mile-per-hour mark…sixty…seventy…

Typical country roads allowed such speeds. Woods on both sides whipped by, the same trees he used to glare at out of the bus window at age ten. They closed in on him like a vengeful spirit, but he stared straight ahead, lost in the long stretch of rural road.

"Um, you just missed the turn." Elena smacked his arm.

Mateo turned into the shoulder. The guy from the tracks laid on the horn and made an effort to flip him off.

"Has it been that long?" she asked, eyes glued on Mateo as if staring would keep him in reality.

He shrugged. "Damn trees have swallowed everything."

Everything but his memories.

Traffic cleared, and he made his U-turn. The private dirt road led them into the trees for about half a mile before the two-story house came into view. Mildew and white, it stood among a closet of trees engulfed with overgrown weeds. A 1998 silver Dodge Ram was still parked in the same place as always—by the porch. The branches near the house created a long patchy shadow, and when the headlights hit the window, the glass darkened.

"Hopefully, he's resting," Elena said as Mateo cut the engine.

In no real hurry to reach the house, Mateo fiddled with his keys and unbuckled himself reluctantly. It wasn't the rotten porch planks or missing shingles drawing his attention, but the wooden cross hanging above the peeling screen door. Last he checked, his dad wasn't Catholic or religious. Agnostic at best.

"That's new."

"What is?" Elena slung her duffle bag over her shoulder.

"The cross. Who put it up?"

"Dad. Who else?"

Moldy planks creaked under his weight. In person, the cross

appeared bigger, as if it could shine a spotlight on both him and his sister. The tip of it nearly pierced the porch roof. Five large nails were hammered deep into the wood. Dad deliberately placed it there.

Four bedrooms made up most of the two-story house. It reeked of cat litter, even though Dad's cats hadn't lived there in over five years. Each room was stuck in the nineties, the old carpet still stained with years of dirt, spills, and a vomit stain at the end of the staircase from when Hector chased Mateo up and down until he puked. The same flowery curtains Mother hung up covered the grimy windows.

The man in the reclining chair was not the same man from five years ago. His limbs were thin, brittle even. The same black boots, only this time, they swallowed his calves. The rough whiskered face of his father bore into Mateo's soul.

After more awkward exchanges, Elena got right down to business.

"I'm staying," Dad spat. "Not dying in one of them old timer camps."

Dad rubbed at his chest and groaned. His attention was fixed on the broken TV, like his kids were not in the same room.

"Mrs. Darcy found you a day after you'd fallen. You broke your foot last year. Went after a stranger in the woods, got lost. You don't remember to take your meds half the time, let alone remember that the remote does not belong in the fridge."

His dad said nothing, only shrunk in his recliner, like a child caught in a lie. Dad could protest his stubbornness all he wanted, but they all knew he was terrified of dying alone, so why the act?

"I told you. That person needed my help."

A chuckle escaped Mateo, and they both turned to glare at him. Mateo wasn't sure what was funnier—that Dad imagined a person in the woods, or that Dad was so inclined to help someone. The man was only capable of helping himself.

"Dad." Elena softened her tone. "You can come and stay with me and Ben for a bit. Just until we get things figured out."

"Your kids are brats," Dad blurted.

Elena's cheeks turned pink, and Mateo rubbed the ache on his temple.

"Fine," she said. "Die here. Alone."

Dad shuddered. Elena ignored him and stormed off to her old room, Mateo assumed, because he heard a door slam, and that sound brought back six years of teenage angst. Now, it was Mateo's turn to shudder. This house needed to stop regurgitating every little memory.

To Mateo's surprise, Dad found a civilized way of asking, "You're taller?"

Mateo chuckled. "I'm the same size as five years ago."

"Hmmm. Must be the boots."

Mateo nodded, not sure of the point of the conversation. "Dad, why is there a cross outside your door?"

Dad glanced out the window overlooking the porch. "Keeps the spirits away."

"What spirits? Thought you didn't believe in that stuff."

"I only believe when something keeps coming through the doors. Moving things. Moving in bedrooms. Sheets are always stirred."

Dad was many things, but not a storyteller.

"Odd assumption, Dad. Sure it's not you misplacing things? Maybe you changed beds and don't remember."

Dad snorted. "Unlikely."

"Or maybe you're just hearing the bone creaks of this old house."

"Hardly sleep at all anymore. Can't stop hearing it."

"Hearing what?"

His father shrugged but not convincingly. "Like bare feet across the floor. Then a wheezy…chuffling."

"Did you check for mice?"

Dad gripped the armrest and propelled himself forward. "Boy, what part of 'bare feet' don't you understand? Someone's getting into the house."

Mateo sighed. "You've been alone in this house for a decade. This is why I think it would be a good idea for you stay with Elena for a while."

"Is that what you think?" Dad growled, his fingernails digging into the old leather. If Mateo didn't know any better, he'd think his father was ready to lash out.

Mateo took a step back. "Dad, think about this from our perspective for once. We can't be here each time you get lost or break a foot. Elena lives three hours away. She's got her life and family. Hector is on the other side of the country. I'm…out of state."

Alone by himself and with no real responsibilities, and now with Lily moving on in life without him, he was forever alone. Regardless, he'd rather live with a banshee than this mule for brains.

"I ain't asking nobody to be here. And I ain't asking for no help." His palm moved in small circles over his chest.

Shuffling in the foyer changed Mateo's focus. Elena reached for the front door, and he caught a glimpse of jagged stitches peeking out from her sweater cuff. No wonder she wore that in the middle of June in Texas.

Mateo gently grabbed her wrist. "Hey, you going to tell me what that's about, or more importantly, why are you covering it up?"

She pulled away. "Let's not do this right now. I can only handle so much drama for the day."

"Did Ben do that?"

"It's handled." Elena let out a sigh of exasperation. "Did you talk Dad into coming home with me?"

So Ben could beat Dad too? No part of this plan was going to work.

"He won't budge."

"Okay. Great. We're only staying for the night. Tomorrow, he's coming with me, whether he likes it or not." She returned to the door. "Give me the keys."

"Where are you going?"

"Fridge is empty. Going into town for groceries. You stay here with him. Don't leave."

Even if he wanted to, Elena took the keys, just like in high school when she picked up her boyfriend in his car for a Sunday drive. Mateo needed to get out of the floodgates of nostalgia before he went insane.

THE LAST VISIT 191

Dad had long gone to bed by nine o'clock. That was Mateo's cue to head up to the second floor. The long hallway led to two bedrooms and a bathroom on the left. To the right was Mateo and Hector's old room. At the far end was Mom's room—used to be Dad's room as well. Now Dad slept on the first floor down the hall from Elena.

The wood popped underneath his feet. The same wood, the same squeaky floorboards that snitched on their late-night childhood adventures into the kitchen to steal cookies. He cast a glance at the closed door down the hall, a faded carving of a rose on its surface. Dad made that for Mom when they first moved into the house.

Twelve years of hell came after. Four years of silence. Then one year of Mateo comprehending the reality of life without Mom.

It happened in there.

With a clammy palm on the handle, Mateo turned the knob and pushed the door. He flipped the light switch on.

Pop!

One of the bulbs in the ceiling fan went out. Mateo would have reacted, had the sight not fused his skin to his bones. Nothing changed—same metal frame, dusty nightstands, a few magazines still lying from a time when people read, a small, littered table next to a suitcase propped against the wall. Same bed with the same faded red and white flowery covers, one pillow, and the carpet runners. It was an ordinary bed, but nothing about this room ever felt ordinary.

Mateo closed his eyes and took a deep breath. He couldn't bring himself to step inside but allowed himself five minutes. Five minutes to stare, take it all in, and feel something other than the horror stirring within the room. Five minutes to be close to the room but not a part of it.

He turned off the one working light and shut the door.

Every muscle in his body cringed. He squeezed his fists together. Mateo hated his cowardice. Hated that room. Hated this house. Hated the memories. Hated how Mom died.

Air. Mateo needed air.

In long strides, he dashed down the stairs, forgetting not to wake Dad. He flung the front door open and sucked in the woodsy night air. He placed his hands on the porch railings, only for them to crack under his weight.

"Come on, Elena," Mateo growled. "Where the hell are you?"

He sent a text to her.

Plan on coming home anytime soon?

It was weird he instinctively typed *home*.

Elena quickly texted back.

U won't believe who I ran into? Greg!

Mateo groaned, not in the mood to indulge in her fond memories of high school sweethearts. He made his thumbs run a mile.

Great. Does he know you are married and leaving tomorrow with Dad?

A few minutes passed before she texted again.

Did Dad cool off?

Mateo rolled his eyes.

See for yourself.

With that, he shoved his phone into his pocket and turned back to the front door.

The cross was gone.

Mateo jerked his phone back out and switched on the flashlight to confirm the empty space. Only the nails remained—all five stuck in the same place with no cross. How could the cross be gone without the nails being removed? He shone the light on the floor.

Wood shavings.

The cross.

Or what was left of it. The cross hadn't looked like it was crumbling when he first laid eyes on it. Would a woodpecker or termites mess with it? Probably a heat reaction to the untreated wood. More likely, the wood was cheap and wasn't meant to be in the humid outdoors.

Screw this. With each minute passing by in hours, Mateo couldn't wait on the porch for his sister. He went back into the house, locked the door behind him, and headed for the living room sofa to call it a night. No money on Earth could make him go back upstairs to his old room. He wasn't getting comfortable in this place.

The sofa reeked of wet rag and old cat piss. He was probably better off sleeping on the floor. Better yet, in the woods.

Mateo stiffened when the second floor emitted a creak.

He scoffed. The house loved to sing at all hours of the night. As a kid, it took him years to get used to it. Now, as an adult, he was annoyed at how fast his rational thinking liked to scurry away.

Another creak, this time at the far corner of the house near Hector's room.

Mateo let out a heavy exhale. The older the house got, the more its frame moaned in protest. Several more creaks followed. He tried to justify each sound, inviting one reason after another, but the creaks became a never-ending chain of excuses. But as the noises had actually been occurring for half an hour, Mateo could no longer be taken in by his apparent imagination.

He counted backward.

Twelve, eleven…

Again. A creak. This time closer to the bathroom across from Mom's bedroom.

Ten, nine, eight…

Multiple creaks closing in on Mom's bedroom. Mateo searched through his childhood memories. Like a homeless man scavenging for food, somehow knowing, confirming, those same creaks were familiar.

Seven, six, five…

Mateo's dad screamed, launching him to his feet with pulse thrumming.

He dashed down the hall, skidding on the floor as he turned into his dad's room. Mateo flicked the wall light on. His dad thrashed and screamed on the bed.

"Dad, what's wrong?"

An unseen stressor pulled his dad's features into tight wrinkles. He clawed at his chest, and for a second, Mateo feared he was having a heart attack.

With a wild gaze pinned on the ceiling, Dad kicked his feet and pounded his fists on sheets. The screams drilled through Mateo's skull. In between breaths, his dad managed a few words.

"Taking…me."

"Tell me what's wrong," Mateo said.

"You...blame me...Elena...blames me." His dad's screams turned into sobbing, and his eyes squeezed shut in pain. "It's payback. Send me away. Want me to die, right? Alone...dead...like her."

Mateo kneeled beside the bed, reaching for Dad's hand. "Nobody wants you to die. Nobody blames you either."

Mateo bit his lip. Lies.

The crying of a thrashing man began to transition back to screaming. He wailed as if something were tearing him in half. Elena once mentioned Dad would get anxiety attacks at night, but Mateo had never seen one up close.

"Dad, you need to breathe." He squeezed his dad's hand. "Breathe with me."

His dad thrust a palm into Mateo's face and shoved him away. Mateo caught himself on his heels and stood, not knowing what to do. The lights of the ceiling fan popped, just like in Mom's bedroom, except they all went out, leaving the glow of the moonlight sliding between the parted curtains to illuminate the old man.

Cold water or an icepack might help.

Mateo quickly turned but stopped when a figure loomed in the shadows of the doorway. He instinctively stepped back, ready to run, but slipped on something. Gravity took over, and Mateo's head collided against the nightstand. His vision blurred for a second. His dad still wailed and screamed, not aware of the stranger watching them.

The figure just stood. Stared. Then it gently turned and walked down the hallway.

Mateo reached for his dad's arm and shook it hard. "Stop it! Someone's in the house."

His dad hadn't reacted. Not to the burned-out lights, or the fall Mateo took.

Dad always slept with a gun, so Mateo reached under the pillow, only to find it empty. He cursed, grabbing Dad's old cane instead. The long wooden cane felt rough, hard, and heavy in his hand. It might work as a last resort to ward off a home invader.

Mateo hurriedly turned on the flashlight on his phone and investigated the hallway. If the uninvited guest wasn't intimidated by a man with a cane slung over his shoulder, he'd hope his dad's maniacal screaming would scare them off.

He poked his head into each room. Nothing but the soft pattern of the windows against the humid night. The doors and windows leading out of the kitchen and living room were as he left them. The front door remained locked. Even the rooms on the second floor were not touched. All except one room he had not checked.

Mom's room.

A curse escaped his lips as he stood in front of his mom's room. The door was cracked open, and he couldn't recall closing it or not. Cane wielded and heart thrumming, Mateo forced himself inside. His light sprayed every inch of the room.

Nothing under the bed. Nothing in the closet but an old chest he couldn't remember from before. As if he was running out of oxygen, Mateo quickly shut the door. His knees buckled, and he slid to his bottom, his back against the door.

It didn't dawn on Mateo that his dad had stopped screaming until a few minutes later. He wasn't sure what that meant. Mateo pushed himself to his feet and raced down the stairs. Forgetting about a possible intruder lurking around the corner with a gun, Mateo sped by each threshold until he reached his dad's room.

Dad rested in his bed, snoring.

Mateo's limbs grew heavy. He leaned against the threshold and let out a sigh of relief.

The headlights of Mateo's car shone between the window's curtains. Elena was finally home.

Home.

There was that word again.

The idea of food made Mateo's stomach cringe, yet he sat across from his dad at the dining table with Elena.

Just like old times.

Two chairs were empty, and it was strange to think there had been a time when all five joined together at the table.

Not a word was said from Dad. He was pale and somehow skinnier than yesterday, like a piece of him withered away each second. Mateo feared his dad's limbs might snap.

The old man acted as if last night's screaming-fest never happened. Dad would never admit embarrassment of it—ignoring things was his gift.

Dad scarfed down Elena's pancakes and it wouldn't have surprised Mateo if it was the only decent meal he'd had in years.

Mateo kept his focus on his coffee cup, head lowered. His mind went numb. The circus show from the night before made logic harder to surface. When he was a kid, he used to see figures in the corners of his room, but then every kid did. He outgrew that. Most people had enough sense to know there was a logical reason for everything. What Mateo saw was just an anomaly he had yet to find an answer for. That did not mean the answer was nonexistent.

One hand on the coffee cup, his other arm laid flat on the table, Mateo forced his attention on the old man.

"How long have these anxiety attacks been happening?" he asked.

Dad didn't break his attention from his plate. "Who knows. A while."

Mateo rubbed his face. "Dad, you said we blamed you. That we're punishing you. Is that why you won't come to live with Elena? Do you really believe that?"

Dad's grip tightened around the silverware. "I belong here."

Elena leaned back in her chair. "Dad, it's not safe here for you."

"I said no, Maria," Dad snapped.

Mateo swallowed. He wasn't sure what kind of person he was, if a part of him took pleasure in the guilt his dad harbored. For Mom, it was deserved.

Mateo looked up at his sister. Maybe she hid it better, but for a split second, he saw it. Elena blamed their father too. There would be no coddling from either sibling.

With a thumb jabbed at his chest, scratching vigorously, his dad stood up. He tilted his body and faced the window, staring out, eyes glazed over. Their dad gazed forward, fixated. If a person looked through the window, they would see the sky.

A part of the sky.

His dad's glass clinked against the table. Even with a rigid body, he swayed side to side, as if in pain.

"Dad," Elena said. "We really need to get you out of this house. Please, just come home with me until we can get a permanent living situation."

Dad said nothing. Elena and Mateo were invisible. He pushed the creaky back door screen open and let it slam behind him.

Elena shoved her plate away. "I'm so tired of this. Why can't he see that he's physically and mentally spiraling downward? He can't do this on his own anymore."

All Mateo could muster was a nod.

She rubbed at her temples. "If it were Mom, she'd come home with me in a heartbeat."

"If it were Mom, we wouldn't be pretending we cared."

"You don't mean that."

Mateo wasn't so sure. Some diseases spread wider than others. The darkness had invaded his household, and it seemed to be growing bigger and bigger. Mom had always been the sunny one, even when Dad pounded on her with his constant insults and narcissistic demands. Sometimes, Mateo wasn't sure how she managed to stay so strong. She was only strong for so long though, until she wasn't, until that day something broke in her. Maybe that's why her heart gave out.

He pushed himself to his feet and met Elena in the living room, but instead of sitting next to her, he pulled in Dad's recliner.

Elena gave him a look, then giggled. "Add another fifty years, and you look just like Dad."

Mateo pulled the recliner back in. "Add in the crazy, and I'm the full package."

He missed the simple laughter shared between himself and his sister. Elena and he always got along that way. They used to tell each other everything.

Mateo leaned forward, pinning his focus on the black screen of the TV. "You really didn't see anything weird last night?"

"No. Just you, stressed out and panicked."

"Dad was screaming like he was being butchered and someone was in the damn house. Can you blame me?"

"No one was in the house, Mateo. I don't know how many times you want to search the place. Yes, I know Dad's attacks are scary. The first time I witnessed him, I was alone, and it lasted for two hours. I didn't know what to do either. Ended up calling the ambulance. When he came to, he refused their service."

"Yeah, sounds like Dad. But why does it happen? What started them?"

"He told me it happened two years ago, the night he went into Mom's room."

"I thought he never went in there."

"He doesn't. But that night, he did." She shrugged. "I think the guilt is just eating him alive. Night time is the worst for him, which is why I don't want him to be alone anymore."

"Yes, but he's...well, Dad. He's kind of done this to himself."

"He's the only parent we have left."

Mateo rose to pace the room. "You can't force him to go with you. He won't budge."

"Well, I was thinking..." she said. "Maybe you could offer...He'd go with you—"

"What? I've already said he can't—"

"Only until he gets used to the idea of being away from his house. I think the real reason why he won't leave is because, in a sense, he's leaving a piece of Mom behind."

"He left her behind when she was still alive. What's the difference now?" Mateo closed his eyes. "What do you want me to do, Elena?"

"Talk to him."

Now, it were his eyes that rolled. "I've been trying that. He doesn't listen."

"Then you need to apply other factors. Care and concern. Not force or resentment."

"Are you really one to talk?" he said, testing her boundaries.

"I am the only one talking about where he will die."

Mateo found Dad outside in the back on his hands and knees, crawling along the dirt.

Mateo cursed. "Dad. What are you doing?"

"It's gone."

"What's gone?"

Dad remained on all fours. "The crosses."

A quick glance over the screen door confirmed the same dirty outline of an absent cross as the one in front of the house.

Mateo operated on two hours of sleep and patience as thin as Elena's pancakes. He had to stop himself from yanking his father off the ground like a child.

"Jeez, Dad. Why does that matter?"

"Keeps disappearing. That's when things happen. It comes back."

"What comes back?"

His dad growled. "Something…I don't know. Bad spirits here."

Mateo leaned over to grab his dad's arm. "Dad, get up, please. There are no spirits here. Just memories. Mold. Decay and pain. That's all we have left from this place, remember?"

His father stumbled to his feet, then yanked away and would have fallen back, had Mateo not reached to stabilize him.

"You don't u—" He turned to the woods, rubbing his neck. "I don't know what I'm saying. Don't know what's happening anymore."

As his dad stumbled like a lost deer, Mateo saw something in him, other than the abusive man he remembered. The old man was broken. Hurt. Frail inside and out. The image had Mateo's gut buckling.

"Dad. Just take it easy. Talk to me."

His father walked out further toward the woods and sat on a stump. He stared long and hard at everything in front of him, yet at nothing at all. Mateo stood in his dad's view.

"Dad. Please talk to me. What's been going on with you? Night anxiety? Is that why the gun is gone? I can't find it anywhere. Where is it?"

"Threw it away."

"What? You threw it in the trash?"

Dad pointed at the woods. "Threw it in there."

"Why?"

For a long moment he said nothing. "Afraid I might use it."

Knots twisted Mateo's stomach. He looked into the woods, wondering where the gun rested. Had his father actually thought about killing himself? Another glance at his dad, who seemed to be sinking further and further into the soil, and it wasn't a real mystery. If his father had actually pulled the trigger, Mateo wasn't sure he'd be able to forgive himself for not stopping him.

The knots continued to expand, choking until Mateo thought he'd be sick. The idea of leaving his father to slowly die by his own misery was a fantasy, rather than a reality he could bring himself to face.

His sister was right. Their dad was spiraling down in every way possible, diminishing faster than the house.

"Figured you would want me gone anyway," his dad said.

"No one wants you gone, Dad. We want you safe. Why do you think we want you out of this house?"

His dad shrugged, still staring at the woods.

Mateo lowered to his haunches. The words were right there in front of him, but he wasn't sure if he should reach for them. They wouldn't slap him in the face. Only his father was capable of that.

"Whatever is happening at night, I know I wouldn't wish it on my worst enemy. I know you don't want to live your last days like this." Mateo sighed, not sure how to find the courage for his proposal. "Elena is not an option. I get that. But, Dad, you have other options. You have me. Come with me."

For the first time, his dad broke his gaze and looked Mateo in the eyes. But he still couldn't get a read on his dad.

His father nodded slowly. "Give me two more days. Then, you will have my answer."

Mateo chuckled. "You want me to stay two more days, is that what you're saying?"

"Is it too much to ask for?"

"What about Elena?"

"What about her? She can leave whenever she likes. As can you."

Mateo would be lying if he said he hadn't thought about tossing his bag into his car and peeling out of the driveway, with or without his dad. He wasn't sure what two extra days would change. If he knew his father, the man would just decide on staying here at the end of the day. Stringing him and his sister along was a large hell to pay.

But the small speck of hope Mateo clung to was enough to make him trudge up the stairs with his bag in hand.

If he was going to hang around this crypt for the next two days, he would go into his old room where, hopefully, the creaking nights could not reach him.

A glance down the hallway to his mother's room had him second-guessing his every decision.

Just two more days, he reminded himself.

Mateo settled in the dusty room. A stench of sulfur and eggs lingered. After a quick spray of Lysol, he rummaged through his old closet. A few plastic action figures, Legos, a kite, and a crossbow were left behind. Mateo smiled. Some good memories still remained. When he grew bored, he lay in his bed and allowed his mind to doze off.

A knock jolted Mateo from his slumber. The door creaked open, and his mom poked her head inside. Still in her kitchen apron, she grinned, her dark flowing hair falling over her shoulder.

Mateo's chest seized. *Mom?*

"Wash up," she said. "Dinner's ready."

The image quickly washed away when he recognized the voice as Elena's. His sister stared back at him. Same hair. Same apron. Different person.

"You okay? You look so...pale."

He rose. His limbs felt weak. Despite the nap, Mateo was still exhausted.

"Fine. Just tired."

Elena gave a sympathetic grin and left Mateo sitting with his legs numb. He felt an ache in his chest. Was it the remnants of anxiety? The idea made him smirk. Anxiety was not *his* monster. But he couldn't shake the feeling of an unseen fog slowly smothering him.

When the ache didn't stop, he lifted his shirt. A faded red oval marked his chest, from collarbone to circling both nipples. It burned to the touch.

Mateo showed Elena the second he could. She encouraged him to not sleep in his room and to rub some Cortizone on it. That might have been useful, had the cream not expired eight years ago.

After dinner, Mateo passed the time by fixing all the busted lights. Without too much complaint, he forced his sister to change the one in Mom's room.

"It's just a room," she'd insisted.

Mateo soon found himself back on the couch. Time passed slowly here, and like clockwork, the creaks returned upstairs. A tremor seized his limbs. When he realized how ridiculous his reactions were, he shook himself out of his semi-trance silence, gripping onto the couch. The ache in his chest returned, and soon, the discomfort spread throughout his body. He tossed and turned.

A good, long piss might do him some good.

He pushed to his feet, surprised by his lack of strength as he stumbled down the hallway. Someone could confuse him for his dad with the way he swayed side to side, gripping the wall for support. Mateo groaned as the chest ache kicked into mild pain.

On his way past his father's room, he heard the old man stifle a sob.

Not again. At least he wasn't screaming.

"Dad?" Mateo poked his head into the room. "Are you okay?"

Mateo couldn't see a thing, but he heard his dad stir in the sheets. His father's words were a mumbled gibberish.

"What's wrong?"

The old man was finally able to muster words. "I dreamed of Maria."

Mateo stiffened. His father never brought up their mom. Saying her name out loud was out of the question.

There was a long silence. Mateo parted the curtains enough to see his dad's gaze on the ceiling.

"I miss her," Dad said, his last words cracking.

"I miss her too, Dad."

His dad fixed his attention on Mateo. "Every night, a piece of her is gone. The memories are fading. I'm fading. Thought I could never forget." His face squeezed in agony. "Oh, God. I can't feel her anymore. Can't see her."

Dad gripped at his chest. "All I see. Pain. It takes her from me. Again, and again. Make it stop." He reached up to claw at his son's collar.

"It's okay, Dad. It will be alright."

This brought a new ache to Mateo. Suddenly, he couldn't catch his breath. His chest felt like it bore an elephant. "It's okay," he struggled to say, but it was becoming harder to breathe.

"It's not okay." Dad coughed out a laugh, though the smile was wiped away with the pain returning. "Not until it ends."

An unseen veil took hold of Mateo as his vision blurred. When he came to, his dad was peacefully asleep, chest rising in even breaths. He slept so calmly, Mateo wondered if he'd imagined his dad's panic state. Mateo stood in a hunch, then exited the room in a hot sweat.

He leaned against the wall. "What the hell is wrong with me?"

In the bathroom, he relieved himself, then splashed cold water on his face. Finally, he took in a strong breath of fresh air. Just as he closed the door behind him, the sobs from Elena's room rang in the hallway.

Mateo groaned. If his family didn't get their shit together fast, he would hog-tie them both and toss them into the back of his car.

Mateo knocked on the door.

"What?" Elena said in annoyance.

Mateo entered, finding his sister sitting at the edge of the bed, a pile of tissue paper beside her.

"You're still awake?" she said.

"You can say that." Mateo sat beside her. "You going to tell me what's going on?"

"Ben is threatening to leave me." Her shoulders quivered.

"Like hell he will."

She scoffed. "Right, because beating him to a pulp will help."

"It would be a start. He still needs to pay for hurting you. How long has this been going on for? Has he hurt the boys?"

"No. Never. They love their dad. He is decent with them—"

"But not you?"

She started sobbing again. "Sometimes I think he hates me."

Mateo placed a hand over hers. "You have to get out of this relationship."

"I know. But I'm so scared. What about the boys? What will this do to them? Mom never left Dad. She should have, and look what that did to us."

"Whatever happens, I will help you. We will sort it out."

"How? You live away. I hardly see you and Hector anymore. I don't have the funds for a lawyer. Ben will fight me till death. I just can't…do this."

Elena whimpered as she leaned into her brother. Mateo wrapped his arms around her. His sister used to tell him everything. How had he missed this? So absorbed in his own misery, he had failed to see the torment his sister and father endured.

"I can pitch in. Maybe selling Dad's home would help."

Elena laughed uncontrollably, pulling away, tears running down her cheeks. "Who wants this stupid house? We don't even have the money to fix it. Life is just falling apart. I just…I didn't think I'd be in this position at this age. I wanted my marriage to be different. Not like Mom's."

She latched onto him again, sniffling as she wept against his chest. He groaned at her touch.

She released him. "Oh, I'm sorry. It still hurts?"

"Burns like a mother…"

"Let me see."

Elena yanked down his collar.

"Hey," he whined. "How about personal space?"
"Jeez! What is that? Looks like teeth marks."
"Uh?"

Mateo jerked his whole shirt off and glanced down. The oval was redder. Within the oval were jagged lines and triangles—some thin, others thick. But none had a defined edge. They were sort of drawn out, more like splinters of a memory than gouges. Mateo shuddered.

Elena peered up at him. "Mateo, that doesn't look like a bite. Or an infection. But it looks like something tried to claw you apart."

"Like what? An animal?" The words of his father returned. *Bad spirits here.*

There was a reason for everything. He couldn't entertain the idea. Mateo chuckled to himself but couldn't stop the arm hairs raising from his skin at each glance he took at his chest.

"I think we should take you to the hospital. What if that gets infected?"

Mateo put his shirt back on. "I'll disinfect it and put on bandages. We should get some sleep. Tomorrow, I plan to take Dad back home with me."

"It would be one less thing to worry about if you could."

"It will be fine. We'll figure this out."

The crying stopped for the time being. If fate would have it, the whole house would be free of sobs so he could get a good night's rest. The silence should give him enough time to figure out how to help Elena exactly, and what to do with Dad. He had a promise to keep for his sister and wasn't sure where to start building the foundation for it to hold strong enough, for both Elena and his father.

The door closed behind him. Mateo found himself swaying in the hallway once more. He gripped at his chest and maneuvered through the shadows, hand stretched out for support. Gravity jerked him to the floorboards. The walls felt heavy, as if they were disconnecting from their frame and pressing him to his knees.

Mateo groaned. His knees buckled, and he dropped to his palms.

He tried to call for his dad, of all people, but his throat was as tight as his constricting chest muscles. His back pressed against the wooden paneling, then his chin slapped against the floorboards.

There was something growing sick in his stomach—a deep root he couldn't see or touch. He needed to puke.

Mateo forced his knees apart and violently heaved. The stink of bile splattered across the floor.

The room temperature dropped a degree by the heartbeat. His head felt sluggish, like the muscles in his chest were collapsing. Mateo couldn't tell the darkened hallway apart from his own blackening vision.

An old spring mattress dug into Mateo's back. The stench of sulfur and eggs returned to make him gag, and he groaned, flicking his eyes open. The two new light bulbs he remembered Elena switching out in his mom's room hung high in the ceiling fan.

The sun slipped past the parted curtains. Same flowery fabric. The same dusty nightstands and dresser confirmed the room he recognized.

He was lying on his mom's bed.

Had his limbs not felt like mush, he would have sprung up faster. His legs dangled from the edge of the bed as he rubbed his eyes. Mom's vanity sat across from him. Attached was the round mirror. A pale Mateo stared back, somehow paler than yesterday.

Burning radiated along his chest. He yanked down his collar, only to have the material rub against his skin and make him hiss.

Two new bright-red ovals lay on top of each other but did not overlap. The skin around the circles blistered. He tried to touch it, but it was like caressing raw skin.

Mateo inched closer to the mirror. "What the hell?"

His cheeks were sunken in, thin veins appearing on the side of his temples. No one got this sickly without some kind of assistance. Something was making him ill. He wasn't getting any better by remaining in this place. Getting out of here might be the answer to all his problems.

Mateo looked around, taking in the very room he fought tooth and nail to avoid. Why would he come back here, let alone sleep in Mom's dusty bed?

To test his brain, he tried to think back on the previous night, and it swept through his thoughts. Details were missing. He had lost time and feared he might have had a stroke. They were rare, but he'd heard of thirty-somethings getting them.

More likely, he was so out of it and had to have confused it for his old room. He'd been feeling as if he was fading, that his sense of reality had become muddled. Mateo winced, panic forming in his chest. He had to get out. Now.

Scratch marks along the runner and floorboards halted him. They led into the closet. Sure those marks were not there before, he opened the door to survey the damage. At the bottom of the closet was the old chest, but Mateo did not remember where he'd seen it before. He kneeled to try and open it.

Locked.

Mateo struggled against the lid. Either it was locked, or he was too weak to open it. He couldn't focus around the fear of remaining in the room for another second. In a panic, he went for the door and flung it wide open. Fresh air filled his lungs. Hand on the wall, he made his way down the hallway.

"Elena?" Mateo called from the top step.

Nobody came—the house was silent. Mateo backed down the steps, the paint starting to flake from the railing. His shoulders slumped, and his legs grew invisible ankle weights. Everything in his body told him he would fall.

"Elena?" he called down.

No reply.

Mateo approached the living room, where his dad sat in his recliner, sipping his coffee. Dad took one look at him and froze, the cup halfway to his mouth. He put it down.

"You look like hell. Sick?"

Mateo set his hand on the armrest of the couch. His legs felt too rubbery to put full weight on them.

Mateo scoffed. "You don't look so great yourself."

If this was a who-was-the-palest contest, his dad had taken the win, without a doubt. Despite his sickly appearance, Dad sat there without much care of what was around him.

"Something in this house is making us sick," Mateo said. "Surely, you can see that. We need to leave."

"About that." His dad took one calm sip, then rested the cup in his lap. "I've decided. I'm staying."

A wire short-circuited in Mateo's brain. "You're unbelievable, you know that?" His fist balled, and he ignored the control he had on his tone. "We came all this way for you yet get treated like unwelcomed morons. Elena takes the brunt of it. Jesus, she's your flesh and blood, not a step kid. Have you even once thanked her?"

When his dad said nothing, Mateo further marched into the storm. "Did it ever cross your mind that you might not have a fucking choice? Unless you choose death, is that it? You're giving up, just like you gave up on Mom? Gave up on us. It's all you know, right?"

"I'm not the only one who's given up on this family."

For the first time, Mateo wanted to take one long stride across the room and sock him right in the mouth.

Instead, he shook his head and released his fists. "I'm walking out of that door today and I'm not coming back here."

All his dad managed was a nod.

A tremor shook the wall behind him, as if a train just passed by the house. Mateo pivoted. A breeze washed over him, and all the adrenaline drained away. A chill started at his feet and extended to his neck. He moved closer to the wall and studied it. A crack the size of a splinter formed.

Mateo turned his attention back to his dad. "What was that?"

His dad shrugged. "Hard to hear with your whining."

A new burst of energy had Mateo pacing the room. "Where's Elena?"

His dad stood up and stretched. "Haven't seen her. I reckon still in her room."

Mateo ran down the hallway. The *thump-thump-thump* of his heart ceased the weakness in his limbs. It no longer mattered whether his dad left this house or not. Mateo would leave, and he would run a marathon to get out.

He reached Elena's door. Without knocking, he flung it open and found the bed made. The same pile of tissue papers remained. He took a deep breath. The same suffocating torment he felt from his mom's room overpowered Elena's. Once more, he was underwater, gasping for air as he searched.

When he came up empty, he checked the kitchen. The bathrooms. The porch. The car. Everywhere except his mom's room. He even called her cell, but it rang and rang—and not within earshot.

On his way down the main hallway to the living room, the stench of sulfur and eggs was so potent, it made him stop in his tracks. He smothered his nose with his hand. A faint tremor seized the wall again. It quivered like a mechanical tool vibrated from within, then the tremor shifted to the outside walls, flickering the ceiling lights.

The ceiling creaked, and plaster fell. Mateo covered his mouth and shut his eyes.

The tremors stopped. A dead silence followed, so deafening he forced himself to speak through it, to say anything.

"Dad?" he whispered.

A series of thuds on the second floor had Mateo scrambling up the stairs.

"Elena?"

The way his legs wanted to collapse had him grabbing the railing. He looked up at the second floor and saw something pressed against the staircase, then followed a wheezy chuffling. Another thud jerked his attention back to the top step. Muffled screaming, so faint he had to pause and still his breathing to hear it. Elena. She was crying for help.

"Elena? I'm coming!"

Mateo ran down the hallway. Mom's door was closed. His hands shook as she screamed back for him from within the room. The second he busted in, he could make out her panicked words.

"Can't breathe."

She was in the closet.

Sweaty hand on handle, he flung it open, but the only thing on the floor was the chest, with Elena's cries coming from within it. A flood of death filled his lungs.

"Jesus! Elena!" Mateo pushed against the lid, but the chest wouldn't open.

Panic seized him. Mateo shoved his fingernails between the seam and dug into it until the nubs of his fingers could get a grip. He lifted. His nail bent back and snapped. Blood trailed down his finger.

He hissed.

"Mateo! Please help. Can't breathe." She kicked and pounded.

"I'm getting you out! Save your air!"

With the dwindling energy he had left, he grabbed onto the chest's handle and yanked it out of the closet to get a closer look. No hole for a key. No buttons. No history of why this damn thing existed. He didn't understand how it was locked so tight, as if nails fastened the lid in place.

"I'll be right back. Stay calm."

"No! Don't leave me. Mateo, please!"

The strain in her voice was enough to cut his heart in two. He had to get her out of there fast.

The only thing resembling a crowbar was the kitchen knife. His dad had asked what was going on, and when Mateo shouted it was Elena, his dad stood from the recliner.

Mateo hurried back to his mom's room. A brief pause of mind-numbing terror seized him when he no longer heard his sister.

"Elena?"

No response.

He jammed the knife into the seam of the chest and tried to wedge it in, sawing as best as he could. Another slight vibration shook the house. Something thudded from downstairs, but Mateo couldn't bring himself to remove his focus. He leaned into his wrists, groaning at the resistance and frustration of his depleting muscles. The chest lid lifted, like a volcano about to spew lava.

Elena was curled into a tight ball, her arms around her knees. Damp hair covered her face. At the top and bottom interior of the chest were symbols Mateo hadn't seen anywhere in history books, or media, for that matter. For a second, he was sure he saw one glowing by her head.

"Elena!"

She slowly turned her head toward him. Mateo picked her up and carefully placed her on the floor. It took her a long minute to cough and welcome a proper breath. He leaked tears of relief as he held her.

Elena looked up at him, first with confusion and then with a terror he'd never seen from her before. A small stream of blood flowed from her nose and down her lip. There were little cuts on the right side of her face.

"Oh, God, Elena. What happened?" Mateo helped her to her feet, trying his best to support her unsteady legs.

"God, it was moving inside…like pulsating. Inside me too. A pulse not belonging to me," she whimpered. "My God, something is in this house. We have to leave. Get Dad. Go!"

Mateo noted the tip of a red oval along her collarbone. He yanked down the collar of her shirt to reveal the same red mark across her chest. Her reaction was late, and when she looked down and back at him, tears crept at the corner of her eye.

Arms over shoulders, the two hobbled down the stairs. Mateo's hands shook, and his heart and lungs labored with the same exhaustion his limbs felt. Together, they burst into the living room.

Dad was sprawled on the floor, his shirt pulled over his head, belly and chest exposed. Elena gasped, and her knees buckled. Unable to hold her any longer, Mateo let her drop. What sucked all the air from his lungs were the multiple red ovals on his dad's chest. Old ones and new ones. Some bubbled up in rough scars. Others spread all the way down to his groin area.

Mateo rushed to the old man. "Dad!"

Mateo pulled his dad's shirt back down. His dad's breaths were shallow, and he was so cold.

"Dad, can you hear me?"

Elena crawled toward them. "What's wrong with him?"

Mateo shook his head. "I don't know. Just help me get him to the car."

A violent storm of vibrations rattled the floor. Mateo lurched to his feet with fists balled. Just as he spun, something clawed at his back and hit him across the room, where he crashed into an old coffee table butted up against the wall.

Had it not been for Elena's screams, Mateo might not have fought to remain with her, but her cries were quickly cut off. Somewhere in the distance he heard her moaning.

Mateo's head felt heavy, like he was being pushed into the carpet. His limbs protested against movement. His eyelashes fluttered open, but he couldn't make sense of what he saw.

Something was on top of his father.

Not a shadow. Not a human. Not a spirit.

A creature.

It locked eyes with him. Brown, dried beef skin. Thin limbs led to four long fingers, with nails stretching into its knuckles. Its shoulder-length stringy hair didn't sway because it was somehow embedded into its skin, as if the creature had rested for eternity on its side, and the skin decided to absorb the hair fibers. Its head was swollen like a rottweiler's, blending into its bulging neck. Its veiny mouth pulsated and stretched, long and wide, into an oval to latch onto his dad's chest.

Knees and elbows bent out, the creature was low, as if taking a drink at a watering hole. This creature stared at Mateo with eyes like shiny eight balls. An awful groaning and guttural growl came deep from within it. A clear warning. *Stay away.*

Mateo recoiled, hair standing on end. The creature slurped at his dad's skin. It wasn't biting or removing the flesh, but rather sucking it like a babe on a tit.

"Stop," he begged.

Mateo tried again, hoping to sound more threatening. "Get off him!"

Though his muscles were unresponsive, he forced himself to stand. Step by step, he made his way across the room, picking up a lamp pole on his way, but his presence didn't bother the creature. When he was within arm's length, he slammed the lamp pole over its bloated head.

The lamp broke. The figure's head bounced off his father. Shrieking and hissing, it scurried up the walls and along the ceiling, toward the hallway on bent limbs, belly low to the surface, faster than any animal he'd seen.

Mateo hung over his dad. "Dad? Oh, God. Dad."

He shook him from side to side, but his father remained motionless. His skin was sunken and cold to the touch. Mateo's gaze went from his dad to the hallway, then back to his dad.

A violent gasp escaped the old man.

"Dad! I'm here."

His dad shivered in the silence, and his eyes flitted around the room. He grabbed Mateo's wrist so forcefully it hurt. Mateo awkwardly leaned into the embrace.

"Saw its eyes," his dad said. "It's real. Wants me." An out of place smile crept at the corner of his mouth.

Elena did her best to crawl over the couch to reach their dad.

"Daddy," she said, in near sobs. Then, she turned to Mateo. "Where did that thing go?"

"I don't know. Help me get him in the car."

"Come on, Dad," Elena said, sliding her arm behind him.

On three, they both lifted him to his feet. Dad groaned with each step. Mateo scanned the hallway and did his best to watch their backs.

A loud thumping scurried above them. Mateo was certain the door of his mom's room slammed, and for the life of him, he couldn't imagine why. A wheezy chuffle followed, deep in the throat of that beast, like the flaps of its vocals were trying to make contact. The sound of it echoed off the walls.

Elena and Mateo scrambled for the door. She turned and froze.

Mateo tried to make a break for it but felt rooted in place by his father's shaking grip. His sister was staring at something on the ceiling.

The creature pounced on top of them and sent both Mateo and Elena sliding across the floor. Mateo's back hit the wall. Elena slammed against one of the half-wall columns. The creature had his dad in a tight grasp. His father's head tilted back, and his neck stretched into an uncomfortable square so he could keep his mouth open. Dad bucked, and the creature's head popped back.

Elena pushed her palms and knees into the floor, bringing herself forward. A piece of skin dangled off her shoulder from a gash. Mateo fought against his nerves and forced himself to stand.

The creature scooped up their father with its front limbs and cradled him, like a mother protecting a cub. It scurried down the hallway and into his dad's room. The door slammed behind them, followed by a series of crashes, like a tornado rampaged through the room.

"No!" Mateo ran after them.

He huffed and rammed his shoulder into the door. It didn't budge, but it wasn't locked. Something heavy blocked it from the other side. Elena cried out and rushed at the door, but Mateo grabbed her by the shoulders.

"The window," he said.

Mateo wasted no time shooting out the front door and rounding the porch until he stood at Dad's bedroom window. Groaning, he lifted a rotten plank and slammed it through the weathered panes. Glass broke away. He twisted the board in the opening to knock the rest of the shards, but not all of the glass was gone—it cut his belly when he climbed through. Mateo hissed, nursing his stomach with his hand.

The scene in his father's room was like a war zone. All the furniture was shoved against the door. The only light was from the broken window.

There, in the shadowed corner of the ceiling, hung the creature with his dad. His dad's shirt was ripped open, his arms and legs thrashing violently as he struggled to break free. The creature's legs held him down in a triangle, as its other limbs kept them glued to the wall. It stretched its veiny neck over Dad's shoulder so it could suckle along his father's chest.

"No!" Mateo shouted. "Let him go."

Panic seized him when he realized the creature was too far up. He grabbed the nearest objects—a lamp, an old radio, anything he could find—and began throwing them.

No impact bothered it. For all he knew, Mateo himself wasn't even there.

The creature's eyes began to squint, and its shoulders lowered as his father went limp. It looked a little drunk, shivering against the walls, its elongated feet flexing in and out.

"Stop." It was killing him. "Let him go!"

Mateo had no choice. He grabbed his dad's cane and hacked away at the lower half of the creature's legs. It freed its mouth from his father and hissed. Mateo kept hammering on its limbs. Shouting and screaming, he rained down on the creature.

A roar he hadn't heard before rang deep from within its throat. The creature dropped his dad. Mateo stretched his arms in time to break his fall, but the dead weight had them both crashing to the ground.

The creature crawled along the walls. Long fingers scratched against the surface. Veins along its skin pulsated blue. Its head and limbs swelled like it was increasing its size. The pulsating continued, like a machine firing up multiple servers. Somehow, it was collecting energy—maybe energy it had already sucked from his father. Mateo felt the pulses run through him, so deep it tickled the back of his throat.

Something Elena said after he freed her from the chest…How she felt a pulse not her own.

Could it be?

The walls rattled from under the creature, spreading to the ceiling and the rest of the room. A crack on the ceiling split open, racing toward the center where a piece of sheetrock hit Mateo's shoulder.

He did his best to pull his dad away from the freak vibrating the walls. The sheetrock cracked in the creature's place. The wall trembled once more and crumbled like a fallen curtain, along with the creature, revealing the other side of the hallway. The house shook in its wake.

Mateo covered his dad with his body. Dust and debris rushed to them.

Out of the white powder leaped the creature. It grabbed Mateo's ankles and launched him through the new opening, where he crashed into the hallway. The creature crawled over the rubble and pounced on Mateo, pinning him. Shiny eight-ball eyes stared down, that mountain of a head enough to swallow his face in one bite. Rolling hisses issued from the creature. It leaned close to his face, staring down. A string of wheezy chuffing rolled in its throat, the rhythm reminding him of laughter. A look in the creature's glare confirmed its amusement. It was toying with its prey.

It dug a claw into the side of his face and peeled a string of flesh off. Mateo's raw screams were cut short when it squeezed his throat, as if the very noise he made irritated the beast.

The creature's head tracked toward the sound of footsteps, and it loosened its grip.

Elena stood at the end of the hall with his old crossbow aimed. The bolt sped into the creature's eye. Black fluid sputtered into the air as the creature shrieked and thrashed along the floorboards.

Mateo coughed, forcing his legs from under him. Hand on the wall, blood dripping down his face, he pushed himself up. Elena quickly dropped the crossbow and slipped her foot into the step bar to reload it. She aimed just as the creature ran toward her. She fired again, this time hitting its chest. The creature crashed at her feet. Its pulsating stopped. The blue veins absorbed back into its body, and it even seemed to shrink a little.

Jaw dropped, Mateo stared at the unmoving creature.

Elena stepped over it and ran toward Mateo.

"Is it...?" he said.

"I don't know—"

The creature's limbs slowly rose and it picked itself up. The bolts she shot into it dropped from its body, as if something from inside was pushing them out. Then, it turned and roared at them, its back skin peeling up and fluttering like the hood of a cobra.

Aim locked on Elena, it launched across the hallway. Before it could reach her, their father stepped in between and tossed a large sheet in its way. The sheet caught the creature midair, and it skidded across the floorboards in a tangled mess. Dad limped over to it with cane in hand and began hitting. Another blow, and this time, Dad stabbed the blunt end of the cane into the creature.

It shrieked.

Still twisted in the sheet, it picked itself up and scurried around the corner. Mateo grasped his dad's arm. The creature was gone, but he knew it would come back. It wasn't going to let them leave this house.

Regroup. Regenerate. Attack. He picked up on that much. It would come back. If he was right, he had to end it. It was a guess, but nothing else was killing this thing.

"Elena," he shouted. "It's the chest. Destroy it. Kill this thing."

"Are you sure?"

"No. But it won't let us leave unless it's dead."

His dad yanked out of his grasp. "You two leave. It only wants me. I'm all it knows."

"Dad, no one is leaving you."

"You two ain't dying for me. Go. Get out of my damn house."

"Dad, stop it," Elena said.

He turned to Elena and rested a shaky hand on her cheek. "Forgive me, daughter."

Dad looked Mateo in the eye. "I can't even remember her name anymore, nor your mother's."

His dad walked down the hallway, banging his cane against the wall. "Come on. Get it."

Mateo rushed behind him and started pulling away. "Stop it, Dad!"

Elena ignored them both and ran across the hallway. Mateo watched her disappear around the corner. Her running footsteps up the stairs confirmed what he'd feared. She was going after the chest.

He cursed. "Dad, I have to help Elena."

His dad nodded, then made it back inside his room and turned on the little radio. Spanish music blared through the rest of the hallway. He swung the cane around wildly at the remaining three walls, cursing and calling to the creature.

Mateo sprinted toward his mom's room.

Elena glanced at him. "How do we do this?"

He'd left the chest wide open. The symbols inside were glowing. The same pulsing he'd felt in his dad's room vibrated within the chest. It reminded him of a machine. And every machine had a cord attached to power it. He had to assume that was the case with the symbols. Separate them and maybe, just maybe, stop the creature.

"Break it," he said.

"With what?" she snapped. "It's as solid as a rock."

Of course she would know. So that wasn't an option.

"Fire."

Mateo turned to the drawers, pulling each out until he found a flashlight. He unscrewed it. Two-D batteries slapped into his palm. His mom kept old foil sheets for whenever she colored her hair. He ran into the bathroom and back out with the sheets and a can of old hairspray; he tossed Elena the can.

"Spray the second this flame ignites."

Downstairs, a loud roar erupted, and the walls shook.

Dad!

Mateo pinched a thin strip of foil over the positive and negative sides of one of the batteries. A small flame ignited in the middle of the strip.

"Now," he said.

Elena sprayed it toward the chest, and with greed, the flames quickly licked at the old wood. The chest itself made a weird creak, like the wood was crying in pain. It cracked, the symbols inside splitting apart and flickering to a dull gray color.

"Let's go," Mateo yelled, pulling his sister behind him.

They sprinted down the stairs, a plume of smoke following them.

"Mateo," Elena warned, freezing.

It wasn't smoke from a fire that followed. It was a rush of black cloud moving like a giant snake, writhing, surging, and undulating as it moved blindly through the stagnant air. It spread in all directions, leaving no room or corner untouched.

"Run. Now!"

She paused by Dad's room. "Dad?"

In the distance, the creature screeched. The lower half of the house was still rattling.

Mateo searched the room. "Where's Dad?"

More screeching from the creature deafened the whole house.

THE LAST VISIT   219

When he looked back, the wall of black smoke was closing in on them.

"Mateo," a faint voice said.

He found his dad on his knees with his head down, eyes squeezed shut, enduring some unmentionable ordeal. The creature held him from behind. Not feeding on him, just gripping him like that was its lifeline.

His dad's brow was locked tight in agony, his entire body hunched over and shaking, tight as a wire about to snap. He panted heavily.

The creature clutched his dad so tight its fingernails dug into his shoulders. Dad groaned.

The blood pooled to Mateo's legs, and his head swayed. Dad had said the beast wanted him, and Mateo couldn't shake the idea that destroying the chest wasn't enough, but losing his father wasn't an option. He wasn't leaving this house without him.

"You can't have him!" Mateo rushed to his father's side.

His dad's stomach buckled. His head slammed against the floor, where he writhed in agony, the creature on top of him like a UFC fighter.

"Get off him," Mateo roared.

He threw a punch at the creature's bloated head. Elena soon joined and tried to pry its limbs off their father, but it was as stiff as a dead body. Mateo knew his words were pointless.

Malevolence...The room reeked of it, and it was closing in on them as the black smoke inched further into the room. Mateo rained down more punches. The creature gave weak hisses, but its strength wouldn't falter.

His dad's head rose, his eyes longing for something Mateo refused to see. Not death. This thing wasn't taking his life. The creature rolled them on their sides, like a dead tree, its nails stabbing his skin. It lips peeled back from its teeth, exposing a chasm of writhing maggots. The creature's skin and blood ran down its chin, dropping on Dad's neck. Each drop burned him.

Dad howled in pain.

Mateo lurched for the creature. He grasped it, intending to rip the thing from his dad, even if it killed him in the process. His hands dug into the creature's arms.

But it was no longer a mass of taut skin and muscle. Underneath, dozens of worms whirred around, as if swimming under a blanket of skin melting off its body. Mateo recoiled. His attacker screeched and rolled them against the half-wall column. The black smoke poured across the floor, on its way toward them all.

Mateo felt its pulse thrumming through him. It beat weaker and weaker. Mateo dug his arms under the creature's head and pulled hard. An explosion of shrieks, then the creature's feet dug into Mateo's shins where he bled. Its front limbs clawed into his hips.

Mateo's arms burned under its chin. He could feel its flesh melting, dripping down his skin. Mateo screamed at the creature's fire. The pain was excruciating.

More skin spotted his cheek, and he yelped. His own grip was waning. The skin on his bones threaten to rip free.

Mateo pulled harder. His hands were going to come off.

The creature's grip was weakening. Mateo groaned words that were not English. Elena tried to rush in for him, but he kicked at her, warning her to stay away.

"No! Mateo," she cried.

The creature's grip convulsed, like a mad dog, momentarily releasing, then clamping down hard enough to make Mateo's teeth click.

Something was different. It was no longer digging its nails into him.

Mateo felt a bit of dust shower up into the air. Weight dropped off his chest. The thing forgot about Mateo's arms and locked its frantic and spasming grip onto his forehead. Mateo screamed again. Now his head was on fire. Blisters formed and bled down to his ears.

The creature's head wrenched back and away. Its blood was

changing, tunneling away from him, into the ceiling, and leaving particle by particle.

Mateo let go, his hands finally catching a break. The creature's blood and skin were spilling in buckets into the air, sucked up into the room's ceiling and vanishing into an invisible vortex.

Without the creature's aid, Mateo stood. He wrapped his arms around his dad and held him. The creature's body was shrinking like a dried slug, and the beast's pulse was slowing.

Crawling along the hall, the black smoke was so close he could reach out and touch it. He didn't know if that blanket of evil would kill them or not. But he couldn't risk it.

"Elena, get out." She didn't respond. "Go," he said.

She dropped to her knees and placed her hand on their dad's arm. Her head dipped, eyes wide in shock.

The smoke curled, circled, and slipped into the room, like oil into water. It swirled in an angry tunnel. Then, it was over them and swelling into the air, taking with it the top half of the creature's head. He could hear the thing weakly thrashing and flailing against the floorboards. An explosion erupted, and the creature's last screeches were cut short.

Mateo could smell it—the smell of a thousand empty pits of despair. The entire house shook. His face struggled to move, his legs and fingers twitched as they fought. His eyes jittered under their lids.

The darkness was birthing something, and Mateo wasn't sure he would live to see another day. The air grew hot. Mist gathered on his arms, then it lifted into the air.

Elena screamed as the roar of smoke bore down through the rest of the house like a stampede. Mateo squeezed her hand. Dad looked up at him. He mumbled something, but Mateo couldn't hear it.

Mateo leaned closer to his dad's head. He tried to mouth the words "I love you," but the sides of his face ached with each movement.

As if a fan was sucking it out, the smoke rushed out of the windows and doors, leaving a clear view of the house Mateo thought he knew.

No creature in sight.

Just Elena, Dad, and himself.

Their dad tensed under his grasp. Mateo scanned every inch, seeking out the creature. They all froze in place, watching every angle for the slightest movement.

A charred circle remained next to them where the creature had struggled. The house was eerily still. No screeching. No whining from the house's bones. No evidence of something living in this place. It was as if they were ghosts who didn't belong.

No one needed their next instructions.

Mateo and Elena weakly pried their father off the floor and stumbled toward the front door. They broke into the light once they stepped off the porch step.

Elena slipped the key into the ignition, and the car roared to life.

Dad and Mateo huffed and puffed in the backseat, Mateo resting his hand on the door.

Elena looked back at the house in the rearview mirror.

"Go," Dad said. "Let it rot."

"We're okay," Mateo stammered, the pain along his head beginning to settle. He glanced at his dad. "Aren't we?"

His dad weakly nodded.

They rolled down the driveway, dust swirling in the path.

They were flying.

In time, the trees would swallow up whatever was left. The concrete would crack. Bricks would crumble, and as the years passed, more and more would deteriorate. The grass would spring up and warp itself around the house, one final embrace before it vanished.

ABOUT THE CONTRIBUTORS

Taija Morgan

Taija Morgan is a horror, thriller, and suspense author with short stories and non-fiction articles published in various anthologies and magazines, including the *Prairie Gothic* anthology (2020) and *Prairie Witch* anthology (2022) from Prairie Soul Press, Tales to Terrify's horror podcast (2022), *Penitent's Gold* (The Seventh Terrace, 2022), and many others. She has degrees in psychology and sociology that contribute realism and insight to her dark, twisted fiction. Taija was the editor of Crime Writers of Canada's 40th Anniversary anthology *Cold Canadian Crime* (2022). She is represented by Oli Munson with A.M. Heath. Find her at www.TaijaMorgan.com or www.linktr.ee/TaijaMorgan.

J. Agombar

J. Agombar resides near the treacherous waters of Southend-On-Sea, Essex, UK where visions of the speculative, criminal and supernatural have taken over his mind (usually alongside a bottle of whisky). He holds a BA Hons in Humanities where the creative writing module inspired his first published work with Luna Press. He is a fan of the short story and inspired by classic authors such as Richard Matheson, Ray Bradbury and H.P Lovecraft. His work has been printed with over twenty publishers to date. His third short story collection is due in 2024.

Glenn Dungan

Glenn Dungan is currently based in Brooklyn, NYC. He exists within a Venn-diagram of urban design, sociology, and good stories. When not obsessing about one of those three, he can be found at a park drinking black coffee and listening to podcasts about murder. For more of his work, see his website: whereisglennnow.com.

Clarence Carter

Clarence Carter is best known for The Rejected Ones, Shadows & Keyholes and Damn Ernie. He has also been featured in a handful of anthologies. Born and raised in Maine, Carter has long appreciated its beautiful landscape and has drawn inspiration from its ebb and flow. Carter is an avid nature lover who tells a terrifying ghost story around the campfire.

Molly Thynes

Molly Thynes has been everything from a student at an all-girl's Catholic school to a nanny, a purveyor of haunted artifacts, and a mental health counselor, but she has been a writer before she even knew how to write. Her first love is the horror genre, but has found inspiration in a few other genres too (just not romance). Currently, Molly lives in Saint Paul, MN with her husband and as many animals as their landlord will allow.

Evander L. Fragoso

Born and raised in New Jersey, Evander Lee Fragoso now lives in Michigan with his wonderful wife Katrina. Creative pursuits were always on his mind, starting with doodles in classes along with short stories. While he works in food production, he spends the time before his "day job" working on his next book. Finding inspiration in horror movies and video games, he enjoys blending genres with a touch of whimsy into the tales he weaves, within universes with intertwined roots.

Phil Keeling

Phil Keeling is a writer and playwright. He is the author of the novella *Juice,* along with a smattering of short stories, essays, and plays that have been published, performed, and politely tolerated all over the United States. He is the co-host of Pixel Lit: the best (read: only) podcast dedicated to video game novelizations. He lives somewhere in the woods with his wife and their family.

Kevin Emmons

When he isn't taking care of family or critters or working, Kevin spends his time writing, gaming, and absorbed in art. He currently resides in Indiana, and works as a remote software engineer.

ABOUT THE EDITORS

Clay Vermulm

Clay Vermulm is a full-time creative writer and editor from Everett, Washington. When not at his desk, he is an avid mountaineer, surfer, and board game player. His debut horror/adventure novella, *Crevasse*, was published by City Stone Publishing in 2022. In 2023, two of his short stories were accepted for publication. One in Jennifer Brozek's upcoming flash-anthology *99 Fleeting Fantasies*, and the other in the *Tales of Sleyhouse 2023* anthology, published by *Sleyhouse Magazine*. Clay is a member of several writing organizations, including the Horror Writers Association, Northwest Independent Writers Association, Writers Cooperative of the Pacific Northwest, Cascade Writers, and Authors of the Flathead. He also curates the annual *Camp Crypticon Seattle* writing contest, reads slush for *Nightmare Magazine*, and writes weekly newsletters for *Grendel Press*.

Tori V. Rainn

Tori V. Rainn, a Texas-based novelist, weaves captivating tales that delve into the darker, mysterious, and sometimes morbid sides of life. Her short stories have been featured in online zines. Tori's passion for writing was ignited when she earned a creative writing certificate, propelling her towards her ultimate calling. When she's not crafting thrilling plots, you can find her immersed in the world of gaming, engrossed in her favorite shows, collecting knives that hold secrets of their own, and exploring the beauty of nature. Amidst her fascination with the shadows, Tori cherishes time spent with loved ones.

Made in the USA
Columbia, SC
16 May 2024